MW01489066

Also From The Author

The Captive Series
Captured (Book 1)
Renegade (Book2)
Refugee (Book 3)
Salvation (Book 4)
Redemption (Book 5)
Broken (The Captive Series Prequel) Coming Spring 2015

The Kindred Series
Kindred (Book 1)
Ashes (Book 2)
Kindled (Book 3)
Inferno (Book 4)
Phoenix Rising (Book 5)

The Ravening Series
Ravenous (Book 1)
Taken Over (Book 2)
Reclamation (Book 3)

The Survivor Chronicles
Book 1: The Upheaval
Book 2: The Divide
Book 3: The Forsaken
Book 4: The Risen (Coming Spring 2015)

Special Thanks

Special thanks to my husband, I don't know what I would do without you. Thank you for putting up with all my craziness.

To my parents for always being so supportive and allowing me to dream.

Thank you to my brother and sisters for giving me little pieces of you to add to characters.

To Megan for all the days and nights spent reading, whispering and dreaming.

To Kayla for being a pain in the butt and not putting on shoes, you slowed us down during our escape. Who knows where we would be living now!

To my nieces and nephews, thank you for making me smile and showing me just what the true definition of strength is in all that you do.

Thank you to all my friends who make me laugh and also add little pieces of themselves to the people in my head.

Thank you to Leslie for all of your continued hard work and support, I'm so glad we met.

Thank you to Christina for your good eye and friendship.

Thank you to all the fans who have become my friends. I don't know what I'd do without. You make everyday an adventure.

To Donna, Michelle, Christina, Cheryl, Tina, and Kathy thank you for the laughs, gentle nudges and countdowns that keep me on my game.

A very special thank you to Jessica for becoming my friend, for all your continued help and support, and for coming to visit me! I hope you find the Jessica in this story to your liking; she is named for you after all!

CHAPTER 1

I ducked low and spun away as the snapping tentacle zipped by my head. The hollow slapping sound it made against the concrete wall resonated within the quiet alley. The creature, frustrated at missing me, made a noise that wasn't quite a roar but more like a growling hiss that made my blood run cold. Whatever it was, it wasn't a sound that had ever been heard on our planet before their arrival.

Taking up the shooter's stance that Darnell had taught me. I didn't have much time, but even so I fired off five quick rounds into the smallest creature. A screeching noise erupted from it as it curled into itself but I didn't intend to stick around and make sure it was dead.

Keep moving, I told myself fiercely. *Don't stay still, just go.*

Leaping forward, I darted in and out as I attempted to stay ahead of the hideous thing pursuing me. I'd been hit once before by one of those tentacles and there was no way I was *ever* going to have that agonizing experience replayed. Grabbing hold of long forgotten trashcans and bicycles, I threw them behind me as I dashed into an empty office building and bolted through the shadowy and cobwebbed lobby.

I could barely hear over my own breath as my lungs labored for air. I grabbed hold of a dead potted plant and spun to heave it behind me as I tried to get enough distance between me and the monster to fight it off. The creature made that strange hissing sound again as the pot connected with its opalescent and mottled red exterior. It wasn't as large as some of the others I'd encountered, but it was faster and able to get through the building better than the bigger ones would have been able to.

My legs were burning as I jumped onto a sofa in the lobby and cleared the back of it in one single bound. There had been a time when I would have tripped over my own feet and ended up in an ungraceful heap on the floor, but things were different now. I wasn't the ungraceful, uncoordinated girl I'd been before The Freezing had occurred.

Cade had made sure of that, though his blood had resulted in consequences he hadn't expected and some he didn't even know about, as I still couldn't bring myself to talk to him about what was going on inside me.

I heard the creature coming seconds before I lurched to the side in order to dodge the tentacle's deadly trajectory. The snake-like appendage struck the wall with a sickening slap that caused my stomach to twist. I didn't know where everyone else was, we'd been separated when these things had emerged from the alleyway, but I knew if I could just stay free long enough, I'd be able to get the upper hand on this thing.

The entrance to the stairwell loomed ahead of me. The door had been half ripped off and hung askew on its broken hinges as I dove under it. I cleared the bottom half of the door and rolled into the gloomy stairway. I launched back to my feet and took the stairs two at a time as I ascended rapidly. My breathing sounded like a horse that had just won the race by the time I made it to the second floor, but I didn't slow down as I shoved through the stairwell door. The creature was only twenty feet behind me when I crashed through the first door on my right into an abandoned office.

My footsteps echoed through the cavernous space as I ran by the receptionist's desk, through another open doorway, and into a room filled with desks and copy machines. The smell of something dead and gone for too long now was coming from somewhere within the room. I prayed I didn't stumble across it as I ran in a zigzagging pattern I was hoping would help me lose the creature. I tried to ignore the blood streaked over the floor and smeared on the back wall but my eyes were drawn toward it repeatedly. The life of human beings gone, and sadly most likely forgotten, coated these walls.

I thrust open another door and plunged back into the hallway I'd just left. The screech of bending metal resonated through the hall as the monster scrambled through the office behind me. I had to get out of this building and somehow lose that thing. *Now.*

The door at the end of the hall was missing as I dashed into a different stairwell. It felt as if my feet barely hit the ground as I used the railing to propel myself down the stairs. My heart was in my throat as I leapt over the last four steps and fell into the closed door. My hands scrambled over the doorknob but it didn't budge as I twisted and tugged at it. A strangled scream escaped me; I slammed my shoulder against the metal, but it did little good as the door remained a solid barrier between me and my quest for freedom.

My lungs strained for air as I slapped my hand repeatedly against the metal and jerked on the knob. The thing's many legs sounded like nails on a chalkboard as it rounded the landing. Its chelicerae like mouth clicked eagerly when it spotted me against the door.

Not like this, not like this, I prayed fervently. *I'm not ready to go now.* Cade would be heartbroken and devastated; he would be lethal if something happened to me now. This time my scream of frustration wasn't muffled, it was a loud and clear shout of pure fury and terror as I kicked and tore feverishly at the barricade in my way.

Faster than I could blink the door was ripped away from me. I gasped as light blazed against my irises and instinctively took a startled step back. Hands seized hold of me and pulled me out of the stairwell. I caught a brief glimpse of Cade before he pushed me behind him. The normal onyx of his eyes had seeped out to encompass his entire eyeball; the veins in his face seemed to have filled with liquid coal as he turned to confront the creature stalking me.

The thing was brought up short by the fact that one of its creators was standing in the doorway staring at it with murderous intent. Before I could react, and before the creature could sense the threat, Cade pulled out his knife and launched himself forward with a vicious snarl that caused the hair on my neck to stand up. The creature hadn't been expecting to be attacked by Cade, but its shock wore off the minute it realized that its life was in danger.

I stumbled back a few feet as squeals of pain and the sounds of fists pummeling the creature's almost mushy exterior surrounded me. My hands fell to my waist and the gun resting there. Pulling it free, I ran toward the doorway. There was no way I was going to stand back and take the chance of something happening to Cade. Before I could make it to the stairwell a low keening sound emanated from the creature but Cade remained eerily silent as the hollow thud of thumps and blows continued from within. My heart was a drumbeat in my chest; I could barely breathe through the constriction in my throat.

Was I already too late?

I was brought up short in the doorway as Cade reappeared. Blood streaked his midnight hair, full mouth and cheeks. "Are you ok?" he demanded as his eyes pierced me.

I opened my mouth to answer but I didn't get a chance to as he whirled away from me and disappeared into the stairwell. I caught a brief glimpse of blood splattered walls, and limp tentacles before he carefully closed the door behind him. I didn't know what had happened to make him retreat until I caught the sound of running feet. Spinning around, I took a step forward to block Aiden, Bret, and Lloyd as they charged across the lobby of the office building.

They couldn't see Cade like this, they simply couldn't. Their breathing was labored and their hair was dripping with sweat as they skid to a stop in front of me. "Are you ok?" Aiden demanded as his mahogany eyes fixed upon me.

Unable to hold his gaze, my eyes flitted back toward the glass front of the building. Aiden had been scrutinizing me ever since Cade had been forced to kill Ian in order to save me. Cade had revealed what he truly was to me that night, but the others didn't know and they could never find out. Aiden didn't know the true depth of the secrets I was hiding from him, but he was my brother and in the past, he'd always known when I'd been keeping something from him. Right now was no different; he knew I was holding something back.

I jumped a little as Cade's hands came down on my shoulders. Twisting to look up at him, I was relieved to see that the black had seeped away from his face to reveal his striking features. He had cleaned the blood from his mouth and hands though I could still see specks of it in his hair.

Knowing that it would help to calm him further, and needing the connection with him, I rested my hand on top of his. "I'm fine," I assured the others. "How is everyone else?"

"They're fine." Bret's clover colored eyes scanned me before settling upon Cade. He'd become a lot more accepting of our relationship, but like Aiden he'd never hid the fact that he didn't entirely trust Cade. If they knew the truth, the looks on their faces would be a lot less friendly, and as it was, the looks they gave him now weren't entirely welcoming.

Cade slid his arm around my waist as he stepped beside me and pulled me against his side. "Are you ok?" Lloyd asked.

I was uncertain what he was talking about until I realized that his focus wasn't on me. My gaze slid to the four round patches of blood, each about the size of a quarter that stained Cade's electric blue shirt. My mouth went dry and my mind went blank as I felt trapped beneath their inquisitive gazes.

"I'm fine. I must have rubbed against something." Cade pulled the shirt out from his body and looked down as if to study the spots of blood. He pulled off the lie and baffled look far better than I would have as he rubbed at the marks before shrugging and dropping the shirt back down.

"Looks like blood," Aiden pressed.

"It could be," Cade acknowledged. "There's plenty of blood marking this city right now."

I shuddered at the reminder and slipped my hands into the sleeves of my sweater to fiddle with the edges of the tattered cuffs. "I suppose." Aiden slid his rifle onto his back, but he didn't seem satisfied by Cade's answer. "We better get back. Darnell plans to try and get out of the city before morning."

"Since when?" I inquired.

"Since it has become apparent that most survivors have either moved on or…"

His voice trailed off but we all knew what he was going to say; or they were dead. We hadn't seen any living, breathing people since entering the city. Blood spattered the streets and buildings and I had seen far too many bodies and random body parts in the past few days. The worst were the children and babies. I tried not to think about them, but the images of the lost young would haunt me for as long as I lived.

Whereas the aliens had turned Cape Cod and Plymouth into a makeshift prison for those who hadn't been frozen, or that had already been reawakened, Boston seemed to have been a zone used simply for slaughter, pleasure, and mayhem. The aliens had come in here and ruthlessly hunted and destroyed any person they'd found, frozen or moving. I assumed there had to be survivors somewhere, that some people must have escaped, but there was no way to know as we'd come across nothing but death and destruction.

I'd asked Cade why they had left one area alone and basically untouched, while completely destroying another. He'd assumed that it was because Boston's population was far higher than the Cape's so there had been more survivors in Boston and more of a chance of a rebellion amongst them. The people within the city had been decimated, and their bodies left behind, as a warning of what could happen to any other survivors that came here seeking refuge or retribution.

However, Cade hadn't expected the complete massacre that had occurred in Boston, he never would have allowed us to come here if he had. He'd expected more aliens in the city, we all had, but the risks had seemed worth the food, medical supplies, and possible help we had hoped to find here. None of us had known that we were walking into Hell on earth, and that the rewards we had been hoping to find here were never going to materialize.

Even though we wouldn't be able to get supplies, a part of me was glad that Bishop wouldn't be able to get a hold of more equipment to test my blood with. I wasn't like the others, my blood type wasn't O, but there was no secret cure hidden within my blood like the one that Bishop hoped for. The secret lay within the fact that Cade wasn't human, and in the hopes of saving me from The Freezing, he had given me some of his blood. His blood could have killed me, but if he hadn't done it I wouldn't have survived at all. I would have been like my mother, who had been lost soon after The Freezing occurred.

Although Cade's blood had changed me and may still be changing me, I would forever be grateful for what he had done for me. Grateful for everything that he had risked for me, and for the pure love he so easily gave when his kind was incapable of such a thing. I couldn't help but return that love as he'd had my heart since we were children.

I would have liked to have been able to get our hands on some more medicine and supplies though, even if it meant we had to come up with a viable excuse for Bishop not to poke and prod at me anymore. We were in need of antibiotics, antibacterial creams, bandages, painkillers, and any other thing that would help keep us alive. Which was just about everything, we didn't have much left if an emergency arose.

However with most of the routes to the hospitals blocked off, and absolutely no guarantee that any of them actually still remained, that part of our mission had quickly been abandoned. Just as the mission of trying to find Jenna's parents had become too hazardous to pursue. The decision had broken Jenna's heart and she had cried a lot of tears, but she had never complained and she hadn't argued with us about it.

Her parents had probably arrived in Boston a couple of weeks before us, when the alien occupation here had been at its highest and worst. Unwilling to not show some kind of an effort on Jenna's behalf, Darnell had managed to get us to her grandparent's house. It had still been standing, but there were no signs of life within the dusty recesses of the home. We'd tried to get to another of the meeting places that Jenna's parents left in their note to her, the science museum, but the way had been blocked. The search was officially abandoned as our own survival became paramount, and the risks too high.

I *hated* being in this city of suffering and death and I couldn't wait to be free from it. I'd expected some of the others to try and stay in the city with the expectation that there could still be survivors out there, or something useful for fighting back, but I was glad they were ready to go. We needed to get out of here before we were all killed, or before the desolation of this place wore us down completely.

"Let's go then," I said eagerly.

Cade slid his hand into mine and squeezed it as we made our way out of the deserted office building. I tilted my face back to take in the fading rays of the setting sun filtering around the buildings. Glass gleamed with rainbows of color that danced across the broken sidewalks and roadways. It should have been beautiful and breathtaking but it just reminded me of times forever lost to us.

I couldn't wait to see open sky and inhale air that wasn't tainted with the stench of death and blood again.

Cade's fingers were strong in mine as we hurried down the street to the small hotel we'd spent last night in. Though the street was desolate, there were still random things like shoes, purses, bikes and strollers left behind by those that had been taken. There was even a doll, missing an eye and soaked in blood, lying on the curb. Vehicles were parked on the side of the road but few congested the streets as driving had been banned shortly before The Freezing had occurred.

I could almost feel the life that had once flowed through here, the people that had once packed the restaurants, bars, museums and hair salons. Almost hear the laughter that had been forever silenced. Now, the once beautiful and proud city would forever be haunted by those who had been ruthlessly slaughtered here.

CHAPTER 2

I dug my heels in like a stubborn dog refusing to go back inside. My heart lurched and kicked as I swallowed heavily and forced myself to breathe. I could barely get any air into my chest as my lungs seemed determined not to work.

"Bethany." Cade's hands were firm on my upper arms as he held me. "Listen to me Bethy; you do *not* have to do this. We can find another way around."

"We'd have to double back…"

"You and me," Cade harshly interrupted Lloyd and silenced the Private with a withering glare that would have made men twice the size of Lloyd take a step back. I gave Lloyd credit for holding his ground, but he didn't speak again. "The two of us will find a way around."

"Be reasonable Cade," Darnell muttered.

Cade shot him a fulminating look as his jaw clenched and a muscle in his cheek jumped. I closed my eyes and grappled to regain control of my body. I hated this inner betrayal, hated this intense physical reaction that still had a hold over me. I opened my eyes to focus on Cade's face as he leaned closer to me. His breath was warm against my face, his hands strong on my arms as he rubbed them reassuringly. I knew he would go out of his way to avoid this tunnel for me if I asked him to.

"Listen…"

"That's enough Lloyd." This time it was Aiden who interrupted Lloyd as he stepped closer to us. He may not be exactly trusting of Cade and me right now but he wasn't going to force me into that tunnel either.

I took a deep breath. They would do this for me, they would both go around and then Abby, Bret, Jenna and possibly Molly would most likely follow. The group would become even more divided. That couldn't happen; it simply could not be *allowed* to happen. Our numbers were already small enough and I couldn't let them become even smaller simply because I was afraid.

Or what if they all decided to come with us and someone was lost? I couldn't take the chance of anyone being hurt because I couldn't shake the persistent phobia that had haunted me ever since I'd been trapped within the wreckage of that ruined vehicle with my dying father.

"I… I can do this," I choked out. I saw the doubt and hesitance in Cade's eyes and I gushed on before he could argue with me. "I *can* Cade. I made it through that pipe I can make it through this."

It was true I had made it through that pipe in the dump, barely. But the pipe had been smaller, it had stunk and been filled with slime, and those things had been right behind us. This tunnel was much larger with plenty of room to move about. I kept trying to focus on those thoughts, rather than thoughts of being stuck underground, trapped between those concrete walls and unable to see daylight or breathe fresh air. If I focused on those thoughts I would *never* make it inside.

"I'll be fine," I said, trying to believe it even when I didn't.

"Bethany once we get in there…"

"I know." I couldn't hear him say the words, I could *think* them, but I couldn't hear him say that there would be no return. "Don't."

His eyes shimmered with uneasiness but he grasped hold of my cheeks and kissed me ardently. My toes curled and for a second I was able to forget about the tunnel as he encompassed my entire world. "I'll get you through," he whispered when he pulled away.

I managed a feeble smile and a small nod. "I know."

His thumbs caressed my face as he studied me before turning away. He kept his strong fingers interlaced with mine as he quickly nodded to Aiden. Aiden hesitated before turning away and entering the gloomy tunnel. I kept my eyes on my feet as I became focused on the oversized sneakers I'd recently traded my old, holey pair for.

I was aware when we stepped into the tunnel as the air temperature dropped a good ten degrees and the smell brought forth memories of my damp cellar in the summertime. My heart rate accelerated but if I kept my gaze down I could almost pretend that I wasn't standing within a giant concrete tube with water flowing above me.

Cade directed me with subtle pulls and tugs on my hand as his body against mine moved me toward the left or right. *It's not so bad*, I told myself. *It's just darker that's all, that's the only difference.* My eyes weren't nearly as good as Cade's in the night, but they had improved over the past few months either from his blood or from the fact we were almost nocturnal now. Either way, I was able to pick out subtle differences in the asphalt I was focused upon.

"Lights." Darnell's whisper caused my head to instinctively come up. I immediately regretted the action. I brought my head back down, but not before the dim glow of the flashlights illuminated the walls around us. I was tempted to glance back at the front of the tunnel, I knew I would still be able to see the fading daylight, but I couldn't bring myself to move. It may be the last of the day I'd see for awhile, but I was too busy focusing on putting one foot in front of the other and not falling apart, to look back.

Coward, I ridiculed myself. *Childish, broken, coward*!

Tears filled my eyes as I took a deep breath and forced my head up. The shadows that played over the walls gave the tunnel an even creepier feel that it did *not* need. Though there was no fog, there was an almost misty quality to the air that caused my skin to crawl and the air to shimmer oddly.

It wasn't the misty air that held my attention though but the amount of vehicles clustered within. There were more vehicles stretching into the tunnel than I'd seen in months. They were bunched in the middle of the road and lined the sides of the walls. My mouth parted as I looked at all of the vehicles before turning to look behind me. There were a few cars stretching back to the opening, but it wasn't until here that they became thicker and more congested. We were going to have to zigzag through and climb over them in order to get out.

"What is this?" I squeaked.

Cade shook his head as he studied the confines of the tunnel. My claustrophobia was briefly buried under my growing confusion and uncertainty as we scrambled through the vehicles. Cade helped me climb onto the hood of a car as we reached an area that was completely blocked. Like a plucked guitar string, his body vibrated with tension as he landed next to me on the other side of the car. The fact that he was so unsettled by this new development did little to ease my anxiety as there was little that ruffled Cade.

I pulled Abby closer to me and held her against my side. Her doe brown eyes were wide as she wordlessly gazed up at me. My hand entwined with her small one as Cade moved before us unflinchingly.

"Wait." Darnell pulled up. He shifted his rifle and grasped it in both hands before him as his mocha eyes surveyed the crowded tunnel. His deep coffee colored skin gleamed in the flashlight beams as he crept forward. Beads of sweat had broken out across his forehead and trickled down his cheeks. He had recently shaved his head completely bald which emphasized his high cheekbones, narrow chin and handsome features. Years of being a soldier had honed his body into that of a well built killing machine, one that we all looked to for leadership.

"Everyone get your weapons ready." I squeezed Abby's hand and reluctantly released it to pull my pistol free of my waistband. "Do not fire unless you have something to hit. Ricocheting bullets are just as deadly," Darnell ordered gruffly.

I could sense Cade's displeasure as he watched Abby and I. He liked this even less than any of us, but what choice did we have? To double back now would take too much time and there was nothing to go back to. As of now there was no threat here, only haphazard cars.

Another fifty feet into the tunnel things began to change even more. Whereas the cars had seemed to have a certain order to them before there was no such order now. They were haphazard and askew, and appeared to be waiting for their final crushing at a junkyard. I gazed in incredulity at the vehicles tossed here and there, the shattered windows, and the twisted metal remains. Abby was shaking as she pressed closer to me and gawked at the wreckage.

It didn't take a genius to know what had caused this much carnage and destruction. The octopus/jellyfish/tick/crab monster things that the aliens had unleashed upon us had obviously been through here. Though it had to have been some of the smaller ones; the larger ones, the ones *full* of human blood, wouldn't have fit through the tunnel. It didn't matter the size though as they were all deadly, and the small ones had developed the uncanny ability to mimic a human being.

Everyone stopped moving as Darnell, Lloyd, Bret and Mick moved cautiously toward the next bend in the tunnel. Cade's nostrils flared with his inhalations, he glanced rapidly at our surroundings as the four of them disappeared from view. I found myself unable to breathe as I awaited gunfire or screams of death. I took a deep breath as Bret returned and gestured for us to come forward to join them.

The next bend in the tunnel didn't reveal any less destruction. It did, however, offer an exit ramp that led to somewhere else in the city. In front of the exit was a large gap with mutilated cars shoved to both sides of it. These vehicles appeared to have already gone through the crusher as they were twisted to the point that they were almost unrecognizable.

"What happened?" Abby breathed.

"Someone tried to use the cars to block the ramp so that nothing could enter the tunnel from above," Cade answered. He pressed closer to me, his head tilted back to study the ceiling. A chill of trepidation coursed through me as I tilted my head back too. I was petrified I would see one of those things hanging above us waiting to pounce. Relief coursed through me when I discovered nothing but concrete and shadows.

I turned back to the mangled vehicles as my throat went dry. "People tried to blockade themselves *within* the tunnel," I croaked.

I couldn't wrap my mind around such a notion. They had tried to keep themselves safe within these concrete walls, beneath the ground, trapped like rats. They'd had no hope if those things ever managed to get in here, which they apparently had.

"They must have repeatedly gone above to steal cars; they had to have been down here for awhile before they were discovered," Cade answered.

"They could still be down here," Molly whispered. She seemed more frightened by that notion than the one that they were all dead as her gaze flitted over the tunnel and she took a step closer to Aiden.

I had to admit that the idea of running into anyone that had been living down here for the past couple of months wasn't that appealing to me either. "Those things broke through though," Abby breathed.

"They did," Cade agreed flatly. "There are other things that could still be down here, besides survivors."

I hated this tunnel more and more with every passing second. Whatever had been so awful up above seemed to have seeped into this underground world of shadows and destruction. I didn't plan to stay down here for one minute longer than we had to, but they had spent weeks, if not *months,* living beneath the earth and skulking through these tunnels like rats.

Cade took a step closer to me. "I don't smell death," he stated.

My head turned toward him as I inhaled deeply. The air was dank and reeked of mildew, gas, oil and something musky and feral, like rodents or other wild animals, but there was no cloying odor of decay within the tunnel. I imagined that within these confines the scent would be overpowering and sickening.

"You're right," Lloyd said.

"Do you think they survived?" Abby asked hopefully.

"Maybe," Cade murmured.

There was something he wasn't saying, something bothering him as he took a step closer to me and Abby. I wanted to ask him what was wrong but I bit my tongue. If he thought it was safe to say it out loud, he would. Instead he slipped a knife from its holster and flipped it into his free hand. Even with my newfound grace I would have sliced myself open if I'd attempted such a thing, but he did it with easy confidence and an elegance that was mesmerizing.

My hand shook on the pistol before I took a deep breath and steadied myself. "Should we try going up?" Bret asked as he studied the ruined blockade before the exit ramp. Somehow, perhaps with pulleys and ropes, it appeared that the survivors had at one point stacked the cars on top of each other. Those things had come down that ramp and torn through the barricade with enough force to scatter the cars like a bomb had exploded beneath them.

I was eager to get out of this tunnel, but I was less than thrilled with the prospect of going up that exit ramp. Death awaited us up there I was certain of it. "I don't think that's a good idea," Bishop's gray eyes were large and troubled behind his Lennon style glasses as he studied the ramp.

Abby began to shake against me as her hand wrapped around my arm. "I agree," I said.

The matter seemed to be settled as Darnell and Lloyd moved ahead again to scout the tunnel with the rest of us steadily following behind. It was a good ten minutes before we came across the obstruction in the tunnel. My heart sank as I stared at the jumbled pile before us. The bottom layer was made up of at least ten to fifteen cars. Some of the vehicles had been tipped on their sides while others were completely upside down. On top of them had been heaped bikes, sinks, toilets, bed frames and mattresses. Twisted pieces of metal, rebar, and steel beams rounded out the assortment of materials comprising the makeshift wall.

"What the...?" Aiden's voice trailed off.

"We're going to have to dig our way through." Darnell didn't look at all pleased by the notion.

"What's on the other side though?" Molly asked.

I crept closer to the mound of junk. It had taken them awhile to do this, and then they had abandoned it. *But why had they left? Why had they done this? Where had they gone and what was on the other side?*

I took a step away from the mounded rubble and doubled back to the bend in the tunnel. A sudden thought occurred to me as I peered around the corner. "What if it wasn't people that built the barricades? What if it was *them*? What if they built it to keep people from using the tunnel as an escape route?"

They all stared at me for awhile before turning back to the pile. "You think those creatures would be capable of doing this?" Jenna inquired.

I looked toward Cade for an answer but he was keenly studying the pile with his hand resting against a beam. "I think they're capable of anything," I answered.

"That they are, but they didn't do this," Cade informed us as he stepped away from the pile. "It was built by humans; there are dirty handprints on some of these things, and footprints all over the ground." He flashed his light over the old prints that marked the floor, and some of the materials in the pile that had handprints on them. "It's going to take awhile to dig through all of this."

"Are we sure we want to?" Molly wrapped her hand around Aiden's arm as she stepped closer to him. I quirked an eyebrow at my brother; I'd noticed that they had been spending a lot more time together recently but Aiden hadn't said anything about it yet, and until she touched him just now I'd thought they were only friends. Maybe they still were, but the gesture seemed entirely too intimate to simply be one shared between friends.

"We'll make a small hole and I'll climb through first," Cade volunteered.

"Cade…"

He shook his head to cut off my protest. The idea of him going through first was enough to make me want to hurl, not when we didn't know what he was going to be climbing into. He may be stronger than the rest of us, faster and deadlier, but he wasn't immortal.

"Give me a hand," Cade said.

Aiden shot me a glance but nodded his agreement. Bret and Lloyd joined Cade and Aiden while Darnell, Mick, and Frank fell back to the curve with me. I listened to the small grunts and muffled curses as they worked to dig a hole through the mound of materials. Metal clacked and clanged and grated on my nerves as I watched the tunnel with a growing sense of urgency.

"Think we're there," Aiden muttered after what seemed like countless hours but was probably only two.

I took a deep breath to steady my nerves before turning around. My heart was in my throat as Cade took off his rifle. "You have to take a gun," I insisted. I didn't realize I'd been walking toward him until I was standing before him with my pistol extended. He grasped hold of my hand

and caressed it before he took the gun from me and handed me his rifle. "Be careful."

He flashed his dazzling smile that never failed to melt my heart. "Always." His cavalier attitude did little to ease the knot of anxiety growing in my chest. "I'll be fine."

He kissed me quickly before disappearing into the small hole they had carved through the rubble.

CHAPTER 3

I anxiously peered into the hole as I watched Cade squirm his way through it. I kept the flashlight focused on him until he disappeared. My breath was trapped in my chest as I waited for some sign that he was alive and well. Aiden's head was bent close to mine as he tapped his foot. I could feel his breath as it heaved in and out of him. His honey hued hair, so similar to mine in color, was longer than I'd ever seen it as it hung about his handsome, angular face in sweat dampened curls.

The light flashed off of Cade's face as he reappeared on the other side. He slipped back into the hole and made his way toward us. I stepped aside when he reached the end and pulled himself free from the hole. Some of the color had faded from his face and his lips were pursed as he reclaimed his rifle from me.

"They barricaded themselves on the other side," he stated crisply.

"Are they still there?" Aiden inquired.

"No. It's safe over there, but I have a feeling we're going to encounter another wall of debris at some point."

I didn't like the look in Cade's eyes as they met mine. "How bad is it?" I asked.

"It's not good," he told me.

"Should we go back?"

"It's a long way back and then we would have to find another route. It would mean crossing a bridge, maybe two. Our best option is continuing on," Lloyd insisted.

"He's right; it's probably our best chance," Cade agreed. "Going back above is unsafe and it will only delay us in the city even more. What's left over there can't hurt us."

I flinched away from his words. *What's left, what's left!* The words echoed in an endless scream through my mind.

"Let's get some more of this stuff out of the way," Darnell ordered. His tone was brisk but there was a catch in his voice that revealed his inner turmoil. "Make the hole big enough for us to get everything through."

"The other wall of debris, it won't still be intact like this one, will it?" I whispered.

Cade touched my cheek as he rested his forehead against mine. "No, it won't be."

"Are they all dead?"

His silence was answer enough. I didn't want to go over there and I certainly didn't want Abby to see what was on the other side, but there were no other options. It took an hour before the hole was big enough to fit all our supplies and Barney, a dog I had adopted in Plymouth, but who had become more of Abby's pet recently, through. It was another half an hour before we were all standing on the other side.

Aiden grabbed hold of Abby as she spun away with a disgusted cry and held her against his side. The urge to turn around gripped me but it was already too late. Even if I never looked again, the revolting images before me would forever be seared into my brain.

This side of the tunnel reminded me of a paintball course straight from a nightmare. The blood sprayed over the walls was nearly black in the beams of our lights as they played over the concrete walls and asphalt road. These people hadn't been killed, they'd been massacred. Rotting body parts littered the tunnel; limbs had been brutally wrenched from the bodies and tossed haphazardly about like they were no more than discarded tissues. Snapped bones, joints and muscles stuck out from the decaying remnants of the lost souls.

My hand flew to my nose and mouth as I tried, and failed, to block the stench. Molly spun to face the pile of debris at my back and vomited. Since The Freezing we had all seen, and survived, horrors that none of us ever could have imagined, but this was the worst. This was the sadistic and brutal destruction of the human body that served no purpose other than to entertain the monsters that had destroyed it. I could almost hear the echoing screams of agony and terror that had, at one time, resonated within these walls.

Aiden comforted Abby the best he could as she started to cry. My eyes burned too, but I found I couldn't master even the simple action of shedding tears right now. Cade's arm encircled my waist, he pulled me against his side as a tremor began to work its way through my system. It was so difficult for me to believe that he was a part of the race that had inflicted this cruelty upon our planet.

"Why?" I whispered.

He dropped his head against mine and nuzzled my hair as his fingers stroked over my arm. I wondered briefly if the tension in his body was from the tragedy surrounding us, or because it had triggered his hunger and killer instincts. He couldn't help what he was but looking at this place made me want to shriek with fury.

"There is no reason for this. Just focus on me, I'll get you through." Cade's words caused guilt to slither through me over my unfair and judgmental thoughts.

"We have to move," Darnell commanded in a clipped tone.

I kept my head bent as I pressed against Cade's side and gained strength from his unwavering determination. I tried to focus on his smell but even his scent of cloves and sweat couldn't block the hideous reek of this place. Molly and Abby were crying quietly, Jenna was as white as a ghost as her lower lip trembled.

Unlike the other stretch of tunnel, the street through here was relatively clean of all debris, except for the human remains. Lloyd's smattering of orange freckles stood out starkly against his pale face as he shifted his rifle onto his back and stopped to pick up a box full of canned food. His orange red hair stood out from his face and his blue eyes were large behind his glasses. There was a rare slouch to his shoulders as he hefted the box into his arms. I didn't particularly feel like eating anything that we'd found here but we couldn't turn down the extra food.

The dead had brought metal barrels into the tunnel and the ash remains of cooking fires filled the bottom of them and lent a smoky aroma to the air. We came across areas that seemed to have been people's sleeping quarters as we moved deeper into the tunnel. There hadn't been much privacy, but blankets and sheets had been hung to delineate small rooms. We moved by a door set into the side of the tunnel, but I had no interest in knowing where it went as I was certain it was only to even smaller places.

Cade's fingers dug into my waist and as I tilted my head back to meet his soulful eyes I saw true sadness there. It wasn't sadness for the dead around us, but for me. He was sad because *I* was sad. Along with his sympathy though, I also saw the hunger I'd wondered about earlier.

I shuddered as he pulled me closer against him and briefly rested his chin on top of my head. He wasn't cruel like the others of his kind, I knew he took no pleasure in the mayhem surrounding us, but he still had to survive. Being surrounded by all of this blood and death was fueling his ever present thirst, and though he wasn't inherently a cruel being, I knew that I was the only one he truly cared about. He would do whatever he could to keep the people I cared about safe, but I was his number one concern.

I was also the one he yearned to feed from the most, though he never did. No matter how often I offered him the nourishment he desperately needed, he refused it. Things were different now though, he had even less opportunities to satisfy his appetite than before. If we didn't get out of here soon he may have no choice but to allow me to satisfy him. I thought I should be troubled or repulsed by such a thing but I wasn't. *He* was frightened he might hurt me but I was positive he wouldn't.

Cade pulled his shirt over my nose as he urged me to move faster. I knew that being near me didn't help with the urges that pulsed through him, but somehow he managed to keep himself under control despite the steadily increasing tension I felt humming through him.

Time was rapidly slipping through our fingers; we had to get free of this awful place soon. It wasn't just the two of us starting to lose it but also the struggling group surrounding us. Even the more experienced soldiers were nearing their breaking point. Mick and Frank were bug eyed as they swung their guns rapidly back and forth. I was half afraid they were going to open fire at the first sound they heard.

Something clattered further down the tunnel. Before I could blink, or even react, Cade was shoving me behind him and whipping his knives out. Movement exploded around the turn at the end of the tunnel as one of the alien's monstrous creations charged out of the murky depths. Liz, a middle aged woman with dark blond hair nearly knocked me over as she bolted past me with the look of an untamed horse trying to escape a wolf.

"Don't run!" Jenna yelled after her but Liz didn't appear to hear her.

I jumped as shots reverberated through the confined space. My ears rang incessantly as my heart beat a rapid staccato against my ribs as another creature barreled around the corner. These monstrosities were on the smaller side, but they were just as deadly as, and far faster than, the bloated larger ones that had gorged themselves on human blood. Cade threw back his arm and released one of his knives. It made a whistling sound as it whipped through the air with swift and deadly accuracy. A sickening squishy sound followed as it punctured through the monsters spongy outer body. Blood, most likely human, sprayed out of the wound but it didn't slow its rapid pace. I aimed my gun at the other one and fired rapidly as it skittered perilously close to Lloyd.

Lloyd swore loudly as he dove out of the way of a swinging, jellyfish like tentacle that whistled as it sliced through the air. It scarcely missed crushing his skull as it slammed down with enough force to rattle the walls and leave a large crack in the asphalt. I suddenly understood what had happened to these people, understood how they had been so violently overrun as two more creatures emerged from the gloom.

Guns or not, they were going to overpower us.

Abby started screaming as my gun emptied and my heart broke. I didn't care what it took; I was *not* going to let them get their deadly tentacles on my little sister. Moving hastily, and with far more calm than I felt, I grabbed more ammo from my pocket.

I had just finished reloading when two strong arms wrapped about my waist and spun me around. My tailbone screamed as I landed on my backside with a solid thud and my hand went numb when my elbow cracked off the asphalt. Cade and I bounced and rolled over the surface. He somehow managed to get my gun and flip over on top as he kept me pinned beneath him.

Sitting up, he fired at the creature looming over us on its hind legs. My blood ran cold at the spectacle of the mouth-like hole in the center of the creature's midsection. I'd never seen one from this angle, and as the blood drained from my brain and face, I wished that I never had. The mouth opened to allow tentacles to slither forth in search of one of us to snag hold of and drain dry. Thousands of bristles that resembled the coarse hair of a wild boar rolled and bowed over like dandelions in the wind. It took me a second to realize that they weren't actually hairs but rather teeth that chattered in eager anticipation of sinking into one of us.

It didn't seem to recognize Cade as one of its masters, and I supposed that most of them probably wouldn't when confronted with him looking entirely human, and fighting for us. When his eyes were black and his veins were filled with whatever alien power that surged through him, they knew immediately that he wasn't one of their victims. Now though, it unknowingly dove at him as it eagerly sought to get at both of us.

It hissed and howled with pain as it fell back beneath the barrage of bullets Cade fired into it. Its legs folded in on itself as it sought to protect the hole in its center. Most of its tentacles retracted but one whipped out at us and almost took off Cade's head. His hand slapped the feeler away as he somehow managed to reload my gun, with inhuman deftness, and fire again.

A human scream of suffering ripped through the air. Panic clawed at me as I fought to see who and where the stricken sound was coming from but Cade continued to keep his body pressed protectively against mine. Another scream split the air as Cade launched to his feet with the grace of a cat, grabbed hold of my arm, and pulled me up so fast that I barely had time to blink let alone register the fact that I was standing again.

Cade's jaw clenched as he wrapped his arm around my waist, lifted me off my feet, and spun us so that we were facing the creature he had just emptied my gun into multiple times. It was still coming, but it was more sluggish now and oozing blood from the many holes puncturing it. Cade pulled his other knife free and deftly released it. The creature reeled back as the knife pierced through its chest region.

Cade bent over me, his hand wrapped around my head as a slashing tentacle slammed into his back. He grunted and was knocked forward by the blow. A cry of alarm escaped me as I clutched at him frantically, I was certain he had been flayed open. The force of that blow would have broken a normal man's back but it barely did more than slightly faze him. His lips brushed over my temple before he abruptly released me.

For a moment I thought the thing had grasped hold of him and was trying to take him from me again, but then I saw Cade's eyes. Black filled both of his eyeballs as he began to lose his firm restraint upon himself. Words escaped me as I was hit by the certainty that something bad was about to happen. Thrusting my gun at me, he spun away and moved rapidly beyond my grasp.

My heart was in my throat as he launched himself at the creature and scurried up to the top of it. In one ferocious motion he ripped the knife he'd flung free from the thing's flesh. Weak from its numerous cuts, the monster stumbled beneath Cade's weight but didn't go down. With a savage cry, Cade raised his knife above his head and slammed it down. Blood drenched his face and clothes as he was saturated in the life force of those that had been lost. I didn't want to see the brutality that encompassed him, but I couldn't tear my eyes away as he ripped the knife free and plunged it down again.

"My God," Bret breathed beside me.

I could barely meet his appalled gaze as he looked between Cade and I. Cade hadn't revealed anything about himself; any of the more physically fit men, including Bret, could have done what Cade had just done. The only problem was that they *wouldn't* have done it.

More motion exploded from the gloom as two more creatures came into view. "Fall back!" Darnell yelled above the growing ruckus.

I turned away to face the fresh blood coating the tunnel. The tattered remains of Private Mick Doogal's body were strewn across the road like some sort of macabre voodoo doll. Sorrow twisted through my chest, I hadn't known him long but he'd been a good man and he hadn't deserved to die like this. No one had. My hands were shaking as I grabbed more ammo and fumbled to reload my gun.

"Bethy, Bethany we have to go! We have to *go!*"

I stumbled as Aiden grabbed my arm and began to pull me back. I tried to tug my arm away from him as I searched for Cade amongst the crush of people pressing against me, but Aiden refused to release me as he relentlessly pulled me back.

Relief filled me when I finally spotted Cade pushing through the horde to get to me. His face was streaked with blood and his clothes were caked with it, but he didn't seem to notice it as he focused on me. Though he looked untamed and savage, he seemed to have regained some control as his eyes were back to normal. I wondered if he'd managed to feed on some of that blood, if only just a little, but I quickly shut the thought down. I loved him, I loved everything about him, but there were certain things I didn't need to know.

"We have to go Bethy," Cade said as he grasped hold of my arm and pulled me away from Aiden. Our feet slapped off of the concrete as we raced down the tunnel but the creatures were closing in on us. There was no way we'd all make it back through that small hole in the wall of debris. I wasn't even sure we'd make it back to the pile of rubble.

"Here! Here!" I could hear Abby's frantic cries, but I had no idea where she was in all of the chaos and noise.

Darnell jerked his head to the left. "This way!" he barked.

I jumped and leapt over rotting body parts as we followed Darnell's zigzagging route through the tunnel. Flashlights bobbed and weaved as they cast shadows over the walls in a disconcerting pattern that made my head throb. Abby and Molly came into view amidst the anarchy. They were standing on the concrete walkway that ran along the side of the tunnel. Barney was pressed firmly against Abby's side, his ears raised, and his hair standing up as he let out three rapid barks. It was one of the few times I'd ever heard him make a sound. Aiden and Jenna grabbed hold of the metal railings and squeezed through the bars to join them on the walkway. Lloyd was standing beside a door, his gun raised as he fired at something behind us.

"Hurry!" Abby screamed. "Bethany *hurry!*"

The urgency in Abby's voice pushed me even faster. Aiden pushed Abby and Molly through the door. Jenna, Bret and Barney were close on their heels. We were still a few feet away from the walkway when Cade grabbed hold of my waist, lifted me up, and threw me over top of the railing. I stumbled, nearly fell, but was held up by the wall I fell against. The breath was robbed from me by the strength he'd just exhibited.

I went to spin toward him, but his chest pressed against my back as he wrapped his arm around my waist and propelled me forward. He was practically carrying me toward the door, apparently more concerned with my survival than with anyone finding his amazing burst of strength strange and out of the ordinary. Although, no one was paying any attention to us as they scrambled through the doorway. Darnell fired another round of bullets from inside the door, Aiden leaned out and grasped hold of my arms as Cade roughly pushed me toward the doorway.

"Wait! Wait!" Liz cried as she emerged from the darkness.

I shook Aiden off and lurched back toward the tunnel. Cade caught hold of me and lifted me against his chest as he pulled me away from the door. "We can't leave her!" I gasped.

I saw the hesitation, doubt and lack of compassion in his eyes when they met mine. I thought he was going to ignore my plea but he turned around and made his way toward the doorway. Darnell and Lloyd stepped closer to the opening. The echoes of their shots ran throughout the tunnel, but it was obvious that their bullets were doing little to frighten the stampeding monsters honing in on Liz.

A wailing scream pierced the air, I'd never thought a human could make that kind of sound as it grew in intensity and reverberated through the suddenly hushed tunnel. Lloyd and Darnell had their fingers still on their triggers but no more rounds were fired. The rising shriek began to hit glass shattering levels but I refused to leave her out there alone. We had given up on so much already; I wasn't going to give up on Liz too. I jerked my arm free and leapt away from Aiden.

Cade spun toward me as Darnell and Lloyd rapidly retreated from the door. "Wait! Liz!" I cried.

"No!" Cade roared as he pulled me back.

Liz's tortured scream abruptly broke off. Tears sprang to my eyes but instead of trying to break free of Cade I clung to his arms as revulsion swamped me. No one drew a breath in the hush that followed as we waited expectantly for something more, but there was only the unearthly quiet and the knowledge of what it signified. Darnell, the first to recover, slammed the door shut. Something bounced against the door and rattled it savagely within its frame.

I couldn't see the door but I didn't think it would hold up under the assault being waged against it on the other side. The heavy breathing of exhausted lungs was loud within the room as people pressed against me on both sides, but for some reason I didn't feel claustrophobic in the crammed confines. All I felt was numb and yet strangely secure as Cade held me closer to his side.

"Who still has a light?" Darnell demanded.

A light flickered from somewhere near the front of the group. A muscle twitched in Cade's cheek as his midnight gaze raked me up and down. His arm twisted within my grasp so that his hands seized hold of mine, he turned them over to examine my skin. A small tremor shook his hands before he steadied himself with a deep breath and his gaze came back to mine.

"I'm fine," I whispered. "Not a mark on me."

"Yes," he murmured but he didn't look appeased. Instead he looked as if he was about to rip this entire room apart as rigidity kept a firm hold on his muscles.

"What is this?" Molly inquired.

I tore my attention away from Cade to take in the room. There was barely enough room to stretch my arms out between the walls as the room was full of pipes and large pieces of machinery. "Appears to be a maintenance room," Lloyd muttered as he pushed through the remaining people in the room.

Darnell clicked a lock into place as another crash echoed throughout the room. He remained leaning against the door for a second before straightening himself. "Is everyone here?" I asked.

"All that are left," Private Frank Smith answered after some hesitation.

I shuddered at the reminder of the loss of Liz and Mick, but one thing these past couple months had taught me was that there was never any time for the dead. There was only time to pick up and move on if we were going to survive.

Lloyd moved further into the room and disappeared amongst some of the machinery. "You see anything Lloyd?" Darnell demanded after another crash shook the door.

Those things were all too big to fit through that doorway, but it didn't mean their tentacles couldn't. My hands tensed on Cade's, I closed my eyes as I tried to control the rolling panic that swelled up my throat. I had been doing well until now; I had to remain that way if I planned to keep control of my sanity and not freak anyone else out. I just had to take it one breath at a time. We would not die in this cramped room, desperate, starving, and God only knew how far below the surface of the earth.

"Lloyd?" Darnell called.

"There's a door back here and some stairs that lead down." The steps led *deeper* into the earth. I opened my eyes to find that Lloyd had returned. Another crash echoed through the room, followed by an ominous splintering sound that caused my jaw to clench. "Let's go."

I could do this. I didn't have a choice. I swallowed heavily, straightened my shoulders and followed Aiden as he shuffled forward. My brother stretched his hand back and I eagerly clasped hold of it. I didn't know where we were going but I was certain that it would only get worse before it got better.

CHAPTER 4

The stairs creaked and groaned like they were some prop in a B horror movie as we slowly made our descent. "What is this?" Jenna asked.

"Must be some kind of passageway for the workers," Darnell answered.

"Where does it go?"

Darnell didn't respond to her second question. My grasp was so firm on the metal rail running beside the stairs that my knuckles ached and my palm was leaving a trail of sweat behind. The dim glow of the flashlights illuminated the damp concrete walls surrounding us. "We're not the first ones to come down here recently," Lloyd said.

"How do you know that?" Molly inquired.

"There's no dust on the railing or the steps."

I frowned at the railing and then tilted my head back to look at the shaded light fixtures above us. They were coated with a layer of dust, and cobwebs hung from the ceiling in straggling, broken strands. Neither of those things was on the stairs or railing though.

"There must have been survivors from the tunnel," I guessed.

"Or the group split before the attack, and some came this way while others chose to stay behind," Cade muttered.

"Or this only dead ends or leads to another trap," Lloyd said.

I frowned at the back of Lloyd's head nearly half a flight below me at the front of the group. I knew we had to be practical, but I couldn't bring myself to think about what the consequences of his words implied. "Who brought Mr. Pessimism to the party?" Jenna retorted.

Lloyd paused and turned to face everyone behind him. "I'm just being realistic. You all have to be prepared for what might be at the end of these stairs."

When I had first met Lloyd his reddish hair, freckles, soft blue eyes, and glasses had made him appear younger than his twenty years. He'd been less jaded than the other battle hardened soldiers surrounding him. That youthfulness had vanished now as the lines around his eyes and mouth made him appear years older and more rigid than a steel beam.

He had changed so much in the past six weeks, but as I looked at the group surrounding me I realized that we had all changed. It wasn't only the streaks of dirt, the tattered clothing, the scratches, bruises, or scars we had all acquired that had altered our appearances. It was the knowledge of what we'd seen and endured, and everything we had lost. Our eyes were haunted, our faces thinner, our bodies leaner and there was an aged wisdom to all of us, including Abby.

Except for the soldiers, and perhaps Cade, none of us had had any knowledge of battle, much less any experience in fighting one. A gun had been a foreign object, and walking was something that the aliens had forced upon us when all modes of transportation had been barred. Now, most of us were at least decent with a gun, if not proficient. Walking miles upon miles had become a daily way of life, and no one complained about blisters or sore feet anymore. Hot showers and meals were a thing of the past. A cold rinse off, a can of peas, and a piece of meat were a new heaven that I often longed for. Homes had become temporary shelters that simply housed the relics of their former owners.

We were all different. We were all more callous. I just didn't know if that was good or bad. We had to be more thick-skinned to survive and in order to keep our sanity. *But did it mean losing our humanity in the process? In order to survive were we becoming more like the emotionless, cruel aliens that had driven us beneath the earth?*

I was struck immobile by the aversion curdling through my stomach at the thought. We were still there for each other, we still protected and cared for each other but would we continue to do so? Just a little over two months had changed us into people that I barely recognized anymore. What would another two months do to us? What would more losses take from us? Would we still care for each other, or would each new loss make us less and less human until the only thing we cared about was ourselves?

I felt weighted down by the questions and frightened by the lack of answers. There was no way to know what would become of us. No way to know if we would live or die, or if we would even be worth saving in the end. I certainly hoped we would be. We had to be stronger, remorseless, but if we were like the aliens in the end I would prefer it if we just simply died out ourselves. I felt that death may be less of a loss than the actual loss of our compassion and everything else that made us human.

If I ever became like that then it would mean that Aiden, Abby, Cade, and every other person with us now would be dead. There would be no point in carrying on after that. I loved life, even this twisted version of it, but when there was no one and nothing left to live for, I didn't think I could continue to love it. It was a future I didn't want to think about, but it was a very real possibility and it could be waiting for all of us at the bottom of these stairs.

Lloyd started moving again. Cade rested his hand on my shoulder and squeezed it as he sensed my sudden distress. "Door," Lloyd announced.

"Large enough for two to go through?" Darnell inquired from the rear.

"Yes. Frank and I will go!"

We were stuck in the middle of the stairwell, completely trapped if there was something beyond that door. I leaned over the side of the railing but I could barely see Lloyd and Frank on either side of the door. There was no way I would be able to see what was on the other side of it. Frank nodded to Lloyd, twisted the handle and flung the door open. They disappeared into the void beyond.

I leaned over the rail, bending awkwardly as my feet came off the ground a little. Cade wrapped his hand into my waistband and held me against the rail as I leaned over even further. I held my breath in anticipation; the only sound I could hear was the loud thump of blood rushing through my ears. Molly and Justin, a young man in his twenties, were pressed firmly against the wall at the bottom of the stairwell.

Mark stood behind them, his sons Sam and Matt were protectively pushed behind his body. They were the only family unit, besides my own, that had opted to stay with us when others in the group had chosen to leave after Ian's unexplained death. Mark, a man in his early forties, had decided that the benefit of staying with the guns and troops was better than the risk that one of us may be a killer.

I was well aware of the fact that a few of them suspected Cade, and though they were right, I wasn't about to tell them that he *had* killed Ian, but he had only done it to save my life. They would understand that, but they would *not* understand that Cade wasn't like us, that he wasn't human and I worried that they would be scared of him and hate him. They may even try to hurt him. Maybe, after time, they would come to understand and accept him but I wasn't going to do anything that would risk Cade's life, or anyone else's.

Matt held a hand back for Abby, who grasped hold of it. He was a year younger than her at fourteen, but he was cute with his light brown hair and twinkling brown eyes. The relationship between them had grown since we'd entered Boston. At first I'd thought I should be concerned, but I'd realized that although she was only fifteen, Abby was far older and wiser than her years. She knew what she was doing, but even still I was going to talk to her as soon as I got a chance alone with her. Aiden seemed to have come to the same conclusion as I'd caught him watching them closely too, but he had yet to say anything about it.

"Bethany!" Cade growled.

I realized that I was nearly flipped over the railing now as I strained to see anything outside of the door. I silently thanked his strength as I used my arms, and his helping hand, to pull myself back over the railing. I cast an apologetic smile at him that he returned with a raised eyebrow and an admonishing shake of his head.

Lloyd half stepped back into the doorway. "It's clear," he announced.

"Move out!" Darnell ordered crisply.

Everyone trudged down the stairs and out the door. I was one of the last ones through and I stopped so abruptly that Darnell slammed into my back with a muffled curse. The force of his body rocked me forward but my feet remained planted in place. Cade stretched a hand back for me and frowned as he realized I wasn't beside him anymore.

I finally managed to move by taking another step back into Darnell. "Bethany!" he barked from behind me. "Damn it, *move*." I stepped to the side to allow him enough room to slip by me. He gave me a disgruntled look that quickly faded. "Bethany?"

I shook my head. My hands fisted so firmly that my nails dug into my palms. It was dark, so enclosed. *So tight!* The walls were within arm's reach and there was no way to know where the passageway went as shadows enshrouded it. The air was so heavy with moisture that my hair stuck to the nape of my neck almost instantly. The smell of it brought to mind images of crypts as mildew and the scent of decay hung heavily in the air.

Darnell took a step toward me, but Cade moved in front of him. He took hold of my hands, but I couldn't get them to unclench even though my nails were digging into my skin and my blood was filling my clamped hands. Cade seemed to blend into the shadows surrounding him. *He was part of the dark,* I realized with a moan that didn't escape my clamped lips.

Closing my eyes, I inhaled deeply. I could do this, I *had* to do this, but once it was over I was going to allow myself some time for the meltdown I was going to have at the end of it.

My hands uncurled. Cade's eyes narrowed and blackened at the sight of the blood trickling from my self-inflicted wounds. I reached out to try and calm him but he took a small step away from me. There would be no comforting him right now. In fact, I was only agitating him more. I closed my hands and pressed them against my side to staunch the blood seeping out.

I knew he was dying to get away from me but he stayed by my side. "I'm ok," I breathed.

He managed a feeble smile. "You're strong Bethany."

"So are you Cade."

His eyes lit with amusement. "Like a rock," he said with a wink.

I couldn't help but smile at him as some of the tension in my chest began to ease. For a moment I could almost believe that we weren't trapped here, that he was human, and that none of this awfulness had happened. I could almost believe that I'd simply caught him watching me in the hall once more, but this time I'd actually had the nerve to smile at him instead of shyly looking away.

Then motion behind him caught my attention. The moment faded as I realized that everyone was waiting for us, and that all of them were watching us with a mixture of curiosity and suspicion. I took a deep breath, wiped my hands once more, and stepped away from the wall I had plastered myself against.

"Well let's see where this goes," Darnell said as he propped his gun against his shoulder.

Cade's fingers wrapped through mine. An electrical current rushed up my arm from where we touched as we made our way cautiously down the dark hallway. It became so restricted in some areas that Cade and some of the others had to turn sideways in order to fit through the winding passage.

"What is this?" I heard Abby breathe from ahead.

"Boston's an old city; I imagine there are thousands of tunnels and passageways we don't know about." Bret's answer was muffled by the concrete wall nearly pressed against his face as he slid sideways.

"Opening!" Lloyd called back.

The breath I didn't know I'd been holding exploded out of me. We stepped onto a platform and fanned out as everyone moved to the side to make room for each other. My eyes widened, my mouth parted on a small puff of air. "What is this?" Jenna whispered.

I stared at the tracks, faded posters, and broken signs in awe. I could barely make out the colors and lines on one sign and had no idea what it was supposed to be. Another sign boasted the faded picture of women in bathing suits drinking beer, and yet another advertised a luxury car.

"It is part of the T line, or it was," Bret said slowly.

"It's nothing like I remember," Jenna breathed.

I'd never seen the commuter line that ran through Boston and the surrounding towns and I definitely never would have come here *willingly*. The station we were standing in was shaded and dirty, but I could picture how different it must have been before the aliens had banned all forms of transportation. I could almost see the people pushing and shoving, jostling about as they tried to get through the daily grind of their lives.

The thought made my skin crawl but at the same time I was filled with amazement. I would have hated being surrounded by all those people, but it would have been wonderful to have the simplicity of the every day, average life once more. It would have been breathtaking to see the train arrive through the underground tunnel and to watch the people move about with the confidence that came from their routine. There was so much that we had all taken for granted, and now it was gone.

"The stairway is blocked." Lloyd was standing by a pile of rubble as he surveyed it. I hadn't even realized that there had once been a stairwell there until now. It was obstructed by concrete and rock that blended seamlessly into the darkness.

"Did the survivors do it?" Frank inquired.

"Doesn't look like it. The walls look like they were exploded inward."

"To keep people out?"

"Or to keep them in," Molly breathed.

I shuddered at the thought. We didn't have many supplies left, if we couldn't get out…

My gaze slid to Cade. His shoulders were thrust back and his eyes narrowed as he stared at the wall of debris. "Can we dig our way out?" Darnell inquired.

Lloyd shook his head. "Even if this was just one flight of stairs, and not two or three, it would still take at least a week."

At most, if we were conservative, we had enough supplies for a week. We didn't have the supplies it would take to fuel us digging through that rubble though. Sweat trickled over my arms and forehead. We were trapped like rats in a maze. It was no surprise those things just hung around in the tunnel up there, they must know that there was a good chance we would reemerge.

"It looks like we're heading for the tracks then," Aiden said. He was staring at a faded poster with squiggly colored lines going across it. I moved closer to him as he wiped the dirt and dust off the glass plating. It appeared to be a map of some kind as he traced one of the lines and nodded to himself before stepping away. "Right now we're on the junction of the red and green line, but if we go down a little bit we can meet up with the orange line. That will either take us out or hook us up with the blue line."

Everyone stared at him like he'd just started speaking French. "Which means?" Bret finally prompted.

"Both those lines lead out of the city and are the only routes that won't have us backtracking into territory we already know is deadly."

"And if they're blocked?" Lloyd asked.

Aiden ran a hand through his tussled hair and shook his head. "There are no other options, at all, unless you want to go back into that crap up above. We have the orange or the blue line."

No one spoke as they absorbed the full impact of his words. Cade was the first to recover. "Which way?"

"I'm pretty sure it's right."

"Pretty sure?" I asked.

"It's really faded Bethy and I don't know the T routes. I can't pinpoint where we are exactly but I'll know within the next hundred yards. If we make it to the next station and it's the wrong one we'll just have to turn around."

"We'll be fine," I assured him.

He nodded, but his eyes appeared distant and unfocused. "We'll be fine."

I squeezed his arm, ashamed of the fact that I hadn't realized just how rattled Aiden was. This was the first chip I'd seen in his armor since we'd descended into this hell. Aiden squeezed my hand, closed his eyes, and took a deep breath before he spoke again. "Right. We have to go right. We're going to have to take a left after and then we'll have a choice of which way to go. There should be other maps along the way."

"Let's go then," Lloyd commanded.

Lloyd jumped onto the train tracks and lifted his gun as he made his way forward. *Well at least it's more open through here*, I thought as I followed them.

CHAPTER 5

"Drop your weapons! Drop them! Drop them!"

I barely had time to register the barked orders before Cade grabbed hold of me and shoved me behind him. I stumbled and had just recovered when the first bullet flew. A startled shout escaped me as Cade drug me down and pinned me to the ground beneath his body. "Stay down!"

"Cade!" He didn't hear my terrified gasp as he pushed himself off of me and disappeared.

I rolled over as another shot reverberated through the tunnel. Abby let out a shrill scream that propelled me back to my feet. My heart was almost bursting in my chest as I ran toward where I'd last seen her. Arms wrapped around my waist and pulled me to the ground. A low groan escaped me, my body protested the impact and I just barely stopped my chin from smacking off the ground.

I was so dazed that it took me a second to realize the gentle doctor had been the one to take me down. I wrestled to squirm free of Bishop's hold as he clutched tenaciously at my waist.

"Abby! Aiden!" I screamed as another bullet zinged off the concrete walls and echoed down the tunnel.

"Bethany!" Bishop grunted as I continued to squirm beneath him.

"Let go!" I spat and forcefully shoved back with my feet.

He let go as I caught him under the jaw with enough force to make his head snap back a little. I felt a twinge of regret but it didn't stop me. I liked Bishop, I really did, but he was keeping me from my siblings and that was *not* going to happen.

I moved forward on my belly as I sought out Abby and Aiden. Another round of gunfire pierced the air. I cried out and flung my hands over my head as the bullets rattled down the side of the tunnel. Sparks flew as they ricocheted rapidly back and forth.

"Cease fire! Cease fire!" Darnell's shout was followed by a dull thud that made my skin crawl. The air seemed even heavier as an eerie hush descended over the tunnel. I lifted my head and blinked against the blaze of light as more flashlights clicked on. Through the smoky haze created by the gunfire I spotted Cade standing about thirty feet away, a gun clasped in his hand as he stared down at the crumpled body of a young man. For one heart stopping second I thought he was going to launch himself at the boy and drain him dry. Then, ever so deliberately, he placed the gun down and leaned it against the wall.

I looked away from Cade to find Aiden five feet away from me. He studied Cade like he was one of Bishop's specimens before he turned toward me. Aiden's brown eyes were penetrating and I found myself frozen beneath the weight of his gaze. He didn't know what it was about Cade that troubled him so much, not yet, but I didn't think it would be long before his mind started to wander down new pathways, and those pathways were sure to bring him to one conclusion.

Cade wasn't human.

I forced my attention away from Aiden and pushed myself to my feet. Lifting my hand, I wiped away the wetness I felt trickling down my cheek. I wasn't prepared for the blood that glimmered on the tips of my fingers when I pulled my hand away. I didn't know what had happened to cause it, perhaps I'd been scratched during my scuffle with Bishop.

"Impressive." Darnell was oblivious to the tension within the tunnel as he made his way to Cade. He stepped over the young man sprawled face down on the ground. The man had been sheltered within a side tunnel, one that was smaller than the one we were in. It appeared to be a water runoff tunnel, or maybe even something for the workers to maneuver through. "Ballsy."

Cade shrugged absently and kneeling down, he pulled some bandages from the bag at his feet before returning to me. "What did you do?" I whispered to him.

"Just knocked him out."

"How did you get to him?"

Midnight eyes blazed into mine as they ran lovingly over my face. "Luck."

I closed my eyes and took a deep breath. We both knew that it hadn't been luck, that he had just risked exposing himself, or getting himself killed. He clasped hold of my chin and turned my head to the side. "I'm fine. It's just a scratch."

"It's pretty deep," he mumbled. Though I knew my blood was as tempting as the forbidden fruit to him, he didn't hesitate to tenderly clean and bandage the cut.

A low moan brought our attention back to the young man. Darnell knelt by his side and fisted a hand in his shirt. "You mind telling me why you shot at us?" he demanded.

The young man just blinked as he opened and closed his mouth. He seemed to have forgotten where he was or what was going on. There was a large bump already forming in the middle of his forehead. By tomorrow it would be completely black and blue and probably the size of a golf ball.

"How many fingers am I holding up?" Darnell shoved three fingers in front of the man's face. The man blinked at them before closing his eyes and shaking his head. "Bishop, I think he has a concussion."

"I'd say you're right," Bishop agreed. He slid by Cade and me to kneel next to Darnell. "You hit him pretty hard."

"Next time I'll be nicer to the person shooting at us," Cade retorted.

Bishop shot him a nasty look while Darnell smirked and even Aiden broke into a smile. "Can you tell me your name?" Bishop demanded as he turned his attention back to the injured man.

The kid just blinked again, opened his mouth and closed it. "His name's Dan."

We all jumped as a woman slid from the shadows of the side tunnel. She was tall and lean, with an athletic grace that reminded me of a jungle cat getting ready to strike. The dim light flashed off of her ebony skin and highlighted the striking beauty of her refined features and chocolate eyes. Her hair was cropped close to her head and a dirty blue bandanna was wrapped around it.

"And I'm Arlene." Darnell grasped his gun as he rose to survey the newest arrival. Cade took a small step forward and nudged me behind him with his shoulder. I scowled at his back but didn't argue with him, it wouldn't do me any good right now anyway. "What did you do to him?"

"Knocked out, probably a concussion," Bishop answered. "He'll be fine."

"You didn't have to hurt him." Though Arlene's posture seemed almost casual, there was an air of tension and anticipation surrounding her. I suspected she was a lot faster than she was trying to portray as she leaned back on her heels and watched us.

"He shot at us, for no reason," Darnell informed her.

"You're in *our* tunnel," she retorted.

"I didn't realize that it had been claimed," Darnell grated.

Arlene grinned disarmingly but the tension in her shoulders didn't ease. "We take what we can get now, you know. Dan didn't mean any harm but we've had problems down here with people trying to steal our supplies."

I felt like a bug that had just walked into a spider's web and I kept waiting for the trap to spring as I searched the shadows. "We're not here to take anything of yours," Darnell assured her.

Arlene nodded but her eyes lingered on the weapons we held. "I'm sure," she finally responded.

"We really aren't a threat," Aiden insisted.

Arlene's gaze flickered to Dan. "You see our weapons if we wanted him dead, he would be," Cade grated.

Arlene's eyes once again searched us before her shoulders relaxed and she lowered the rifle to her side. "Have you seen any aliens down here?" Darnell inquired.

Arlene shook her head as she rested her hands on her slender hips. "I haven't seen them since we were driven down here."

"You were in the tunnel above?"

Something sinister slithered through her eyes as her lip curled in a sneer. "Until they broke through. They don't seem to be able to make it down here though."

"Yet," Lloyd said.

Her head bowed. "Yet," she agreed. "But we're better prepared for them now. You were also in the tunnel?"

"Unfortunately," Bret said.

"I know what you mean." She studied all of us again. "You look like you could use some rest, a shower maybe."

I grasped hold of Cade's arm; excitement spurted through me at the possibility of a shower. "You're willing to trust us now?" Lloyd demanded.

Arlene shrugged absently. "Well if your uniforms are any indication than you're a couple of soldiers, shouldn't I trust the military?"

"I'm not sure I'd trust anyone anymore," Lloyd muttered.

"That's true, but you don't seem like some of the gangsters, druggies, or thieves we've run into. If you were like any of them Dan *would* be dead. You look like you need a break. We've been there before."

Three more people emerged from the shadows as she finished speaking. They had blended in with the dark so completely that I hadn't noticed them until they moved. The only one who didn't take a step back from them was Cade as he remained unmoving before me. "We have a place where you can stay for a bit. Eat, rest, if you would like."

"Sounds good," Darnell agreed, but he kept hold of his gun as he studied the three men behind Arlene now. She was willing to trust us, but were we willing to trust them? "How many of you are there?"

"Not as many as you. Come on."

"Arlene," one of the strangers grumbled at her.

"It's fine Lyle. They're just looking for a safe place. You might want to help out Dan though; he's going to have a bad headache come morning."

"That's for sure," Bishop agreed.

CHAPTER 6

I dropped the towel on the pile of blankets that had been set up in my "room." Really, it was just a small space blocked off by sheets hanging from the ceiling in order to offer some form of privacy. It was the most I'd had in months though, and it was fantastic. Cade had set it up while I'd been in the shower. It wasn't a real shower in the technical sense of the word, but a broken pipe that spit out luke warm water that felt like heaven. As had the single bar of soap I'd used to wash my body and hair with. I smelled like lavender, a scent I normally despised, but I found myself inhaling deeply and repeatedly now.

I'd handed my stench laden clothes over to be burned afterward. There was no washing the filth or blood out of them. Arlene had given me a set of relatively clean clothes in exchange. The jeans had a hole in the knee, and they were too big on me, as was the plain maroon shirt, but I didn't care. I almost felt human again, almost felt like a *girl* again.

It had been a long time since I'd experienced either of those things.

Cade had set the blankets up apart from the others at the far end of the tunnel, but there was no one around now anyway. They'd all been gathered in the main room, getting to know each other, when I'd left. The tunnel was lit every thirty feet by flashlights that had been hung from the ceiling. They cast a circle of yellowish light on the floor and constantly swayed in a nearly imperceptible air current. I tried not to think about the walls surrounding me, but I was acutely aware of the stale air and the ground pressing above me.

I settled onto the blankets and savored in the simple act of being alone. It had been so long that I'd almost forgotten what it was like to simply just *be*. I wasn't fooled into thinking that we were safe down here, but it was the safest I'd felt since all of this had started.

I knew Cade was there even before the sheet was pulled back to reveal him. I'd know the nearly soundless tread of his step, a step I was certain most of the others would never pick up on, anywhere. A tread I was certain I never would have picked up on before consuming his blood.

I refused to think about it, refused to acknowledge the changes within my body. I hadn't spoken to Cade about them yet, I knew I should but I couldn't get the words to leave my throat. I'd just gotten him back; I wasn't ready to put a damper on the joy that still came with that reunion.

We'd spent many nights wrapped in each other's arms, but there had also been twenty other people with us. We were alone right now, in my simple sheeted room. The half smile slid from his face as something else sprang forth and he began to stare at me like I was the last peanut butter cup on earth.

A shiver raced up my spine as my throat went dry. He didn't move, didn't come any closer as he stood in the "doorway." There would be no turning back after this, if I reached out to him now things would never be the same, but it was going to have to be me that made the move. He wouldn't come unless I offered myself to him, not because he didn't want me, but simply because this had to be my choice.

I knew what he needed from me; I could see it in the lines on his face and the harsh set of his jaw. I'd offered myself to him before, but this time I knew he wouldn't turn me down. This time there was nowhere else to go, nothing else to turn to for the soul and blood that he required.

I savored in the harsh beauty of his carved cheekbones, full lips, and midnight hair and eyes as I tried to control my leaping excitement and alarm. I forced the lump in my throat down as I stretched my hand out to him.

"I didn't come here for this," he grated out from behind clenched teeth.

"I know." The corded muscles in his lean arms stood out as his hand clenched on the sheet and he glanced behind him. I rushed on before he took off on me. "It's only a matter of time Cade before it happens anyway. I... I want to know what it feels like and I'm here. There's no one else..."

"There are others," he whispered.

"Cade." I wasn't going to spend time arguing with him. "This wasn't why you came here but it's why you're still standing here."

He eyed me like a deadly cobra as I rose to my feet and took a step toward him. I was convinced he would bolt as I moved closer to him, rested my hand on his arm, and pulled it toward me. There was so much strength in the corded wrist I held before me, even more than met the eye as I knew what was inside of him, I knew what he was capable of, and what it took for him to suppress it as he stood before me. *If he ever let himself go...*

I broke the thought off. There was no room here for fear. Though he resisted it, he finally allowed me to pry his fist open and lift his palm to my cheek. "Bethany..."

I stood on tip toe to press a kiss against his compressed lips. He remained unrelenting for a moment and then the sheet fell into place with a rustle as he released it. His hands grasped my waist with the speed of a striking shark. A startled sound escaped me as he lifted me up. Instinctively, my legs wrapped around his waist as his hand entwined in my hair and he kissed me with an urgency that stole the breath from me. His tongue swept in to taste the deep recesses of my mouth in sure, strident thrusts that left me trembling and aching for more as I pressed closer to him.

Inhaling deeply I relished in the fresh scent of him. His hair was still wet and tussled from his shower as my fingers slid through it. On him however, the scent of soap was faint as it mingled with the enticing aroma he emitted. We were far from outside, yet the scent of the outdoors clung to him, making him seem even more wild and dangerous.

Those eyes were entirely black as he pulled back to look at me. The veins in his face were visible as the darkness residing within him spread throughout his body, but instead of finding it hideous or frightening, I found myself loving him even more as my fingers trailed over a vein that ran from his forehead, down his cheek, to his lips. All of this was always within him, he could easily kill any one of us, and yet he was still looking at me as if I were the most priceless artifact in the world.

My chest heaved as I struggled to catch my breath and control the desire thrumming through me. I knew what he needed from me, but right now all I craved was *him*. His hand traced over my cheek and skimmed down to the base of my throat. His breath was warm against my cheek, his body slid tantalizingly against mine as he slowly lowered me to my feet.

Tingles slid over my skin as his fingers traced my collarbone. My heart lurched with excitement, my body yearned for something more, something I instinctively knew that only he could ease. I didn't see the walls surrounding us, didn't smell the stale air as everything in me was focused on *him*.

"Lovely," he whispered against me. "*My* lovely."

"Yes," I breathed. I felt disoriented and out of my depth as my head spun. I didn't know what I was saying yes to anymore and right now I didn't care.

His lips were a bare whisper against my cheek as they moved over me. I leaned closer to him, my hands clenched upon his arms as I sought something to help keep me grounded. Touching him though was like seizing hold of a lightning bolt as it had the absolute opposite effect on me. I had to swallow in order to wet my suddenly parched throat.

I was tingling all over, my body felt strangely malleable. I was putty in his hands and he knew it.

A low growl escaped him, his hand wrapped around my neck as he held me against him. With my cheek pressed against his chest I was able to hear the forceful beats of his heart. His scent was stronger, heightened by his passion as his fingers caressed the nape of my neck and his muscles stood out rigidly against me. He was still fighting his urges and I didn't understand why.

"Bethany."

"It's ok." He had come here in order to satisfy one hunger but I knew now he would be taking two things from me tonight. "I want this. I want *you*."

"It wasn't supposed to be like this. Not here."

"I know."

"Somewhere else…" He said the words, he meant them, but his restraint was unraveling. "Somewhere better. Somewhere special."

"There may not be somewhere else, or some other day."

It had been the wrong thing to say as black raced through the veins in his arms and his hand clenched briefly on my neck. The midnight of his veins was stark now as he pulled back to look down at me. It was such a disconcerting thing to see, but I didn't find it ugly or frightening. In fact, I now found the color in him beautiful even though I knew that it meant the man standing before me, the man I loved with all my heart and soul, wasn't human.

"I'll keep you safe," he grated.

I nibbled at his full bottom lip as I sought to ease his ire and bring back the passionate man that had just been embracing me. We both knew he would die to keep me safe, just as we both knew there was a chance that we wouldn't survive this; that our time together may be coming to an end. I intended to savor every second we had and hold onto him for as long as I could.

His mouth yielded to my kisses as his tongue swept back in and he deepened the kiss. A low moan escaped me; goose bumps broke out on my skin as his hands slid under my shirt and stroked over my stomach before traveling upward. He caressed me until my muscles were nothing but liquid and I was certain that I was going to fall apart or scream from the sheer wonder of it all.

"Bethany," he groaned as he lifted me up and laid me down on the blankets. I had the strangest sensation of falling apart and coming back together again as his warm body settled over top of mine. I couldn't get enough of touching his supple skin that bunched and flexed beneath my palms as my hands roamed over his body.

His breathing was harsh in my ear as his lips left a trail from my collarbone to my ear. We had never let things get this far before, and yet I felt no apprehension or hesitance as he sat back and pulled my shirt off. I fought the instinctive urge to cover myself from his heated gaze as it raked me from head to toe.

Though, I fought not to let it, heat flared into my cheeks and crept over my body as I looked away from his intense gaze. To me, Cade was nearly perfect with his carved body and stunning face. I was plain in comparison, too thin from lack of food. Scarred and battered from everything that had occurred over the past few months. I knew that he loved me with everything he had; I just didn't want him to see all of my blatant imperfections now that I was bared to him. I felt raw and exposed in a way that I never had before.

He pulled my hand away when I finally gave into my embarrassment and tried to cover myself. "Cade…"

"You're beautiful Bethany." I shook my head and bit my bottom lip as I fought against all of my insecurities. "Simply beautiful."

I shivered as his mouth left a hot trail across my raw skin. I forgot all about my uncertainty as he loved and kissed me into blissful oblivion again and made me come alive in ways that I never knew I could. I couldn't possibly know loss or terror here. Not even when he lost partial control of the darkness inside of him, and his eyes became entirely black once more. I eased the torment within him as I took his darkness into me and allowed him to lose himself completely within my body, as I lost myself in his.

I lay shaken and awed afterward, humbled by the love I sensed within him as he kissed me tenderly and rubbed my skin in tempting swirls that made me sigh with pleasure. He produced one of his knives and looked at me questioningly as he held my wrist before him. My heart raced but I managed a small nod.

He pressed the blade to my skin but didn't draw it across as his hand began to tremble. I wrapped my hand around his. "Bethany..."

"It's ok."

I winced as I pushed the blade into my skin. The muscles in Cade's arms stood out as his body was swamped with black at the sight and smell of my blood. Any rational human being would have tried to move away from him, I moved closer.

I felt no revulsion as his heated mouth wrapped around my wrist and his eyes lifted to mine. My fingers twitched and I couldn't stop myself from stroking the black lines coursing through his face. He drank my blood in deep, gulping pulls that made my heart race while his eyes remained locked on mine.

He pulled away from me and wiped the blood from his mouth. His hand fisted in my hair as he pulled me closer and kissed me with a passion that made my fingers curl into his flesh. I was trying to catch my breath when he pulled away and pressed a tender kiss to my nose.

My muscles quivered as he curled around my back and pulled me snuggly against him. Even beneath all the concrete and earth I felt secure within the arms wrapped around me. I'd never felt so whole, so complete, and so humbled and vulnerable as he whispered that he loved me.

I'd felt the darkness creep out of him, and though I knew he would never do anything to injure me, I'd felt it slip into me and latch onto my soul. It hadn't hurt though, not like it had when Ian had attacked me and forced his blackness into me. It had felt entirely right and complete with Cade. I would have to ask him about why it hadn't hurt with him, but I was too warm and comfortable at the moment, too secure to think about anything other than the wondrous joy suffusing me right now.

I was certain that Cade had taken a piece of my soul but even more disturbing was the realization that I had willingly given it to him. I had just eased all of Cade's hungers but what would happen when mine reawakened. I'd been able to get my hands on raw meat once in awhile up above but down here there may not be any way to do so. A shudder ran through me, my hand tightened around Cade's, I opened my mouth to tell him what was going on within me, to finally unburden myself when he released a small snore.

CHAPTER 7

Cade's body seemed to fairly vibrate with tension as he stood before me with his arms folded over his chest, his jaw clenched and his eyes hooded as he listened to Arlene. "There is only one way out," Arlene was explaining. "Unless you would like to go back into the tunnel above. About ten miles from here the line splits. You're going to have to go to the right; the left is blocked after a mile. The line used to go above ground again, but that way is also blocked now."

"Then how do we get out?" Lloyd asked.

"There's a ventilation shaft." My heart pounded out a rapid staccato against my ribs as my breath rushed out of me. It was bad enough being down here, but to be trapped within a *shaft*. Just the thought of being in yet another small, confined space made me break into a cold sweat which was now trickling down my back. "It leads into a manhole. You can access the street from there."

"How do you know this?" Cade inquired.

"We've been up through there. Some people have chosen to move on, and we send out a scouting party once every two weeks for food and supplies. It's taking longer each time to find things."

"Why do you stay here?" I asked.

"Why not? We're safe here; we have shelter, running water and a shower. It's not ideal, but nothing is ideal anymore. Why do you want to go so badly?"

I glanced at the people surrounding me but no one seemed to have an answer other than living beneath the earth wasn't exactly the life that any of us aspired to. However, neither was being sucked dry by one of those monsters either. I couldn't embrace this world of shade, tunnels, walls, and rats. They may have security, no matter how temporary, but they had no freedom, no sunlight and no *air*. The last thing I wanted to do was stay down here, but I could tell that some of the others would like to.

"We're sending a scouting party out again next week; if you would like we can show you the way then, or you can go today. You are also welcome to stay, we could always use help with gathering supplies and defense. Things some of you appear to be very good at."

Looks were exchanged as muffled conversation filled the air. "Winter *is* coming," Justin said.

"We'll wait the week and then go up with you," Darnell suggested. "Perhaps we should at least stay for the winter, but we'll have to decide what we want to do together."

Cade's hand slipped into mine. He stepped closer to block me from everyone in the room as I fought to retain control of myself. I took a deep breath as my fingers clenched around his.

"There's no rush," Arlene said.

Cade nudged me toward the doorway. Neither of us was eager to stay in there and listen to what else was being said. He led me down the tunnel and into the smaller hall that housed the separated rooms. "Would you prefer to stay down here?" I whispered when we arrived at our sleeping area.

He took a deep breath as his fingers wrapped around my wrist. His thumb brushed over the mark the knife had left there as he pressed closer to me. Memories of him within me last night, touching my body and soul, came rushing back as I swayed toward him. I was suddenly frantic to have him enshroud and embrace me once more.

"It does seem safer," he said as his hand slid up my arm.

I had to force myself to pay attention to the conversation as his fingers trailed over my cheek. "They'll come here eventually. We can't stay hidden underground forever. Cade…"

"Not forever Bethany, but winter is coming and we have nowhere safe to stay right now."

He was right, I knew he was right, but I couldn't quell the panic rising up in me. "I want to go up with them."

His hand stilled on my cheek; I knew he didn't like the idea of me going, but I couldn't stay here when others were going to crawl to freedom in a week. I shuddered at the reminder that I would have to crawl through a vent, but I had gone through worse things before.

"We'll see…"

"I'm going Cade. I'll be fine," I added when he looked like he was getting ready to argue with me.

"Don't you think you're in enough danger with me around without throwing yourself into even more?"

I was taken aback by the question. "You're not a danger."

He rested his hands on either side of my head as he leaned closer to me. "I know what happened, Bethany. I know what I *did*. Do you honestly think I wouldn't know that I tasted a part of your soul?"

My heart raced as chills swept up and down my spine. I could barely breathe I was so spellbound and excited. "I'm fine."

His lips almost brushed against mine as he leaned closer to me. "You *know* what I did and yet you show no fear."

"There is nothing to fear, I wanted you to take a piece of my soul Cade. I offered myself to you and I wanted to know what it felt like."

He frowned severely at me as he moved back a little further. "I could kill you Bethany. I could drain you dry and there is nothing that you could do to stop me."

My hands fisted as I glared up at him. "You haven't hurt me Cade; it was nothing like when Ian had hold of me." I wrapped my arms around myself as I attempted to ease the sudden chill that crept through my bones at the memory.

I was so swamped with my own memories that I didn't notice the wrath that had crept over Cade until I felt the edges of it against my skin. I took an involuntary step back as my gaze landed on him. The veins in his face stood out starkly as they filled with black. It seeped down his neck and disappeared beneath his shirt only to reappear on his arms and the backs of his hands.

"That *never* should have happened to you. He never should have been able to touch you in such a way."

The snarled words caused the hair on the nape of my neck to stand up. "Cade…"

A gasp escaped me as he clutched my waist and lifted me against him. I barely had time to take a breath before his mouth claimed mine and whatever it was inside of him slipped into me. I arched against him as he filled my cells and seemed to pulsate through my blood. Warmth pooled through me and my toes curled as I felt part of him slither through my muscles and heat every atom it came in contact with. I drifted into him as I lost myself to his possession of me and the pleasure that came with the swirling combination of our souls.

His breathing was ragged as he pulled away and dropped his forehead against mine. "No survival instinct," he groaned.

My fingers drifted over his beloved face as I traced the contours I knew so well. "You didn't hurt me, you wouldn't."

"Bethany…"

"You didn't even take anything from me Cade."

His head shot up. "How do you know that?"

"I felt it when you did last night, here." I pressed his hand against my breast bone and held it near my heart. "I could feel that small bit you took…"

"I didn't mean to," his fingers curled in my hair as his lips brushed over mine.

"I was happy you did. Why doesn't it hurt with you when it did so badly with Ian?"

His muscles tensed at the reminder of Ian. "Because you're so damn willing to let me inside of you," he grated. "You don't fight me."

I shuddered, not from dread but from a burst of pure excitement. I took pleasure in the scent and feel of him as his arms slid possessively around me. "You're so easy to let in," I breathed.

I melted against him as I lost myself to the miracle that was everything about him, even the darkness that lured me forth like a clear pool on a hot summer day.

***

I couldn't see anything when I woke later, it took my eyes a few seconds to adjust to the little bit of light filling the tunnel. I shifted and reached for Cade but my hand came up empty. Bolting upright, I clutched the blanket against me as I rapidly searched the shadows.

Cade was sitting on his heels by the doorway. If it wasn't for the gleam of his eyes I never would have been able to pinpoint him amongst the gloom. There was something feral about him that caused me to grasp the blanket more firmly against me as he watched me through the shadows.

"Cade?" I was ashamed by the small squeak of my voice.

His mouth parted as he leaned closer to me before quickly moving backward. "I can't," he croaked.

"Can't what?"

His head bowed, his shoulders trembled and though I didn't understand why or how, he seemed to be in pain. "So tempting," he whispered.

Realization hit me like a knockout punch and I almost laughed but the sight of his hunched shoulders froze the sound in my throat. I pushed the blanket aside as I moved toward him. "Then take more. It's fine, I'm fine. You haven't hurt me and I don't feel any different."

"No!" I couldn't stop myself from recoiling as his head snapped toward me and an inhuman snarl curved his mouth. "No more, I can't take anymore from you without taking the chance of hurting you. Stay away!"

I opened my mouth to protest but before I could even inhale to start speaking he shoved aside the blankets, lurched to his feet, and bolted out of the room so fast that I wasn't entirely certain he'd been there to begin with. I sat, speechless and immobile as I gaped at the spot where he'd been.

I grabbed my clothes to follow him but sat back with them crumpled in my lap. Something hadn't been right, his face, his eyes... I knew the death that lurked beneath his surface, but I'd never seen him look like *that*. For a heart stopping minute I'd been certain that he was going to launch himself at me and drain me of every ounce of blood and soul I possessed.

I hastily threw my clothes on and scrambled from the makeshift shelter. Cade had vanished as I'd already known he would. A sheet at the end of the hall swung slightly back and forth but there was no other movement within the tunnel. Grabbing a flashlight, I cautiously made my way forward but I had no idea which way to go or where to begin looking.

I may not know which way he had gone but I refused to give up as I turned toward the right. He had fed from me but it hadn't been enough, a fact that he'd kept hidden well until tonight when he seemed to have lost all control. I wasn't sure there was anything that I could do to help him, but I couldn't leave him out here all alone. Not when I *knew* that I could handle him taking more from me.

CHAPTER 8

"Bethany."

I turned and lifted the flashlight to reveal the tunnel behind me. I'd heard Aiden approaching before he'd spoken but I'd hoped that he would go away. I turned back around and focused on the tunnel before me. When I hadn't found Cade by what I could only assume was morning judging by the single watch hanging in the larger tunnel opening that had been designated as the meeting room, I had volunteered to take over the position Dan had been holding when he'd opened fire on us. The idea of disappearing into the tunnels had actually been appealing for a change as my chest felt as if it were being squeezed by a boa constrictor whenever I thought of Cade.

"Aiden," I greeted as he stopped beside me.

"Are you ok?"

"Fine."

He removed the rifle from his back and placed the butt of it on the ground before him. "Where's Cade?"

His guess was as good as mine but I wasn't about to say that to him. He already didn't trust Cade; a snippy retort wasn't going to help with that. I knew Cade would come back to me, I just didn't know when, and I was scared that it may be days if not weeks before he felt he was in control of himself enough to be around me again. The thought made me feel like crying at the same time that I wanted to punch a wall and scream against the unfairness of it all.

I wish he had listened to me before he took off, but what difference would it have made really? I already knew what he was going through, what he was frightened he would do to me. There was no changing what he was. I just wanted to relish in the joy and beauty of everything we had shared, instead I was sitting here wondering when he would return to me.

"Bethany?"

I turned toward my brother and managed a dismissive shrug. "Around."

"Is he coming back?"

I turned away from him again. I didn't know how to answer that but I knew Aiden wouldn't leave me alone unless I gave him some solid answer. "Of course."

"When?"

My jaw clenched as I grappled with the same question. I could lie to myself about when, but I couldn't lie to Aiden. "I'm not sure."

Aiden released a loud sigh and ran a hand through his shaggy hair. In that moment he looked so much like our father that I was rocked by the realization that though both our parents were gone they would always live on in us. I blinked back the tears that filled my eyes as Aiden continued to question me.

"What is going on with him Bethany?"

I swallowed heavily as my mind searched for a possible escape from this line of questioning. "I don't know what you mean."

"Did he kill Ian?"

I felt like I'd been dumped in an icy pond as my mouth dropped. "Why would you ask that?" I managed to choke out.

"Bethany something is not right with him, I can clearly see that."

I forced myself to maintain eye contact as I uttered my next words. "Cade is not a cold blooded killer."

At least it wasn't a lie. Cade may be a killer but he'd done it to save me, he hadn't planned to kill Ian and he hadn't enjoyed it.

"You really believe that?"

"Yes."

"Because you're sleeping with him?"

I didn't think there was anything that could have shocked me more than his question about Ian, but I realized now that I'd been completely wrong. Like a trapped animal, I came back fighting as indignation filled me. "That's none of your business!" I hissed.

"I know," he muttered as he focused on his shoes and his face started to flush. "I just… ah… I just don't want you to get hurt."

"I know," I assured him as I tried to regain control of my indignation. He wasn't trying to be nosy, he wasn't trying to be mean; he was simply trying to care about me. "He loves me."

"I'm sure you think he does." He held up a hand to stall my angry retort. "Hear me out. You're young Bethy, and you're trusting. I don't know if mom ever talked to you…"

"I had the sex talk with mom Aiden."

"Uh… ah… yeah, yeah sure." He nervously ran a hand through his disordered hair again as he shifted uncomfortably. "I mean… um yeah. I'm sure mom told you things, but she wouldn't have understood how men are."

I folded my arms over my chest as I stared at him. If I wasn't so annoyed I probably would have laughed at the look on his face. "Is that how you are with Molly?" I retorted.

His eyes came back to me as some of the color drained from his face. "No, absolutely not. Molly and I are just friends."

"I have eyes Aiden."

His shoulders slumped as he nodded. "Yeah, ok you're right. I like her, a lot, and she likes me." I couldn't help but melt at the smile that tugged at his lips. "She's a good person."

"She is," I agreed.

"But we're not as serious as you and Cade..."

"*Yet.*"

"Ok, *yet*, but Molly is a lot more open and easier to trust than Cade."

"We've known Cade since we were kids," I protested.

His eyes were so forceful that I felt pinned to the spot. "We don't know him though, or at least I don't. I still don't even know where he was or what happened to him when the aliens took him."

"I do."

I could sense his growing frustration with me as he inhaled deeply and let it out in a low rush. "Ok, but..."

"If you can't trust him than trust me. He would never do anything to hurt me or anyone I love, please believe me. I love him Aiden and he loves me."

"Then where is he?" Aiden demanded. "Where did he go? What did he *do* to you!?"

"He didn't do anything to me Aid," I assured him.

"You're young, you're innocent, you don't even know…"

"Stop it Aiden! Just stop! You don't know what you're talking about."

"I know that he took advantage of you!"

I shook my head as I tried to figure out how to proceed. He was completely wrong but to stand here and butt heads with him would only irritate the situation more. We were both stubborn and bull headed, this would only spiral into both of us not talking to each other, and him resenting Cade even more if I wasn't careful. However he couldn't continue on in his beliefs when they were so wrong.

"I'm not as weak or gullible as you insist on believing. I survived watching dad die; I lived through losing mom, and this whole awful mess. My heart was broken when I thought I'd lost Cade, but I still managed to pull myself together and continue on. I'm stronger than you think Aiden and *no* one is taking advantage of me."

I was worried he would continue to fight me but he finally gave a grudging nod. "You're right," he admitted.

"It's difficult for me not to see you as a little girl, but then you haven't been a little girl in years. Not like Abby."

I smiled at him. "Abby's not a little girl anymore either."

"No she's not," he said sadly. "Are you sleeping with him Bethany?" I couldn't look at him. This wasn't a conversation I'd ever expected to have with my brother, just as I knew it wasn't one he wanted to have with me but for some reason he felt like he had to. "I know you love him, but you have to be careful. The world may be upside down but there is still the risk of pregnancy..."

"I'm well aware of the consequences Aiden, I won't get pregnant," I interrupted briskly.

"Diseases." Jesus, he was determined to have this big brother, protective speech with me no matter how red the two of us turned. "We don't have the medicine that we used to have, or the tests."

"There's been no one else," I said before he could steer this conversation into even more embarrassing waters.

"I know there hasn't been, for you," he gushed.

"For either of us," I whispered around the lump in my throat. I felt like I had the worst sunburn of my life as sweat began to bead on my forehead and my cheeks felt like they were on fire.

Aiden did a double take as his mouth opened and closed and he tried to assimilate what I'd just told him with everything we'd always believed about Cade. In school, Cade had been rumored to be unruly and dangerous and all the girls had chased him around. His air of mystery and aloof persona had only fueled the gossip that had run rampant through the halls. Rumors of Cade having lurid affairs with everyone from college girls to married women had been spread around but none of them had been true.

I forced myself to meet Aiden's astonished gaze in the hopes that he would finally believe what I was saying. "He's loved me since the first time he came to our house, loved me years before I even realized how much I loved him. There's never been anyone else, for either of us."

Cade had first appeared in our home as Aiden's friend, but he had continued to come back because of me. I hadn't known the true depth of his feelings for me until all hell broke loose with the aliens though. Feelings he hadn't even known he could be capable of experiencing until he met me all those years ago.

He would be back soon, I told myself fiercely.

"I see," Aiden said after a lengthy pause.

"I hope so."

"There is still pregnancy Bethy," he pressed. "You have to be careful; a pregnancy now could be devastating."

"I know Aiden."

There were more extenuating reasons why I couldn't get pregnant but there was no way I could go into those with him right now. He couldn't possibly know that Cade wasn't human, and I couldn't bring myself to think about what a baby we created might look like. Cade didn't have scales, but it was suddenly all I could picture covering our child and I shuddered at the thought.

"He scares me Bethany."

I tilted my head to study Aiden. "Why?"

Aiden shook his head. "There's just something about him that frightens me. I'm concerned about you."

"He would *never* hurt me."

"Maybe not *you*, but I can't shake the feeling that he would hurt someone else, especially if they were a threat to you."

I couldn't bring myself to lie to him by denying that. Cade *would* hurt anyone he thought was a threat to me, he *would* kill them. I had already seen that, and Cade was far more treacherous than Aiden could even begin to imagine.

"You wouldn't be a great big brother if you didn't worry." I tried to sound light and airy, but I could hear the tension in my voice.

He snorted softly and managed a small smile. "I suppose not. Do you think you two will get married?"

I laughed as I gestured around the tunnel. "I don't think marriage has much place in this world anymore, do you?"

"No," he admitted. "I suppose it doesn't."

I nodded as I turned my attention back to the tunnel. I'd never really thought about marriage to Cade. To me, our bond was solid and impenetrable already and I didn't need the added bond of being married on top of it. Until a few months ago though it was always something that I had pictured in my life, always something I'd assumed would happen one day. I didn't feel like we *needed* to be married, but I'd also like it if we were. It would be something so normal and wonderful in a world that was neither anymore.

"I would marry him though," I told him. "But I don't feel like we need it. We *are* committed to each other."

His smile was small and fleeting. "That's good to know. Do you mind if I join you or would you prefer to be alone?"

I had come here in order to be alone, but I found that it was the last thing I wanted now. It had been awhile since we'd spent any time alone together. "I'd really like it if you stayed."

We settled onto the ground beside each other, our shoulders touching and our heads bent close as we stared into the impenetrable gloom.

CHAPTER 9

Aiden's shoulder was warm beneath my head and his breathing was even when I woke later. I couldn't see him, but I knew that he was awake as he shifted against me. There was a tension in him that hadn't been there before I'd fallen asleep. "Beth…"

"I'm awake," I whispered so low that I was sure it was my breath he felt more than my words he heard.

He lifted his arm and pointed down the tunnel. My eyes narrowed as I strained to see. One of the changes Cade's blood had rendered in me was better eyesight, but sleep was still making my lids heavy as I tried to pick out whatever it was that had caught Aiden's attention.

Then something skittered from one side of the tunnel to the other. My breath froze; I bit my bottom lip as I lifted my pistol from my lap and adjusted my position. I was afraid if I moved too fast I would draw the attention of whatever was out there. A muted rattling noise rolled off the walls as something else skittered through the shadows. It sounded like hundreds of legs skittering over the walls but the concrete threw the noise off and caused it to echo.

Aiden's rifle was still against the wall but he was holding two pistols before him. His breathing was faint but rapid in the close confines. I couldn't move as another creature skittered forth. They were small ones; they had to be in order to make it into the tunnel. They would be easier to kill than the larger ones, but a horde of them would overpower us in an instant. I grabbed hold of Aiden's arm as the hair on the nape of my neck stood up and a cold sweat broke out on my body.

Amongst the shadows there was something hidden as it watched us, and I was gripped by the certainty that it was focused on the back of my neck.

Ever so slowly I tilted my head back. I could almost hear the world grinding to a halt as I fixated on the creature perched above us. Every horror movie I'd ever seen, and there had been many, flashed through my mind; not the horror movies that had a maniacal villain or ghost, or even the ones with aliens, but the movies that contained bugs and creatures far too awful to exist in this world.

A repugnant creature with spiderlike legs and a compact black body was perched above us. Black eyes stuck a good foot off the top of its head, like a crab's eyes, but the eyes at the end of the stalks were segmented into a hundred different pieces, like that of a flies. Even though it was dark I could see hundreds of *me*, staring back at *me*, with a dropped mouth and the cornered look of one who was about to die. Its mouth, if that's what it could be called, was two sharp stinger looking things that jutted out from the sides of what I assumed were its cheeks. As I watched they pulsated and a drop of some milky substance appeared at the end of each stinger.

It took everything I had to force my mouth closed again. I couldn't stand the sight of my slack jaw and bulging eyes reflecting back at me in the creature's own beady eyes. Aiden jerked me out of the way as the thing launched itself at us with a strange hissing pop, the likes of which I'd never heard before and knew I'd never forget. I expected something to shoot out of it, webbing, acid or some other abysmal thing that would melt the skin off our bones and leave us a goopy, screaming mess on the floor. Thankfully, none of those things happened as it landed with surprisingly little noise on the tunnel floor. Those stingers seemed to pulse and throb with more eagerness as its eyes twisted on top of the stalks to face us.

I pressed closer against Aiden as the eight legged monstrosity eyed us from those awful, segmented eyeballs. I'd never seen anything like it and I'd seen some weird and grotesque things over the past couple of months. I'd seen creatures morph from humans into blood sucking monsters that could destroy the human body in an instant. I'd seen giant creatures that could demolish trees in their relentless pursuit of us. I'd seen my own boyfriend turn into something that could explain nearly every horror legend out there, but *this* thing had me gawking like an idiot and virtually on the edge of pissing my pants.

What *was* it!?

Was it simply a smaller version of the larger monsters that hunted us and drained us dry? Is this what they looked like when they were newborn or something? Or was this some new monster that was just waiting to unleash a new host of disasters upon us? Either way I didn't want to be this close to it.

In an instant it launched at us. It didn't hunch down, didn't gather momentum, it simply sprang forward with the speed of a springing mouse trap. My eyes latched onto the jagged points of its mouth as drops of the milky liquid fell off of them in eager anticipation of the kill. A kill that was imminent if my immobile body had anything to do with it.

Cade's blood had made me faster, had honed my senses and my instincts, but faced with this thing I was suddenly the awkward girl I'd been most of my life. Faced with this thing, I found my muscles useless and my body a shaking mass of nerve endings.

Thankfully, my instincts didn't feel the same way. Seconds before that thing could smash into me, stab me with that tusk-like mouth, dig its razor-sharp legs in, tear off my face, and rip out my heart (because I knew that was what it had in mind to do), I swung my gun upward forcefully. An awful noise that reminded me of water bubbling over on a hot stove escaped the creature as my brisk thrust knocked it away. The thing bounced off the wall and staggered drunkenly on its legs before scurrying toward us once more.

"Move Bethany! Move!" Aiden shouted.

I spun and lifted my pistol up, but the thing wasn't rushing down the floor of the tunnel toward us. It was running up the walls at a diagonal angle that was taking it back toward the ceiling. I tried to train my gun on it but it was fast, far faster than I had expected as it reached the roof. It was scurrying over our heads when I finally got a shot off.

The bullet reverberated down the tunnel as it completely missed its mark. The thing hissed again and then launched forward with a scream that I was certain was just within range of human hearing. In fact, I wasn't even certain that Aiden had heard it until he winced against the piercing sound. I fired again and caught the thing in what I assumed was its belly. It squealed as the force of the bullet threw it back. It fell to its feet and scuttled into the gloom surrounding us.

"Run!" Aiden grabbed hold of my arm as the sounds of scuttling feet rapidly approached us.

He fired two shots behind him but I could tell by the ricochet that neither bullet hit one of them. The slap of our feet echoed over the metal and pounded around us. I didn't recall the tunnel being this long before, but it suddenly seemed endless. The others had to have heard the shots; they had to be coming for us, but what good could they possibly do?

Abby.

The word was a moan in my head. I had to get to her, we *had* to save her. Abby was the best of us and there was no way I would let one of these things touch her. If it was the last thing I did, she would *never* know death by these creatures.

Hands snatched me up, a startled scream half tore from my throat as I was spun around and thrust to the ground. My vision blurred as I tried to get my bearings. Aiden was shoved down beside me, his eyes were just as wide and stricken as I knew mine were.

"Don't move and stay down!"

Though we were trapped in a nightmare, a hot wash of relief filled me as Cade's harsh words and warm breath tickled over me. His hand pressed firmly into my back for a second and then he was gone. Aiden gaped at me for a moment before gathering his arms beneath him and pushing himself up. I took hold of his hand and yanked him back down before he could shove himself to his feet.

"Bethany…"

"You heard what he said," I breathed.

"He needs help." My fingers curled into his wrist as I gulped. Everything in my body was screaming at me to go to Cade, to help him, but he'd told us to stay here and to stay down. He knew what these things were, he knew what he was doing; we would only be a distraction to him. "Bethany!" I closed my eyes against the spine-chilling scream that filled the air from one of those *things*. Cade grunted loudly, the sound was a mixture of pain and exertion that caused my heart to twist as my fingers dug even further into Aiden's flesh and tears burned my eyes. "Damn it Bethany! What is *wrong* with you!?"

I jerked Aiden back down when he tried to lurch to his feet again. I forced my eyes open; I had to make Aiden understand why we had to stay here, why we couldn't look. Everything in me longed to help Cade, but I had to stay here and make sure that my brother didn't do anything reckless, that he didn't see what was happening back there. There were some things that Cade would always try to keep hidden from me, and whatever was happening in that tunnel was one of them. I could feel the hum of violence, the brutality of the battle within these walls even though it was an eerily silent fight that raged on behind us.

"There are some things that we don't need to see," I whispered.

"*What* things Bethany?" I shook my head and closed my eyes again as I labored to keep breathing and not bolt to my feet and rush down the tunnel in search of Cade. I didn't care what I would see, what I would find, but Cade did. He was already standing on a perilous precipice when it came to his control and his sanity. I couldn't push him over it. "Bethany…"

"Aiden stop," I moaned.

"What *things* Bethany?" And then he inhaled a loud breath as his mind finally traversed down pathways I'd hoped it would never travel. "What *is* he?"

I didn't know what to say or do. I loved Aiden, he was more than a brother, he was my friend, and I had been keeping this huge secret from him. I would love nothing more than to unburden myself to him but it was Cade's secret to tell, or not to tell. Yet Aiden was looking at me as if he didn't know me, looking at me as if I'd just kicked his kitten over a cliff.

I released my death grip on his hand and slid my fingers into his as I tried to reassure him that I loved him. That no matter what secrets I kept from him, he was still my brother and I needed him. He didn't react at first and then his fingers tensed around mine. I was just managing a wan smile for him when I heard the sound of slapping feet.

Releasing Aiden I launched to my feet. The others *had* heard the shots and they were coming. I had to stop them, or at least slow them down somehow. I was stepping forward when hands seized hold of my arms from behind. Before I knew what was happening I was pulled backwards and pressed against a solid chest. I knew instantly it was Cade that held me as my skin came alive at the feel of him.

He must have found a smaller tunnel or nook to slide into as he pulled me out of the main tunnel. His chest heaved against my back as his breath sounded ragged and fast in my ear. Even through my turtleneck and sweater I could feel the dampness of his sweat soaked body, and then the tangy scent of his coppery blood hit me. A sense of dread washed over me as I realized that was what was soaking through my clothes.

"Two left. There are two of them left," he grated in my ear. "The others can't see me like this."

My heart leapt as my skin tingled with dread. We needed to get away, I had to get him somewhere that I could look at him, that I could see the extent of the damage that had been done to him. He took another step back and bent to try and hide behind me a little more. I felt walls around me now but my concern for him far outweighed my claustrophobia.

How far back did this small passage go? Would we be safe inside of it? Would *he* be safe and sheltered inside of it? His grasp on my arms became painful but I didn't protest it as I knew he wasn't hurting me on purpose. In fact, I didn't think he was aware of the fact that he was holding me so tightly.

Aiden took a step toward us. His eyes went behind me, but I was certain that he couldn't see Cade within the shadows. "Two," I whispered to Aiden. "There are two left." Aiden's gaze was full of fright and turmoil as he came toward me. "Please don't tell the others we're here. *Please* help us Aiden."

Aiden's eyes closed as the footsteps came even closer. Cade's fingers curled more firmly into me as I glanced nervously toward the sound of approaching feet. We had to get away, we couldn't be standing here when they arrived; I didn't know what would happen if we were, what Cade would *do*.

Aiden shook his head and then began to nod. "Go."

I spun in Cade's grasp and propelled him backwards into the small tunnel. I didn't know where it went and I didn't care. I had to get him somewhere safe, somewhere that I could see the extent of his wounds. Aiden's muffled voice sounded behind us as the others arrived to help him with the monsters. I jumped and urged Cade to go faster as shots echoed throughout the tight confines.

I wrapped Cade's arm around my shoulders as he stumbled and nearly fell. *Please*, I prayed. *Please be ok.* I'd never seen him like this, never known he could be so weak and vulnerable. He was always so strong, so self assured and powerful. I knew he was only mortal like the rest of us, but I'd never expected to see him this way and it spurred me on even faster. I could hear the riotous beat of my heart in the silence that followed the gunshots.

"Opening." I didn't know what he meant until the walls gave out. The walls had been helping me to support him, but without their solid presence I nearly tripped and fell but managed to catch myself before we both tumbled to the floor.

Leaning against the wall, I helped to ease him down. My hands were shaking as I pulled the flashlight hanging at my side free of the loop that held it there. A strange calmness settled over me as I flipped the flashlight on. I could do this, I *would* do this. My hands were far more stable as I placed the flashlight down and focused my attention on the gashes that crisscrossed his stomach and chest.

His skin had been sliced open and blood had turned what remained of his gray shirt red. A jagged cut ran down his cheek so deeply that the skin had peeled back to reveal the flesh and bone beneath. The blackness that seeped through his veins was still running through his face and arms as he struggled to regain control of himself after the battle he had just waged. I found it disconcerting that though black seemed to fill his veins when it appeared, his blood was red.

I wasn't overly squeamish, I never had been, but I had never seen injuries this severe and life threatening before, and they were on *Cade*. Thoughts scrambled through my mind as I pulled the tattered remains of his shirt from him to take in the full extent of the wounds. His muscles instinctively recoiled from my touch no matter how gentle I was in my ministrations. There was so much blood...

"You need me," I stated flatly.

"No," he grated from behind clenched teeth.

I was grateful he didn't pretend not to know what I was talking about. I refused to back down though. "*Yes* Cade. You need my blood and you need my soul."

"I said no!" he retorted.

"It will help you heal, you know that. *I* know that." He shrank away from me as he shook his head. "It won't hurt me. I'm *giving* it to you." He was still shaking his head when I grasped hold of his chin, the only part of him that didn't appear to be coated in blood. "It will hurt me more if you die!" I snapped.

His grasp on my hand was surprisingly strong, yet tender, given his condition. There was a fire in his eyes as he leaned closer. "In the condition I am in I will *not* stop Bethany, not if it's *you*. I would rather die than do such a thing to you." The hair on my neck stood on end as his gaze flickered past me. "Now get her the *hell* away from me Aiden!"

I spun at his words and instinctively leaned closer to Cade as I tried to shield him from Aiden. There was no hiding what Cade was right now, there was no way to deny the darkness within him as it pulsed and swirled throughout his entire body.

"Stay back!" I cried as I pushed myself more firmly against Cade even as he tried to hold me away. "He'll see," I whispered.

"It's too late Bethany. Please, you *have* to get away. You're smell, ah you're smell..." His fingers wrapped into my hair as he drew me closer and inhaled deeply. My pulse quickened as I thought he would finally see reason and give into the needs of his body. Give into the one thing that would save him. Instead, he recoiled from me as he shoved against my arms. "Get her away. Aiden get her *away* from me!"

A protest rose in my throat as Aiden grabbed my arms. I fought against him but in the end it was the tormented look on Cade's face that caused me to relent to his wishes. Tears slid down my face as I allowed Aiden to pull me away. "Get Bishop," Aiden commanded.

"I'm not leaving him," I said forcefully. "And Bishop can't know."

I expected to see condemnation in Aiden's gaze; instead I found only hopelessness as he glanced between Cade and I. "You're presence is upsetting him Bethany, even I can see that. I'll do what I can, but he's going to need *medical* help. Get Bishop."

Cade's breathing was rapid as he gazed at me from under lowered lids. Blood continued to seep from the brutal wounds in his chest and stomach. No matter what Cade was, Aiden would keep him safe, I knew that, but everything in me was screaming against leaving him in such a vulnerable state.

"I'll be fine Bethany, go," Cade urged.

I couldn't withhold the tears that slid down my face. He was in worse shape than I'd realized if he was willing to let me bring Bishop here. "Don't leave me."

Cade forced a weak smile. "Never."

"I love you." I spun on my heel and fled down the tunnel before I lost all resolve and courage.

CHAPTER 10

I returned with Bishop to find Aiden giving Cade his blood. The scene stopped me dead in my tracks and Bishop bumped into my back. Aiden withdrew swiftly and tried to use his hand to cover his cut but blood seeped between his fingers and Bishop was too astute to have missed what was happening.

Bishop's dove-colored eyes were practically bulging behind his glasses when I turned toward him. "You *have* to help him," I pleaded, desperate for Bishop to understand.

Bishop's mouth finally closed, but his eyes were still frantic as they bounced between Aiden and I. "He told me my blood would help, before he passed out," Aiden said quietly. "I think he still got some after."

"What…" Bishop's voice was garbled as he tried to find words. He was probably the smartest person I'd ever met, but I was fairly certain his brain wasn't computing what he was seeing. Though he had passed out, the veins in Cade's arms and the backs of his hands were still more defined against his paler than normal skin. "He's not human." Bishop looked as if someone had punched him in the gut and stolen all his money as it completely sank in. "He's one of *them*."

Aiden grasped hold of Bishop's arm before I could. "I was stunned too, but I don't think he's a danger..."

"He's not!" I blurted.

Aiden's eyes flickered to me before he focused on Bishop again. "He saved me. He saved *us*." Aiden looked at Cade in bewilderment and then at me as he tried to reconcile the fact that although Cade was one of the things that had forced us into these tunnels, and taken our mother from us, he was *not* our enemy. "He loves *her*, more than anything."

I couldn't breathe as I watched the play of conflicted emotions that flashed across Aiden's face. "Please," I begged as I turned my attention back to Bishop. "Bishop, *please* help him."

Before my eyes, I watched as Bishop resolved himself to do what he had to. He may have been mostly a research doctor, but he had stitched and sewed and treated live patients before, myself included. Setting the supplies he'd brought with him down, he set to work immediately on treating the numerous cuts and gashes that marred Cade's body.

Unable to watch, I turned away as I tried not to cry. Cade moaned repeatedly as Bishop worked on him but I couldn't bring myself to look. A loud shout echoed through the room and caused me to spin around. Bishop's hand was knocked aside, the needle and thread bounced against Cade's chest as a vicious snarl erupted from him and he bolted upright. His eyes were completely black; his veins flooded with ebony color once more. Bishop was gaping as he fell back and scrambled to get out of the way.

Aiden grabbed hold of me as I launched forward. Cade's gaze swung toward us, and though I felt it latch onto me, I knew that he didn't see anything. Ice pooled through me as I realized he might just rip us all to shreds, and he would never even know what he'd done if he remained trapped within the depths of whatever delusion held him.

I ripped away from Aiden as Cade launched at Bishop with his hands curled. If he got a hold of Bishop he would shred the thin doctor. "No!" I shouted as I thrust myself between them.

Cade fell against me, his face was warped and cruel as it hovered just inches over me. I barely recognized the man I loved as his face lowered toward mine. He would hate himself for doing it, destroy himself because of it, but as of right now the creature hovering above me knew only that it sought my blood and soul. I turned my face away from him as he pressed closer against me. His fingernails scraped against my skin, a growl of pleasure escaped him when the scent of my blood hit the air.

I was barely able to move my hand for fear that it would draw an instant attack from him, but I was able to do so enough to wave Aiden back. If he tried to attack Cade there was no way that I would be able to stop Cade from destroying us all. Aiden froze as he looked between Cade and me.

"Cade," I whispered. His hand trailed over my throat, the fingers that had once caressed me so lovingly and with such reverence were now poised to kill me. "You don't want to do this Cade." His hand stilled around my throat, my breath froze, I couldn't move. "It's *me* Cade. I love you."

His eyes remained unseeing and as cold and distant as outer space. Then, the blackness seeped out of them as they fixed on me in utter dismay and revulsion. A moan of anguish escaped him as he flung himself backward. He hit the wall with a heavy thud that caused the walls to shake and the room to echo with the hollow sound. He was panting, his breath rapid as his eyes crazily spun around the tunnel.

I turned over and pushed myself to my feet. "Stay *back* Bethany," he sneered when I took a step toward him. "Knock me out. Bishop give me something to *knock me out!*"

Bishop was shaking as he dug through his bag of supplies for a syringe and bottle. Filling the syringe with the clear liquid in the bottle, he looked nervously at Cade whose breathing had become even more rapid. Taking a deep breath, Bishop hurried toward Cade. He fell next to him, grabbed hold of his arm, and shoved the needle in before Cade could change his mind.

Cade bucked, his legs kicked out, and then he went completely still. His eyes locked on mine before his lids reluctantly fell closed. What little strength I had left fled my body as I collapsed onto the floor.

Bishop sat back on his heels beside Cade, the color had left his face, and lines I hadn't noticed before were now visible around his mouth and eyes. Yet I could tell his curiosity was piqued as his head tilted to the side and he glanced between the two of us. I leaned into Aiden as he sat beside me and wrapped his arm around my shoulders. With a trembling hand, Bishop leaned forward and reclaimed the needle lying against Cade's chest.

***

"He's the reason why your blood is different."

I lifted my head from my knees and blinked Bishop into focus. It felt like I had bits of sand in my eyes as I slowly pressed and rubbed my fingers into them. He was almost done stitching Cade's skin back together. I'd lost count of how many it had taken to get this far. Bishop's eyes were focused on me, his eyebrows raised as a look of dawning betrayal began to creep over his features. I liked Bishop, he'd saved my life, and he was helping to save Cade's life. I *hated* that look on his face.

"I didn't know that. Not until recently," I hurried to assure him.

Thankfully that look of me just having stolen his last morsel of food began to leave his face. "But it *was* because of him," he murmured as he rubbed his chin thoughtfully. "He *is* the reason."

"His blood won't help anyone else Bishop," I informed him before he got too carried away. "He took a chance with me, but he told me that mixing the blood kills most people."

Aiden's nostrils flared as fury crept over his face. "And he still did it to *you?*"

I shook my head as I bit my bottom lip. "He had to take the chance Aiden; otherwise I would have been frozen too. There would have been no saving me then." Aiden's eyes burned into mine, I could sense his logical side waging a war against the side that was irate because Cade had done such a thing to me. "He'd never do anything to harm me if he could help it Aiden, there wasn't any other choice."

Aiden shook his head. "Bethany..."

"If my blood was like yours he wouldn't have done it, but it's not. *I'm* not. He saved me Aiden, many times. I know it's hard to understand, I was angry and thrown off by it too, but I'm *alive* and I wouldn't be if it wasn't for him. If I can understand that, then so can you."

"I want to Bethany I really do, but he's one of them and you didn't tell me."

He'd been listening to our mother more than I'd realized as he really knew how to drive the guilt nails in. "I know Aiden and I'm sorry, but that's my fault. Don't hate him; he did what he had to."

"I understand that."

I felt like a chastised child but I refused to back down. I'd been protecting Cade, I'd done what I had to do, but I knew I wasn't in the right here either. "We both did what we had to do."

Aiden shook his head and glanced at Bishop. The doctor snipped off the thread and sat back on his heels. "We can't undo what has already been done and truth be told it's probably good to have one of them on our side. I've seen some of what he can do and I imagine that's only the tip of the iceberg. He's done nothing to hurt us." Bishop's intense eyes pinned me to the spot. "And I don't think he would do *any*thing to hurt you."

"He wouldn't," I agreed. "He got us off The Cape, Aiden, and he has done absolutely *nothing* threatening to any of us."

Aiden still looked torn as he shook his head. Heaving a large sigh, he tossed his hands in the air. "He needs more blood," he relented. "And I assume a transfusion won't help. I doubt any of us have his blood type."

"When will he wake up?" I asked anxiously.

Bishop shook his head. "I gave him enough to knock out a small elephant, but there is still no way of knowing. I don't know what his metabolism is like. It could be another day, it could be an hour."

I began to roll up the sleeve of my shirt; I was grabbing for my knife when Aiden stopped my hand. "What are you doing?" I demanded.

"It can't be *your* blood." I opened my mouth to protest but he cut me quickly off. "We saw how he reacts to you Bethany; he refused your blood before because he was nervous about what he would do to you. We don't know how he will react now. He could kill you; he could kill *all* of us before he ever realized what he'd done."

"He's drugged."

"And if your blood happens to wake him there is no way to know how he will react."

"But the two of you won't be enough, and you've already given him yours!"

His jaw clenched as his warm brown eyes flickered. "I'll find someone else."

I rebelled at his statement. I already felt as if Cade had been too exposed, that he was far too vulnerable right now. I didn't like the idea of even more people knowing about him. Bishop bent over Cade and pressed his fingers to his neck as he checked his pulse. Concern for Cade's life swiftly buried my dread of revealing what he was to anyone else.

"Go," I managed to choke out.

"Stay away from him Bethany."

A single tear slid free as I nodded mutely and Aiden disappeared. I turned as Bishop wordlessly made a cut on his wrist and pressed it against Cade's mouth. Even through his drugged stupor Cade reacted to the blood as he sluggishly began to swallow it. My hands folded against my chest as I fought the urge to go to him, to comfort him in some way. I wanted so much to help him, but there was nothing that I could do.

A noise from the tunnel caught my attention and for the first time I paused to think about who Aiden would bring back. I hoped that it wasn't Abby. I trusted her completely, but I despised the thought of using her in such a way, of having Cade feed from her like that.

Aiden stepped from the tunnel first, followed by Bret and Jenna. I instinctively stepped in front of Cade as a million protests surged up my throat. "It will be ok Bethany," Aiden said.

It couldn't possibly be ok. We had gotten closer but I still wouldn't have trusted Jenna with this and Bret had never liked Cade. However as my ex-boyfriend I thought Bret had every right to dislike the man I'd broken up with him for. No matter how much he didn't like Cade though, I didn't believe he would do anything to hurt him, or me.

"What's going on?" Jenna inquired.

"Is he ok?" Bret demanded brusquely.

I tried to find words but they got stuck on the lump in my throat. "He will be," Aiden said.

Confusion swirled within Bret's green eyes as he glanced at Cade. "What happened to him?"

"Those things," I managed to choke out. "When he killed them."

"He killed *those* things!" Bret exploded. "How is that possible?"

"Bret," I breathed, I was terrified of how he was going to react. Until Cade had reentered my life, I'd lived with the simple acceptance that I would probably spend the rest of my life with Bret. I loved him, but not in the same way I loved Cade, *never* like Cade. Bret had been upset by everything that had happened between us and for awhile he'd hung onto the hope that we would, one day, get back together. He'd accepted the fact that it wasn't going to happen, but I had no idea how he was going to react to this revelation.

Jenna's hand went to her mouth as her vivid green eyes widened. Her strawberry hair curled around her petite face in delicate ringlets that emphasized her beauty. She stared at Cade for a few minutes, then at Bishop, and finally at me again. I simply stared back at her, willing her to understand, willing her not to freak out.

"Bethany?" Bret inquired.

I turned back to him. "He needs your help," I pleaded. "I can't do it."

Bret was unblinking as he stared at me. "I expect an explanation."

"You'll get one," I promised. I no longer cared if it was Cade's secret or not. If they were willing to do this than they would get the explanation that they deserved.

"What do we need to do?" Bret asked.

Bishop approached with the freshly cleaned and sterilized knife. "I have him heavily sedated but he's still swallowing the blood. He needs more if he's going to survive."

Bret eyed the knife warily before holding his arm out to Bishop. I focused on the wall above Cade's head as I wrapped my arms around myself. "I'm sorry." I was repulsed by the fact that I was allowing my friends to be hurt in order to heal and sustain Cade. There was no way around it, it had to be done, but I felt as if I were using them. "If there was another way…"

Jenna tenderly touched my arm. "It's ok."

"No one…" I broke off and swallowed back the tears that burned my eyes and throat. "No one else can know."

"No one will know," she promised.

"He's never hurt anyone." Jenna nodded and smiled listlessly as she pushed a stray hair off of her face.

"What about Ian?" Bishop inquired apparently having already put two and two together. "It was Cade that killed him, wasn't it?"

I braced myself as I turned toward the doctor. I couldn't look at Bret as he knelt before Cade. Jenna's hand clenched on my arm as her breathing escalated. "Ian was trying to kill me," I whispered.

I felt their eyes latch onto me. "What?" Aiden demanded.

I gulped as my hands began to fidget before me. "I found Ian in your workroom Bishop; he was drinking my blood samples."

Jenna shuddered as Bishop frowned sternly. "So Cade wasn't the one who destroyed the samples?"

"No, but I think he would have found a way to destroy them eventually." It seemed as if everything lately had been nothing but a lie, but I refused to lie to them now. "He didn't want you taking any more samples, but I didn't know the reason why at the time. When I discovered Ian in that room he attacked me. He knew that Cade had given me some of his blood; he must have tasted it in my blood somehow. Ian was set on taking me and keeping me in order to punish Cade."

"Why did he want to punish Cade?" Jenna inquired.

"Cruelty I suppose. Cade said that his kind doesn't have emotions, at least not like we do. They don't know love. They only know death and destruction and the pleasure that those two things bring to them. They only know how to take, and Ian was determined to take what Cade had."

Bishop nudged Bret away from Cade and bandaged his arm for him. Jenna released my arm and took Bret's place. "But Cade loves you, I've seen the way he is with you," Jenna said. "He couldn't fake the way he *looks* at you."

I couldn't look as Bishop made a slice across her porcelain skin. For some insane reason, jealousy filled me as she was able to do what I couldn't. That strange new hunger twisted through my belly but I was able to suppress it as I focused on my words. "He's not like the others," I choked out as a way to distract myself from what was happening with Jenna and Cade. "For some reason he fell

in love with me when we were children, he said he's never
heard of it happening before, but that if it had happened to
someone else they would keep it hidden. The aliens thought
that it was his adopted parents he was coming to care for,
that's why the Marshall's were killed, and why he avoided
me after."

"Jesus," Aiden muttered.

"Cade killed Ian to save me, but he wouldn't do that to
anyone else."

"Unless they're a threat to you," Bret said.

There was no denying the truth. "Yes."

"And the reason your blood is different is because he
gave you some of his blood," Bishop guessed correctly.

"Yes, there is no secret in my blood. I can't help awaken
the frozen people."

"We haven't run into any of them in awhile, I don't think
there are many left for us to save." It was something we
had all suspected for awhile, but to hear Bishop confirm it
was disheartening. "But there could still be answers in your
blood Bethany. You say many don't survive, but *you* did. I
was looking in a completely different direction before but
now that I know, there could be answers."

"Bishop..."

He held up a finger and shook his head. "It's something
we can discuss later, when he's awake again."

I didn't argue with him, there was no point and if he was
right than maybe there was something that could still be
done to help the others. I was relieved to see the subtle rise
and fall of Cade's chest and the color returning to his pale
face when Bishop gently pulled Jenna away from him. I
took a step toward him; I was desperate to touch him, to
brush the hair back from his face.

Aiden shook his head at me. "No."

Frustration tore through me; I had to fight the childish
urge to kick him. "He killed some of those things, on his
own?" Bret inquired.

"He killed *most* of them on his own," Aiden answered. "There were more than just the two you saw within the tunnel."

"Shit," Bret snorted as his gaze turned back toward Cade. "What could he do to us?"

"He'd never hurt you!" Anger rapidly swelled through me as my hands fisted.

Bret didn't tear his eyes off of Cade. "If you say so but those things were fast as lightning, and it took at least five bullets to kill them. The fact that he did it on his own…" Bret shook his head as he broke off.

"Glad he's on our side," Jenna muttered. "But if the others are like him…"

"We're fighting a losing battle," Aiden said.

"We just have to stay ahead of them, and maybe we'll find a way to beat them or maybe they'll just move on after they've taken all that they came here for, but we *have* to stay alive if we're going to see either of those things happen," I told them.

"We can do that," Bishop said as he rose to his feet. "Now that I know about his blood in you I can tell you that your blood wasn't contaminated. His blood changed you on a cellular level."

"That explains some things," Aiden muttered.

"What do you mean?" I managed to squeak out, troubled that he suspected the secrets I harbored.

"You were never exactly a graceful or coordinated person Bethy, until these past couple of months. Six months ago you would have shot yourself multiple times in the foot by now, and probably someone else, instead you're a better shot than almost everyone else." I scowled at his assessment but I had to admit that it was probably true. "I'd assumed it was because you were finally growing into yourself but it was more than that."

Bret nodded his agreement as his eyes raked me from head to toe. "What is going to happen to you?" Jenna asked.

My gaze fell back on Cade. "I don't know," I answered honestly. "Cade said there were others that had survived the initial blood intake but that the aliens killed them soon after."

"From what I saw of your blood samples there were multiple changes taking place. His cells are invading your DNA and changing it. That's probably the reason why most people don't survive the initial intake of blood; it's too much of a shock to their system, and to their molecular structure. I would have to study samples of his blood, and yours, in order to know exactly what is going on, but unfortunately I don't have the equipment for that." Bishop's hand dropped from his forehead as he focused upon me. "Is there anything else?"

My throat was suddenly as dry as the Sahara. "Like what?"

"He drinks blood Bethany, but is there anything else he feeds on?"

I shifted uncomfortably. I didn't want to reveal all of Cade's secrets, but I had promised them no more lies and after everything that they were doing here, after the way that they were handling this, I couldn't lie to them. "He also feeds on souls."

The sharp inhalations of their breaths were loud in the tunnel as they exchanged nervous looks. "He won't hurt you," I gushed out. "He doesn't hurt any humans when he does it."

I thought of Cade within me, brushing against my soul and touching the deepest depths of it as he took a piece from me. I had *needed* him to do it. Even now, just thinking about it, caused something to stir and awaken within me. Although something inside of me craved it, I hadn't taken anything from him, he would have noticed if I had. Wouldn't he?

"Bethany?" I was pulled from my thoughts as I forced myself to focus on Bishop. "I've noticed changes in you too."

I nodded. "I can see better at night and hear better, but that could also be because of the situation we've been thrust into now. We have to hear and see better if we're going to survive."

"I suppose we've all noticed a change with certain senses, and our bodies," Bishop muttered. "It could be entirely possible that what you are experiencing is only because of our current environmental conditions, and not his blood."

That could be, but I knew that it wasn't. My vision was too good, my hearing far more acute, and my yearning for things that were far from human, was too intense.

"Does he have to have human blood to survive?" Bret asked.

I buried my strange new hunger in order to answer him. "Not regularly. He said he can get it from meat or animals too. He needs it now though, when he's so badly wounded."

"He'll be ok Bethany," Aiden said as he squeezed my arm.

My gaze fell back to Cade as his fingers twitched on the ground. His eyes began to move behind his lids. I hoped they were at least peaceful dreams as I prayed for him to awaken soon.

CHAPTER 11

Cade,

Dust, kicked up from the hard ground, drifted up to clog my nose. The thousands of feet stomping across here had ruined all of the grass and turned the one time lawn into a field of dirt. Normally such things wouldn't bother me but after the events of this day it irritated me. Just when I was finally able to have my chance to be with Bethany, when I was finally able to touch and feel her like I had yearned to do for years, they had taken me off of that beach and deposited me in this hellhole.

I wound my way through the crowd of people huddled together in search of comfort and security. They wouldn't find either of those things here. Turning sideways I was able to mostly avoid having to touch them but my flesh brushed against theirs more times than I would have liked it to. It wasn't right, it definitely wasn't something Bethany would have approved of, but I felt the thirst stirring within my belly as the scent of their blood and fright drifted over me.

I could almost taste their warm blood in my mouth; almost feel the pleasure of their souls feeding mine. It was all so close and I could take it from them here without any worry of being caught, or of any other consequences. I wouldn't though, this was not my thing. I understood the cruelty that ran through us all, I lived with it every day, but this was far too easy and disgusting for my tastes.

A woman's hand fell to my forearm, halting me in my tracks. Her pretty features were obscured by the grime that streaked them as she pulled herself closer to me. "Do you know what they are going to do to us?" she asked in a tremulous voice.

I stared as I tried to ascertain if she was asking because she was frightened or if perhaps she wasn't really all that bright, but her question appeared to be serious. "They're most likely going to kill you," I told her.

Her hand fell away from my arm as she took a quick step away from me. I shook my head at her and continued on through the crowd. Did she really believe she had a chance anymore? Not all of these humans would be killed, but most of them wouldn't survive to see another week.

But then humans were different than us, they fought and struggled and continued on when it all seemed bleak and hopeless. Bethany had shown me this, and standing amongst these people I sensed the hope beneath their desolate despair. My kind never fought and struggled, we didn't have to. I supposed it was the benefit of being on top of the food chain.

I made it to the steps at the end of the massive encampment and rapidly climbed them. A guard stepped forward to block me but another one stepped forward just as quickly and pushed him back. "Sir," the second man said with a bow of his head.

So they knew who I was then. It wasn't unusual for one of my kind to recognize me; I would see it in their eyes and the subtle lowering of their heads when we would pass each other, but this open acknowledgment was new. I nodded back to him and continued forward when they stepped out of my way.

The massive wooden doors with gold etching on the glass panes in them opened before I could reach for the brass handle. The low sobs of the people drifted into the distance as I made my way into the massive and elaborate lobby of the hotel my kind had established as their residence. More people nodded and bowed to me as they stepped aside to get out of my way.

I barely acknowledged their presence until a woman moved forward to greet me. "I will show you to a room sir," she said to me.

I had no intention of staying here for one minute longer than it took for me to find a chance to break free. I wasn't going to take the chance of having one of them follow me out of here though. No, I couldn't rush out of here now, but the last thing I wanted was to stay amongst these creatures, especially when I could feel Bethany's suffering teasing at the edges of my mind. I had to ease that, I had to make it better for her; she was the only thing that mattered in this world. She was the *only* good thing about it.

"Fine," I stated flatly.

The woman turned on her heel and led me to the stairs beyond the elaborate reception desk. Though we climbed numerous flights of stairs to the top of the hotel neither of us were winded when we arrived at the top. "This is the best suite," she said as we walked down the dimly lit hall to the room at the end.

She turned the knob and stepped back to allow me to enter. The room was more of a suite as we entered the living room with two matching blue sofas and a projector screen that slid down from the ceiling. From here I could see the flames from the fires outside as their light played over the walls in a dance that almost made the shadows seem alive as they moved.

"I'm glad that you found us sir."

I glanced over my shoulder at the woman. She didn't attempt to hide the lust radiating from her as her gaze raked me from to head to toe. Revulsion curdled through me and I couldn't stop the curve of my lip as I sneered at her. There weren't many things my kind enjoyed outside of blood and death but though I had no firsthand experience of it, I knew the other thing they found pleasure in was sex. Something I hadn't even one ounce of desire to have with this woman. There was only one woman that had ever stirred me in such a way, only one woman I even remotely yearned to touch.

The woman took a step back as my gaze seemed to make her realize that I had no interest in her. "Me too," I lied smoothly.

Though the monster that had taken me had been killed, it had already led me to this encampment before it realized its mistake. A mistake I had made it pay for by destroying it before it managed to get me all the way to one of my kind.

I turned away from the woman and made my way over to one of the large windows. Stepping up to it, I surveyed the world beyond the glass. Fires had been lit in metal trashcans; people were huddled around them as they sought heat even in the humid summer night. I thought perhaps the fires offered them some sense of false security, a light in the dark, but I didn't know or care what it was they sought from them. Beyond the smaller trashcan fires a much larger blaze loomed on the horizon. I didn't need to smell the burning flesh to know what fueled that fire.

From here, I could hear their sobs as they held onto one another and sought comfort upon the rough, dirty ground. I didn't know where they were going to the bathroom but judging by the smell out there they didn't have appropriate facilities. I had come to this hotel in Plymouth once before, for a meeting about when The Freezing would occur. It had been a beautiful, thriving park with trees and lush grass as far as the eye could see. All of that was gone now, like my kind was so successful at doing, they had taken something beautiful and destroyed it. It's all we ever did.

My thoughts turned to Bethany as I surveyed the wreckage before me. If it hadn't been for her, this is what I would be. This is the nothing that I would *still* be. This is where I was supposed to belong, with the murderers that had created me and yet I felt no affinity for the woman behind me and the monsters outside that window. Bethany deserved far better than what they had to offer this planet and as soon as I was sure it would be safe for me to leave again, I was going to do everything I could to make sure she got it.

I'd never known sorrow before, or misery, but there was something in my chest now that was making it difficult to breathe as I thought of having to spend an unspecified amount of time away from her. It had been difficult enough to stay away from her before, it had taken everything I had not to return to her after that night in the garden, but at least I'd been able to see her still. I'd known that she was alright, that she was there, and I'd been able to take solace in the glow of life she radiated far more than any other person I'd ever met before. A glow that had entranced me and had made me feel alive ever since the first time I'd met her.

Yes, there was definitely something wrong with my chest as I rubbed it absently.

"Is there anything else you would like?" the woman asked.

I'd forgotten she was even there. "No," I responded in a clipped voice. "Get out."

She wasn't offended by my tone but simply stepped out of the room and closed the door. I turned my attention back to the ruined world beyond the glass. My world, a world I was supposed to help rule now, a world that I was supposed to help destroy now.

She will be fine, I told myself. She was tough and she would survive her broken heart until I could see her again.

I felt wetness on my cheek and lifted my hand to wipe it away. I stared at the clear liquid trembling on my finger in confusion. I'd never seen it before. It was the first and only tear I'd ever shed. I hadn't even known we were capable of such a thing, but there it was, the evidence that I was capable of such a human thing. It didn't make any difference though, I wasn't human.

***

The haunting memories of that time and place drifted away as I gradually began to become aware of my body once more. Every part of me was tender when I moved and I could feel where the needle had repeatedly pierced my flesh but I knew that I would be fine. There was a haze clouding my mind and I recognized it as the enduring effects of whatever drug Bishop had given me.

It must have been the drug that had triggered the memory of that time and place. A time that I hadn't thought of since I'd finally escaped that hideous encampment. There was nothing about it that I had ever wanted to recall, not the endless crying of broken humans, the repugnant smell of burning flesh, or the blood that I had consumed while trying to pretend that I was still one of *them*. I hadn't killed anyone; there had been no need to as the blood supply seemed endless, and the cups of it overflowing. Though some of my kind had taken pleasure in torturing and slaughtering the humans, most of them were content to listen and watch their misery unfold without getting their hands dirty.

I could taste blood on my tongue now, fresh blood, *human* blood, but it wasn't Bethany's. Her blood was better than the finest wine or sweetest chocolate. Her blood infused me with even more strength and made me feel as if I could conquer the world. No, this blood wasn't hers but it had helped, as I already knew the thread that had been required to knit my skin back together was no longer necessary.

I could sense Bethany nearby though and the scent of her was enough to drive my thirst to nearly epic levels. The other blood should have been enough to dampen my appetite, but just the thought of her was enough to make me spiral nearly out of control.

I had stayed away from her and in that hideous place to keep her safe, and if I hadn't felt her intense agony through the bond that we shared when she'd been injured, I might have waited even longer before returning to her. I had been tempted to let her live her life so that I didn't damage her, but after feeling her pain I hadn't been able to stay away. I'd told myself I would be able to control myself around her, but I'd *never* be able to control myself if I felt our bond irrevocably severed by her death and I hadn't been there to save her.

Now however, as my eyes cracked open and landed upon her I knew that I couldn't control myself. The golden aura or halo that encircled her, and none of the others, instantly drew my attention. It seemed to pulse with vitality as it called to me, begging me to taste her, to take from her what I had denied myself for years and had only just recently got a brief taste of.

That brief taste hadn't been enough, I wanted more. I wanted it all and I wasn't sure I could be denied anymore as my veins lit with fire and hunger blazed to life within me.

CHAPTER 12

Bethany,

"Bethany?"

I jolted and nearly fell over as my head flew up from my knees. My eyes burned from lack of sleep and my body ached from sitting on the concrete floor. Aiden and Bret stirred and blinked against the light as Jenna subtly moved away from Cade. I leapt to my feet as his face twisted in his sleep. He muttered my name again and his eyelids fluttered open. Aiden rested his hand on my arm as Cade stirred even more but didn't completely awaken.

The breath I hadn't realized I'd been holding exploded out of me as he remained asleep. I wanted Cade to wake up; I wanted to know that he was going to be ok.

I swore as I spun away. Jenna gasped loudly; I was turning back around when hands grabbed hold of my arms, lifted me off the ground, and pushed me into the wall. A startled cry died in my throat as Cade's mouth seized hold of mine. His grip was firm, and the wall bit into my back, but I didn't feel the pain as it was quickly buried by the sensation of his tongue sweeping into my mouth.

The darkness rose up within him to brush against my soul and I gave myself over to it. He supported my weight when my knees buckled. Something inside of me seemed to twist and turn as I felt him latch onto my soul. A slight tug pulled at the very core of my being but instead of fighting against it, I gave myself over to him as I relished in the feel of him within me again.

He pulled away abruptly and dropped his forehead against mine. His ragged breathing caused his shoulders and chest to heave, his hands eased their grip but he didn't release me. Threading his fingers through my hair, my body instinctively pressed closer to his as his mouth trailed over my cheeks. His breath was warm against the hollow of my throat as he buried his face there.

So vulnerable, I realized.

He'd always been so strong, so sure, and fast. However he was clinging to me like a squirrel clung to an acorn. I was his weakness. I was his downfall. I was the one that could push him over the thin precipice of control he maintained, the one that could make such a powerful man unbelievably weak. He never would have been injured if it hadn't been for me, he never would have left our makeshift room, and he never would have gone after those things alone if he hadn't been trying to protect me.

I knew in that instant that there wasn't anything I wouldn't give to him, even parts of my soul.

I bent my head to his and tenderly kissed the stitches on his cheek as I savored in his scent and lost myself to the feel of him. He shuddered as he lifted his head. His eyes were filled with black, but they didn't appear unseeing or enraged as they searched my face with reverence.

"Are you ok?" he demanded in a raspy voice.

"Yes."

"I didn't hurt you?"

"Never."

I smiled at him, but the tension didn't leave the chiseled planes of his face. His eyes slid closed before they opened to the clear onyx depths I knew and loved so well. "Never say never," he murmured.

"Cade…"

He didn't give me a chance to finish as he wrapped his arm around my waist and turned to face the other people crowded into the room. "Thank you."

Their expressions were wary as their eyes darted between the two of us. *Please stay ok with this*, I pleaded silently. I didn't know what Cade would do if they turned against him now but I knew that we would have to leave. We couldn't stay here when there was a possibility they would hurt him, or he would hurt *them*.

He stood proudly before me but I could sense the fatigue that still held tight to him. I rested my hand on his arm as I pressed closer against him.

Aiden cleared his throat as some of the astonishment faded from his face. "You're uh... welcome," he stammered.

"I told them everything Cade. They had to know," I said.

I held my breath as I waited for his reaction and prepared myself for a fight. "I understand," he assured me as he kissed my forehead. His lips lingered on me before he turned to Bishop. "Can you take the stitches out?"

Bishop's eyes flew rapidly over Cade's bare and stitched chest before resting on his face. There were enough stitches in him that he could almost pass for Frankenstein's monster. "They should stay in for at least another week," Bishop informed him.

Cade's midnight hair fell across his forehead as he shook his head. "They can come out now, I'll be fine." Some of the color faded from Bishop's face but he didn't complain as he bent to pull a pair of scissors from his bag. "There's no need for that," Cade told him when Bishop began to heat the scissors under a flame to sterilize them. Bishop frowned but didn't protest. "Or a sedative."

I clutched his hand as Bishop placed the syringe back in his bag. Bishop approached with the care someone would take with a wounded dog but his hand was steady as he began to cut the thread away. Cade's muscles flinched and flexed every once in awhile, but he didn't protest as Bishop worked on him and eventually the doctor began to relax. I somehow managed to keep my mouth clamped shut and remain immobile, but no one else hid their amazement as the stitches from his chest, face and abdomen fell away. The wounds weren't completely gone, but the deep gashes had faded to little more than just scratches with a few deeper gouges.

Bishop finally took a step away from him. I couldn't believe what I was seeing and was briefly tempted to pinch myself as I stared at the place where bone had once been exposed but now it was nothing more than a deep scratch on his cheek. I had known how formidable he was, but this was beyond even my comprehension. The cuts would have been deadly to a human, but within hours they would be gone from him. His eyes were unreadable as they met mine, his fingers stroked over my arm as he leaned closer to me.

"My God," Bret whispered. "How..."

"It's only flesh," Cade said when Bret's voice trailed off.

"It's *your* flesh," I breathed as I traced one of the lines across his sculpted abs.

His jaw clenched and unclenched as his hand took hold of mine and he pressed it flat against his chest. I managed to swallow but I didn't have any words. "Did our blood do that for you!?" Jenna blurted, able to voice the question that remained lodged in my throat.

"It helped," he said.

"Shit," Bret said from between his clenched teeth.

"We need to leave here. There will be more of those things coming down; they'll search these tunnels until they've covered every square inch of them. They won't leave any place unchecked. There are probably more already on their way."

"What are those things?" I asked.

"Scouts. They've been sent out to search the areas that the others can't get into. If there are too many humans down here, or too high of a threat to their creators, they possess a paralytic agent that will hold a person immobile for twelve hours, sometimes even a full day." I recalled that milky liquid dripping from those tusk-like things and shuddered. "The fact that they haven't reported back has already alerted the others that there is something worthwhile down here. The Seekers will be coming for you, for *us*, themselves."

"The Seekers?" Aiden inquired.

"The larger ones, the ones you've been running from this whole time. We need to get out of here; more Scouts will be coming soon." He shook his head as he ran a hand through his disordered hair. "I was out for too long."

I hated the self condemning tone of his voice. "That's not your fault," I told him.

No matter what I said though, he would blame himself if those things came back. "It doesn't matter. We need to go."

Bret and Jenna looked as if he had just told them that the sun was going to stop shining tomorrow. Bishop picked up his bag while Aiden rubbed his chin and calculated Cade's words. "How much time do we have?" Aiden inquired.

"At the most a day, at the least an hour."

My hand flew to my mouth as dread coursed through me. "We need to find Abby and warn the others!"

"How are we going to explain this to them? How are we going to tell them what is going to happen?" Jenna demanded.

I closed my eyes as I clenched Cade's hand. "They don't know where we've been for the past four hours. We'll tell them that we went back into the tunnel above to see if there were any more of those things around and that we saw more of them coming," Bishop said flatly.

"But what if some refuse to leave?" I asked.

"We can't save everyone Bethany." I would have expected such a callous response from Cade, but not Bishop and his words knocked all further protest from me. "We have to save who we can, and we have to go now."

"Are you ok around me now?" I asked Cade quietly when the others moved ahead of us in the tunnel. His eyes flickered away from me, his jaw clenched as he gave a brisk nod. "Cade..."

"I'll be fine Bethany, I promise. Their blood helped to ease some of my thirst."

"But it hurts you to be around me."

"It hurts me far more to be away from you. I can control this Bethy; I can do anything for you."

A lump formed in my throat but before I could shed my tears Cade's nudging hand in my back got me moving toward the exit.

***

I was struggling not to scream as I burst free of the air duct and inhaled heaping gulps of fresh air. I was shaking and my muscles felt like I'd run a marathon from being tensed while crawling through the duct. The sweat on my back had the effect of an ice cube sliding down my spine as the chilly October air hit me. Cade clasped hold of my arms and helped lift me to my feet.

"It's ok, it's almost over," he whispered in my ear. I couldn't open my eyes to look at him; I could only bite on my bottom lip as I managed a small nod. "Only a few more feet, keep your eyes closed if you want."

I desperately didn't want to see anything around me again. I could feel the walls, but at least I was out of the air duct. I'd been able to make it through the tunnel systems for the past week so I knew I could do this.

"I'll be fine," I whispered as I forced my eyes open. I recoiled involuntarily as I caught sight of the walls pressing against me, but somehow managed to gather the last dregs of my courage for the remaining leg of our journey.

Swallowing heavily, I tilted my head back to look at the manhole cover twenty feet above us. We were almost free, almost back into the real world. I should be thrilled but instead I was terrified. We didn't know what awaited us up there. Not anymore.

Cade squeezed my arm before he slid his rifle over his back and grasped the metal rungs of the ladder. I wrung my hands before me as I watched him. Cade didn't hesitate as he grabbed hold of the metal cover, lifted it up and kept it low to the ground as he pushed it aside and slipped free of the tunnel.

"He has no fear," Aiden muttered as he stepped closer to me.

"None," I agreed in a low whisper. I glanced over my shoulder as Lloyd and Darnell pressed closer to us.

Cade's face was highlighted by the radiance of the sun as it reappeared above us. "Clear."

"Let's go," Darnell ordered.

Aiden nudged me to go first and I happily took hold of the first rung and began to climb. Cade grabbed hold of my hand and helped to pull me from the hole. I blinked rapidly against the influx of light as I attempted to take in the world up above again. Scraps of garbage blew across the road in the breeze that swirled down the street. The sunlight glinting off the fragments of glass littering the streets didn't help to make it easier to see.

I went to my knees on the asphalt and tried to get back up before anyone could see me, but my vast relief at being free again caused me to go back to my knees. "Bethany?"

I shook my head as Cade knelt by my side and brushed the hair back from my face. I slipped my hand into his. "I'm ok. It's just so wonderful to be outside again."

The air, oh the amazing air. I breathed it in gratefully as I savored in its crispness, and the scent of the rotting leaves that littered the tree beds. Even the scent of death seemed to have abated during our time underground and it was wonderful to breathe air that didn't harbor the aroma of mildew, rats, and body odor.

We were *free*!

Cade pressed his palm against my cheek as he turned my head toward him. He was beautiful and tempestuous as he grinned at me before kissing me forcefully. I embraced him as I savored in this one small moment of hope and perfection in a world that had none of those things anymore. He caressed my cheeks as he pulled away from me and I was finally able to fully take in our surroundings.

We had emerged on the outskirts of the city as row houses spread out before us. They were mixed in with stores, businesses, and a playground that was missing a few swings and its slide. The road curved around some homes on a hill before disappearing around a bend. From what I could see, Arlene had been right in her assessment that the survivors had all moved on from here.

I stepped away from the hole as the others began to file out. Though none of them had been enthusiastic, and some had even cried as they packed their things, no one had chosen to remain below after the emergence of those new, frightening creatures. I didn't know how we were going to move so many people, but we'd have to do it quickly if we were going to make it out of this city alive.

We had agreed to head north. The winter would be more challenging up there and we would have to find decent shelter soon, but to move south would only bring us into more populated areas. There were far more cities to our south and west than there were to our north. Cade kissed me once more before releasing me and turning to help some of the others emerging like moles from their holes as they blinked at the bright world around them.

I didn't care where we ended up just as long as I was free of this awful city and every hideous thing that we had witnessed here.

CHAPTER 13

The descending dusk was a deeper twilight in the shadows of the forest that surrounded us and I worried about what those shadows hid. I felt like I was asleep on my feet as we trudged through the woods. Right now all I wanted was to sit and put something in my rumbling stomach. Darnell, Lloyd, Cade and Bret moved ahead of us, keeping lookout for any source of danger. We'd made it out of the city with relative ease but I couldn't decide if that was a good thing or a bad thing. It seemed almost too easy, yet Cade didn't appear overly concerned.

Everyone stopped moving as Darnell held up his hand and Cade became still in only the way that he could, in only the way that his kind could. My hand adjusted its hold on the gun I held by my side as I studied the huddled group surrounding me.

"What's going on?" Aiden demanded in a low whisper.

I shook my head, but I couldn't take my gaze away from Cade as he began to move with the lethal speed he kept hidden from the others. Aiden gasped, I went to take a step back, but Cade's arms were already wrapping around my waist and he was lifting me up and spinning me around. My hands fell briefly upon his shoulders but even as I was touching him, he was releasing me.

A lethal growl issued from him and a rock settled in the pit of my stomach. I knew there was no way to deny what had just happened, the speed he had just exhibited, or the look that was creeping over the other's faces. My blood ran cold, my mouth parted as he pushed me backward, nearly pinning me to a tree with his back as his arm swung out to keep me behind him.

I was barely registering what was happening with him when lights began to blaze to life from the woods. The people that had been falling away from Cade now scrambled away from the flickering torches pulsing from the forest like some kind of overgrown firefly. All my dread over what Cade had just revealed vanished as more lights came to life and shaded figures began to emerge from the trees. The dusk enshrouding them, and the bouncing torches, lent a strange air to their presence, one that made it almost seem as if they were walking through a fog.

"Cade?" I whispered.

His hand twitched toward me, but his eyes didn't flicker in my direction. His muscles rippled beneath his shirt as he pressed closer against me. My heart leapt into my throat, I rested my fingers briefly on his back as I inhaled a shaky breath.

"People," Aiden whispered.

"*No!*" Cade hissed. "Not all of them."

I could barely breathe through the constriction in my chest and I thought my heart was going to burst through my ribs as Cade's words sank in. I brought my gun forward and rested it in front of me in a two handed grip as the shadows began to coalesce into people, and apparently aliens.

Though the aliens were darker in hair, skin, and eye color there was no way to differentiate them from a human. They blended in seamlessly with us, a trait that we didn't share with them as they could spot each other immediately, or at least Cade could. There were so many of them, they outnumbered us at least two to one, and those were only the ones that I could see. I was certain there were more lurking within the forest waiting to pounce upon us like a pack of hungry, rabid dogs. The comparison didn't make me feel any better as a woman about our age, and a middle aged man separated themselves from the others and took a few steps forward.

It wasn't their nearly black hair and eyes that helped me identify their race, but the fact that their eyes immediately latched upon Cade. The pretty young woman's head tilted to the side as an amused smile tugged at her full lips. The man beside her didn't appear at all amused though as he eyed Cade up and down before turning toward me. His bushy eyebrows shot into his receding hairline as his gaze raked me from head to toe.

A low snarl escaped Cade as he took a step to the side to try and cover me more. It was useless though, they could all see us and no matter how strong he was he was no match for the numbers we were facing. He would fight to the death in order to protect me but that was something I was determined not to let happen.

"Hello Cade."

Everyone in our group's head shot toward us as the young woman greeted him with a small nod. I straightened my shoulders and thrust my chin out as her coffee colored eyes slid to me. Her deep brown hair had been pulled into a loose knot that sat against the base of her slender neck. Her thin nose and high cheekbones reminded me of a fashion model, yet there was something about the angular shape of her face that somehow detracted from the aura of beauty she seemed to radiate. I found my eyes riveted upon her as questions and doubts bounced rapidly through my mind.

Cade's jaw clenched, a muscle in his cheek jumped as he surveyed the crowd gathered before us. I didn't know when he'd done it but I spotted a knife in his hand as the light from a lantern gleamed off of the steel. "Hello Jessica," he responded blandly as he shifted so that his shoulder was against my chest.

Aiden glanced at me but I kept my face impassive as my stomach twisted into knots. *Who was this girl, and how did Cade know her?* She had to be an alien, but there were definitely a few humans surrounding her if the fairer color of their hair and eyes was any indication. Unless they were altering their looks now, which would be the easiest thing out of all the deceptions they had unleashed upon us.

"Who are you?" Darnell's rifle was raised and at the ready as he leveled it at the woman. Jessica didn't answer though as her eyes slid between Cade and me and back again. "Who is she Cade!?" Darnell barked. "Someone answer me before I put a bullet in both your heads!"

"That wouldn't be a wise idea," the middle aged man with the receding hairline said in a flat monotone voice that somehow managed to seem more menacing than if he had shouted the words.

I knew exactly how Darnell felt but the worst thing in the world would be for him to pull that trigger, I knew that as surely as I knew that the tide would rise and the sun would set. *Please don't,* I pleaded silently. Although I wasn't as concerned about Darnell as I was about Lloyd. Darnell's rifle was trained on Jessica, but Lloyd had his aimed straight at Cade's heart.

"Lloyd," I breathed.

"It's ok Bethany," Cade murmured. "Just stay behind me." The tip of Lloyd's gun briefly swung in my direction. Cade pressed more firmly against me, my heart sunk as I saw the black beginning to creep through his arms and into his face. "You don't want to do that."

"What are you going to do about it?" Lloyd demanded.

"You won't like seeing what I can do," Cade grated.

"Lloyd," Darnell said in a low voice. "He's not our main concern right now."

Lloyd seemed unwilling to turn the gun away from us though as he continued to eye Cade with an expression that made it clear he would pull the trigger if Cade moved even a centimeter. Lloyd's hand trembled as the black encompassed all of Cade's eyes. "What are you?" he whispered.

"He's one of us," Jessica said in a tone of voice that set my teeth on edge. Darnell released a low curse; a startled squeak escaped one of Arlene's people and more than a few of them looked like a rabbit ready to bolt from a coyote.

"We mean you no harm," receding hairline informed us.

"Than what do you mean?" Darnell demanded.

The man's eyes remained on Cade and I as Jessica began to smile. "Judging by the look of things, we can help each other," she said.

"I highly doubt that," Lloyd retorted.

"Don't be so doubtful, not all of us have ill intent where you humans are concerned. In fact, all of us here are looking to find a way to help you, to save the human race."

My fingers curled into the back of Cade's shirt as hope filled me. More of them filed out of the woods and as I watched a tall blond with piercing hazel eyes and broad shoulders stepped forward. If he was an alien in disguise it was a *really* good disguise. It took everything I had to keep my jaw from dropping when his hand slid into Jessica's.

"To save *all* of us," Jessica continued, her eyes locked upon Cade's. "We have a lot to discuss."

Cade relaxed a little but the black lines didn't leave his face or eyes as even more people began to move from the woods. "It seems we do."

My breath rushed out of me as I watched the shadows continuing to emerge from the trees. We had no choice, even if they were here to hurt us; there was nothing that we could do to stop them. We were outnumbered by aliens and humans alike. I was tempted to grab hold of Cade and bury myself in his chest in case I didn't get the chance to hold him again after this.

I snatched hold of my brother's hand and squeezed as Cade took a step away from me. I used the opportunity to grab hold of Abby and push her behind me. "Bethany..."

"Shh Abby," Aiden hushed her.

"You knew about Cade too," Abby accused.

I was tempted to stick my hand over her mouth but I knew it wouldn't do any good. "Later Abby," Aiden told her.

I could almost see steam coming out of her ears as she folded her arms over her chest and glowered at the two of us. Cade stared at Lloyd as the young soldier kept his rifle focused on him. "Stop pointing that thing at me," he informed him coldly.

"Lower it Lloyd," Darnell commanded. The young soldier hesitated for a minute before finally lowering the gun. I breathed somewhat easier but Lloyd wasn't even a tiny bit of the problem as my attention turned back to the hundred or so people and aliens gathered across from us.

Cade remained standing in front of us but Jessica and the man with the receding hairline moved across the clearing. "It's nice that we finally get a chance to meet," Jessica said as she held her hand out to him.

Cade stared at her hand before briefly glancing back at me. Abby's resentment and annoyance seemed to fade as her arms fell to her sides and her fine boned hand slid into mine. My gaze slid back and forth between Cade and Jessica as my curiosity grew, but I held my tongue. It wouldn't take much for someone on our side to pounce or bolt into the woods. I couldn't shake the feeling that if someone tried to run they would be chased down like a gazelle fleeing a lion.

Cade finally took hold of her hand and shook it briskly. "Hopefully I'll be able to say the same of you."

"You will. We have a lot to explain."

"So it seems."

The man stepped forward and extended his hand. "Timothy Athens."

"Cade Marshall."

"I know."

That only caused my frown to deepen as Jessica turned toward me. "Jessica Leonard," she said as she thrust her hand out.

I released Aiden's hand and went to take hold of Jessica's when Cade not so subtly stepped in between us. Jessica's mouth quirked in amusement but she didn't say anything as she turned her attention back to me. "Bethany Lake," I told her.

"It's nice to meet you Bethany. We have shelter nearby that we'll take you to," Jessica told us.

"Do we have a choice?" Lloyd muttered.

"You do, but I can almost guarantee if you leave here you won't make it out there for much longer. The choice is yours though." She pinned Cade with her eyes. "I'd suggest hearing us out before you leave; we *do* have a common goal here."

Hope spurted through me as I glanced at the people across from us and then the ones surrounding me. Bishop strode forward to stand beside Aiden. "I'd like to hear what they have to say," Bishop asserted.

"Have you lost your mind?" Lloyd muttered.

"I can see as clearly as you that there are humans standing willingly amongst them, unless you have the ability for mind control?" Cade shook his head in response to the question Bishop directed at him. "I'd like to know what is going on then."

Lloyd was fairly sputtering, "You're going to trust *him*?"

Bishop stared at the both of us before giving a brisk nod. "I am, but like the lady said, it's your choice."

"I'd like to hear it also," Jenna said as she stepped forward. "I'm assuming that if Cade hasn't killed Bethany yet than they can't all be bad. We're not going to win this battle hiding in tunnels, moving around, and on our own."

"It's settled then," Timothy said. "Follow us."

I glanced nervously at Cade as Timothy turned and headed back toward the crowd in the woods. "Can we trust them?" I whispered.

Cade stared after them. "You're the only one I trust, but I think they have something to tell us and I'm willing to listen."

"So am I," Darnell said as he stepped forward. "Let's go."

I took hold of Cade's hand as I tried to ignore the resentful stares focused on us as he led me forward.

CHAPTER 14

My head tilted back as the massive gates loomed out of the forest before us. The large wooden poles on either side of the gates were wrapped with barbwire and adorned with what appeared to be blood, but I couldn't be sure in the dim light. People began to hold back around us and I felt my own heels dig in as my heart began to hammer with trepidation.

I was convinced this had been a mistake as my gaze traveled up and down the chain link fence that stretched as far as the eye could see in either direction. Razor wire curled around the top of it and I knew the minute we stepped inside those wooden gates there would be no getting back out. Jessica made some sort of intricate hand signal that reminded me of a baseball coach signaling to steal second. The massive gates before us swung open with a groan of hinges badly in need of being oiled.

Light flared over us as torches were brought forth. More figures appeared and the torches were raised high to reveal the six men and women that had emerged from the darkness. There were at least two humans amongst them, but I suspected there were more as inviting smiles spread over their faces.

"You found more," a woman with deep brown hair who appeared to be in her mid to late thirties said.

"Better than that Rosemary." Jessica stepped aside to reveal Cade standing behind her.

A shiver of foreboding crept down my spine when Rosemary's black eyebrows shot into her hairline. "That *is* an interesting turn of events," she murmured as she rubbed her chin.

My hand tightened around Cade's as I stepped closer to him. I knew he'd told me everything he'd thought I needed to know but there was so much he'd kept hidden from me. I sensed I would get some of the answers to the many questions running through my mind from these aliens standing across from us. *Curiosity killed the cat*, I reminded myself, but the cat also had nine lives and my curiosity was clamoring to be eased.

"Well come along everyone," Rosemary invited.

She turned away but Cade's words stopped her. "I'm the only one that will be coming."

The woman lifted her torch again as she turned back around. "Everyone will be safe here."

"You're not going in there alone," I told him.

"I don't even know where or *what* here is," Cade said to Rosemary.

"It's a prison encampment for the humans, or at least it was," Jessica explained. "We took it over a couple of weeks ago, freed the prisoners, and claimed it as our own."

"Did you now?" Darnell inquired dryly. I couldn't help but feel a little skeptical too. Darnell rested his rifle against his shoulder as he stepped forward. "The last thing I want to do is step foot in there, and I'm not so sure I trust you." His gaze was relentless as it settled upon Cade and though he knew what Cade was now I saw no fright in his eyes. "But Bethany is right; you're not going in there alone, someone else will hear what they have to say too."

"I'll go," I volunteered.

"Someone besides *you*," Darnell sneered.

I felt as if I'd been slapped but managed to keep my face as impassive as possible. I deserved his condemnation, I'd kept a secret from them, a *big* secret, but I admired Darnell and looked to him for leadership and guidance. He'd helped me when I needed him most. I wanted to apologize to him but now wasn't the time and I didn't think he was willing to hear it. I'd chosen my course of action and now I was going to have to live with the consequences of it.

"I'm going," Bishop said.

I didn't think there was anything that could have kept the curious doctor from going in there, not even the threat of being locked in there for good. "I'll go too," Lloyd offered. "You should stay with the larger group, in case something goes wrong," he said to Darnell.

Darnell studied the rest of our group before giving a brisk nod. Cade tugged me to the side and pulled me up against the fence. "I want you to stay out here with your siblings."

I shook my head and thrust my shoulders back. "I'm going in there with you."

"It could be dangerous in there."

"Look around you Cade; it's not exactly open arms and musicals going on right now. They distrust us both."

He glanced at the people we had come here with as they grouped closer together. They spoke in whispers as weapons were exchanged amongst them. "Bethany..."

"I've already assumed that there's more you haven't told me."

His eyes narrowed. "I've told you everything that pertains to *my* life, here. I've told you everything that matters to me. Those things up there don't matter to me and they *never* have."

"I understand that."

He groaned as he ran a hand through his hair and nervously glanced back at the crowd gathered outside of the gates. "I don't think you'll be safe on either side of these gates but out here you could at least still have a chance to run."

"I've seen you take down two of those bloodsucking things with only a knife, I don't think I'd be getting far even if I did run."

His eyes flickered away from me as he shook his head and his shoulders slumped in resignation. "Stay close to me Bethany; don't let them separate us, no matter what."

"I won't," I promised.

"No matter what happens, know that I love you. There are things you're going to hear..."

I smiled as I squeezed his hand. I was certain there were things I wouldn't like hearing, but I hadn't shied away from the revelation of what he was, and I wasn't about to start now. "I know. I love you too."

I went to turn away but he tugged me back. "You have to know this first. Jessica is the woman I was supposed to marry."

If a ghost had floated before me and yelled 'boo!' I wouldn't have been more shocked than I was to hear those words. I hadn't known what to expect once we got in there, but what he'd just said was the absolute last thing I had expected to hear. I opened my mouth to respond but no words came out. I closed my mouth and swallowed as I glanced back at the young woman standing by the gates with the blond haired man at her side.

"I thought you'd never met her," I finally managed to get out.

"I haven't, but I've seen her picture."

"Oh, of course." Who hadn't met their future spouse, the alien they were supposed to spend the rest of their life with, by a picture?

"Bethany..."

I held up a hand and shook my head. "They're waiting for us."

I turned and hurried away before I became too disturbed by his revelation, before I thought too much about it and decided the last thing I wanted was to step foot in there with him and his ex-intended. Or was she *still* his intended amongst their race? I didn't know and I wasn't going to sit around and try and figure it out. Cade and his fiancée were the least of my problems right now.

My head tilted back as I took in the wooden gates before us. Yes, it was definitely blood that stained the wood that bleak color, my nose pricked at the scent of it, my stomach rumbled but I ignored it as I focused on Abby, Aiden, Jenna, Molly and Bret standing near Bishop and Lloyd by the gates.

"We're coming with you," Aiden said before I could protest. Molly remained unmoving beside him, her hand entwined within his as she stared at Cade and I. "We all know it's just as safe in there as it is out here and we'd rather be with you."

I knew exactly how he felt. Cade stepped back beside me as Jessica nodded for us to follow her. Lloyd stayed in the back, the rifle pressed against his chest as we moved through the gates and into the cleared area of the forest that had been created to house the encampment. I didn't know much about acreage, but the cleared area seemed to be as large and in the same shape as a baseball field as it spread out around us. I wasn't sure if the trees had been used to create the rickety shacks that sat around the outer edges of the fencing but they had at least been cleared to make room for the small houses. The forest floor had been tromped down enough that it was now hard packed dirt beneath our feet.

"Is this what it looked like when you took over?" Bishop inquired as more people and aliens appeared around us and Timothy slipped away to join a small woman. The crowd whispered amongst themselves as they gazed curiously at us. The mention of Cade's name amongst them did little to ease the turmoil twisting through my stomach.

How did they all know who he was?

Torchlight flickered over them, highlighting their raggedy clothes and dirty features but none of them appeared frightened or any more bruised and disheveled than any of us were. A child with her brown hair in pigtails tentatively waved at us. Jenna waved back until someone grabbed hold of the little girl and pulled her away. Jenna's hand hovered for a second before it fell back to her side.

"We've removed the execution building, the chains and body parts since we've arrived, but for the most part this is what it looked like," Rosemary answered.

They were leading us toward a building that was larger and sturdier than the other buildings surrounding us. I moved closer to Abby and Aiden as Cade stepped in front of us. Rosemary hurried forward and threw the door open, she disappeared inside and a second later light spilled from within the shelter. I exchanged a look with Aiden, but followed Cade up the three steps to the doorway.

The floor was nothing more than plywood with a single table set up in the middle of it. There were a few rolls of documents sitting in the corner of the room and a full size bed with an old gray comforter next to the rolls. I tore my eyes away from the bed as Rosemary hung a lantern above the table. She pulled the gloves from her dainty hands and dropped them on the bed.

Shadows played over the delicate planes of her face as she approached the table. I'd become accustomed to what the aliens looked like and their attitudes toward us, but there was something different about Rosemary that I just couldn't place. She had crow black hair and eyes the color of obsidian but there was a warmth about her that wasn't present in the others, not even in Cade.

Her gaze focused on me before shifting toward Cade. "Yes a very interesting turn of events," she murmured.

Cade took a step closer to me, his chest pressed against my shoulder as a shadow fell across the doorway. I turned as another man stepped through the door. He was tall with shaggy brown hair and blue eyes that crinkled at the corners when he smiled at Rosemary. I looked to Cade but his attention was focused on the man as he hurried across the room and took hold of Rosemary's hand.

"Did you think you were the only one?" Rosemary's question was little more than a whisper as she met Cade's unflinching stare. "Did you think it was an accident, a stroke of fate, or perhaps a curse that had befallen *only* you?"

"I never thought it was a curse," Cade replied. "I suspected there may be others but to actually find them, to see them..." his voice trailed off as he studied Rosemary and the man before turning his attention toward Jessica. "I never expected this."

Rosemary nodded as she placed her hands on the rickety card table before her. "None of us did."

"What *is* it?" I asked.

Rosemary smiled at me. "It's love."

I glanced at Cade before focusing on her again. "I know that, but why? What is it that is so different about me, or him," I said with a nod to the man beside her. "That makes you feel something for *us*?"

Rosemary frowned thoughtfully as she glanced at the man beside her. "I knew the second I saw Greg that there was something different about him, something... more." Cade remained immobile but Jessica was nodding enthusiastically. "It's not something you could understand as a human. It wasn't until this past year that I began to understand it more, and only because I've finally had a chance to discuss it with others that it has happened to."

I glanced at Cade as she stopped speaking. He remained rigid at my side, his hands fisted as a muscle in his jaw twitched. His eyes slid to me briefly before he focused on Rosemary again. "And what is it that you've begun to understand?" he inquired.

"There's something about certain humans that entangles us. There's something about them that we react to, and it is *only* one of them for each of us." Cade grabbed hold of my arm and pulled me back a step as Rosemary stepped around the table. She held her hands up and didn't come any closer as color began to seep through Cade's face.

"We don't see auras as people commonly think of them but I see something around Greg that is almost similar to an aura," Rosemary continued. "I believe it is the soul of the one that we belong with, the one that can change us that we are able to see. Their souls are stronger, more vibrant and powerful than other human souls and the people that possess those souls call to us. I cannot see yours," her gaze focused on me before sliding over the others. "Or theirs, but I see something around Greg. Jessica tells me it is the same with Leo and the others have reported the same thing to me. I assume it was no different with you, am I right?"

Cade's fingers slid over my arm as he pulled me back another step so that I was pressed firmly against his solid chest. "Something like that," he stated.

"Your souls are stronger, or at least they are to *us*," Rosemary said. "And they draw us in, but its more than that, we can feed off of them and it actually nourishes us and it satisfies us without draining them completely. It also seems to somehow change us physically."

"That's why you look so different," I guessed. "You're softer than Cade and Jessica, almost more... human?"

"Yes, perhaps that is the best way to put it, you make us more human. Your souls bring out a side of us we never even knew existed, a human side, a side capable of love, a side that our kind would destroy us for possessing."

"If you truly feel the same way about Greg as I feel about her than you should realize that moving any closer is risking your life," Cade grated when she took another step toward us.

"There's no need for that," Greg said coldly.

Cade didn't bother to respond to him as he remained focused on Rosemary. "How long have you been together?" I asked quietly, hoping to break the tension in the room.

"I met Greg five years ago. Thankfully I was in a position where I was able to choose the husband I wanted to marry as long as we didn't have children. I was of little importance amongst the ones of us placed here, other than to be a spy," Rosemary continued.

Despite my best intentions I felt my gaze slide toward Jessica. Her gaze was focused on Rosemary as Jessica nodded along with her words. *Of what importance were she and Cade that they had been chosen to marry each other?* I wondered as I looked toward Cade. It was something I would have to remember to ask him about later.

"When I met him, I knew. It was like being hit with a lightning bolt, I was flooded with a wash of emotions that I'd never experienced before. All I wanted was to get closer to him, to know him, and to be near him. To be away was a physical ache and I tried to stay away in the beginning as I was convinced I was going to hurt him, but it was impossible to do so. Eventually I couldn't take it anymore and gave in. We've been together ever since."

I noted the ruddy color in his cheeks and his solid build as I focused on Greg. "You appear healthy," I stated.

He nodded. "I am."

"They're stronger, the humans that effect us, much stronger than any of the others, but it's more than that. When we feed on their souls there is an exchange between us. We don't only take from them but we also give them pieces of our souls so that they're never depleted. I didn't even think I had a soul until I met Greg. I realized afterward it was just hidden and deadened without him, but he alerted me to its existence by awakening it within me. Our humans are able to stay strong because we also supply them. It's how some of the ones without type O blood were able to survive The Freezing; they were cloaked from it by having pieces of us inside of them."

I remained motionless, my arms by my sides as her words ran through my mind. It wasn't Cade's blood within me, or at least not *only* Cade's blood that made me seek out a piece of his soul when he was within me, but something that he was inherently giving to me to begin with. My relief was so profound that I felt tears burn my eyes and it took all I had to hold them back.

"You said *some* of them?" I asked. "How did the others survive?"

Cade shot me a look but I ignored him as I took a step forward. Jessica's face fell as she shook her head. "None of us knew that the soul thing would work for sure and very few of us knew of each other's existence before The Freezing. Some tried a more radical approach to keep their loved ones alive."

I was as still as stone as I awaited her explanation of what this more radical approach was. "What was that?" Molly inquired when Jessica didn't continue.

"They tried to exchange their blood with their Soul, which is what we call the people that we are drawn to." I felt like I was on the edge of a tightrope as I bit back the questions that threatened to spill from my mouth and forced myself to remain as calm as possible. "You have to understand they were desperate to try and keep them alive, it was a risky thing to do, but they saw it as their only option. Their last chance to save the only person they had ever loved."

"What happened to them?" Bishop inquired.

"Most died, our blood isn't typically at home in the human body," Rosemary said. "We have almost fifty of our kind here that have lost the ones they loved. They're surviving, but they're broken, lost without their Soul. They still have no interest in returning to our kind though, or at least the ones we've met don't plan to return."

My hand found Cade's. I couldn't imagine how he would have reacted if I had died. He would have hated himself.

My curiosity got the best of me and I wasn't able to keep silent. "And the ones that survived getting the blood?"

Rosemary shrugged. "Some felt no changes from it, but others claim to have better vision and hearing. Those that claim they have enhanced abilities have also found that their desire for blood has increased, or at least their craving for red meat. There have been no other ill effects reported though."

Unable to keep their faces impassive, I felt my friend's and family's eyes finally flicker to me. I could feel Cade's eyes on me, urging me to remain unspoken, but there were so many questions running through my mind. "There are absolutely no side effects from the exchanging of the souls?" I asked.

Rosemary frowned as she glanced at Cade. "No. Do you not feed from her?"

For a second I didn't think Cade was going to answer but he finally spoke. "Not until very recently."

"You've just met?"

Cade shook his head. "We've known each other for twelve years."

Rosemary stuttered over a few words and even Jessica's mouth dropped. "I don't understand, for all of us it was an instantaneous connection. We *had* to get as close to the people as we could as fast as we could," Rosemary finally got out.

"Perhaps because he was so young when they met," Jessica suggested. "He didn't realize it until he was old enough for The Calling to occur."

"I knew it instantly," Cade told her. "I knew what she was to me, I saw her in a way I'd never seen *any*one before."

"And you were able to resist for *twelve* years?" Jessica blurted in disbelief.

"I had to make sure she stayed safe."

"That's amazing, but you are a part of The Ancient Line and perhaps that is why you were able to resist," Rosemary pondered.

"I'm of The Ancient Line and I wasn't able to resist for more than a month," Jessica admitted.

"So if you've only just recently fed..." Rosemary's voice trailed off as her gaze landed on me and realization dawned in her eyes. "You're not a type O, you survived the blood exchange." I tried not to fiddle with the sleeves of my sweater. "And you're one of the enhanced ones, that's why the questions."

I could feel my friend's and family's gazes burning into me. Most of all though, I could feel Cade's gaze burning into me like a laser beam, as they all realized that I hadn't revealed everything about the effects of his blood within me. I should have told Cade before this but then I never could have expected to run into this group and it was too late at this point. They knew, and now so did he, and this group may have some answers for me.

"Yes," I whispered.

Cade's jaw clenched, a muscle twitched in his cheek, I could actually *hear* his teeth grinding together. "You'll be fine," Rosemary assured me. "The others are all fine and have reported no recent developments."

Bishop seemed to regain some of his composure as he tore his attention away from Cade, who looked like he was contemplating throttling me. "What is The Ancient Line?" Bishop inquired as he stepped forward.

"The Ancient Line consists of Isis, Osiris, Agrona, Forseti, Kali, Raijin, Malsumus, and Sedna." The names Rosemary listed off tickled at the edges of my mind but I couldn't quite place why they sounded so familiar. "They are the most powerful of us and there are only four of us that are directly descended from them."

"Your ancient line named themselves after Gods and Goddesses from different ancient *human* religions?" Bishop's voice cracked a little.

Rosemary shook her head and moved back to the other side of the table. "No, your ancient religions named themselves after *our* Ancients."

Bishop's mouth dropped. "But some of those religions are thousands of years apart and completely different."

Rosemary nodded. "The Ancients are immortal."

I felt as if someone had punched me in the gut as I took a step back and my eyes flew to Cade. His hand pressed more firmly into my back to keep me close to him. "You're immortal?" I blurted.

He shook his head. "No, only The Ancients are immortal. I am only a progeny of theirs."

"Of two of them," Rosemary expounded. "Something that only happens once every one hundred years."

My head spun as I tried to process everything that they were saying. I thought I could have months to try and sort through it all but it would still be impossible to do so. I had to sit. I almost sat on the floor but the second the urge hit me I decided I'd prefer to stand.

"You have one *freaky* ass history that is *completely* messed up!" Bret said as he ran a hand through his hair and began to pace. "How is it even possible that eight of you somehow managed to become immortal?"

"The Fountain of Youth." There were a thousand things running through my mind, but that most certainly had *not* been one of them as Rosemary's words stopped Bret dead in his tracks.

"Oh of course it was," Bret responded sardonically. "What else would it have been? I mean that just makes complete and utter sense. Where did they find it, under Atlantis?"

Though I was just as overwhelmed and baffled as he was, I had to bite back a smile at his words. His sarcasm was apparently lost on Rosemary though. "No, they found it on our home planet, Tintagel."

Bret shook his head. "So The Fountain of Youth was on *your* planet?"

"All legends start somewhere," Bishop muttered.

"Yes they do," Rosemary agreed. "The Ancients discovered The Fountain and kept its location to themselves. It's rumored that when our planet dried up they found a way to keep it with them. They've been our leaders for over seven thousand years.

"Our kind, the Tintagelians, have been coming to this planet for about that same amount of time. They helped to advance the human species and helped to ensure their survival, and our food supply. Many of your legends and Gods emerged from The Ancients as over time humans noticed that The Ancients didn't age and that they seemed to possess powers. Though the stories of those powers were heavily exaggerated, other than immortality, their abilities are no different than ours. They can't control thunder or the oceans, or bring down lightening from the sky. Though, they did bring themselves down from the sky. They do drink blood, they do eat souls, they are stronger and faster than us even, and they haven't aged a day in seven thousand years."

"I knew we didn't build the pyramids," Bret muttered. "And I guess that explains Stonehenge."

"No Stonehenge was all you guys," Rosemary waved her finger as she answered him. "And believe me none of us have *any* idea what they were thinking, or doing, at that time."

Bishop rubbed a hand over his face as he lifted it to look at us. "No wonder you know our languages and can fit in so well. The languages on this planet are probably based off of yours. I mean even the name of your kind, Tintagelians, shortened would be elians or aliens."

"Your languages *are* based off of ours," Rosemary confirmed.

"I feel as if everything we've ever known has been a lie," Abby whispered.

"In a way it has been," Bishop agreed as he finally gave into the urge I'd been resisting and slumped onto the bed. "It really has."

"They destroyed your planet that long ago?" I asked.

"No, that is a more recent development, but they've always been a hungry species that has sought to curb that hunger in many ways. Cultivating species as a food supply became almost a game for them."

I'd already heard something like this from Cade so it wasn't as distressing to me as it was to some of the others, but even still my blood ran cold and I had to swallow in order to wet my very parched throat. "Yeah I mean between destroying lives and a rousing game of rummy I would definitely go for the ruining of lives on that one," Lloyd muttered.

"Lloyd," Aiden said in a low warning tone.

"No, he's right. I didn't see it until I met Greg, but he's right," Rosemary said. "We were wrong. *They* were wrong, but it is what they are. There is nothing to return to on our planet, not anymore. They've drained it dry. What was once a thriving planet with many different species, and lush rivers flowing throughout, is now dry and desolate; the rivers had divided the land into different masses that would be considered something like countries here. When our people expanded into these outer countries and began to eradicate species necessary for the survival of the planet, the rivers began to dry up as the suns baked the land."

"Suns?" Aiden asked.

"There were three of them," Rosemary explained. "Beautiful suns that all rose within an hour of each other, and set an hour apart from each other, so that the sky was alight with color for six hours every day. Not just pinks and oranges and yellows but also the most beautiful greens, blues and magnificent purples. There were even colors that you don't know exist and could never imagine within a sky that was the most pure turquoise color you'd ever see.

"For awhile they tried to save Tintagel, they even imported species from other planets, but it was already too late for that. When the air became too bad for them to breathe they finally admitted defeat and left the planet behind for good."

I was so ensnared by her words that it took me a moment to close my mouth and process what she was saying. "It sounds like it was beautiful, you must have been sad to leave," Jenna whispered.

"Oh, I've never been there," Rosemary responded flippantly. "None of us have. I was born on Planet Earth to two Tintagelians who were born here also. In fact, no one other than The Ancients has ever seen our planet. Each of us is given a crystal that will show us pictures of what Tintagel once looked like when we hold it, but no one has returned to that planet in a hundred and fifty years."

CHAPTER 15

Cade,

Jenna sat down beside Bishop and put her head in her hands. "Jesus," she muttered.

Beside me I could hear the frantic beat of Bethany's heart and smell the increased scent of the sweat on her body. I remained immobile, my face impassive. I knew all of this already, what I hadn't known about was Bethany's newfound thirst for blood.

Why hadn't she told me?

I studied the gentle contours of her face and the freckles covering her cheeks and nose. There was nothing malicious or sneaky within Bethany. All she ever worried about was other people, and I was one of her highest concerns. She hadn't kept it from me to be secretive, she had kept it from me because she had been concerned about how I would react, how I would feel. She had kept it from me because she knew that anything involving her could push me over the edge.

My teeth clenched, I took a deep breath as I cursed my temper and my inability to remain calm around anything that even remotely threatened her life. That would have to change from now on. I had to get better control over myself around her or I had to ensure that nothing was able to threaten her life anymore. I didn't know how I was going to do that, but staring at the group gathered around us now, I had a feeling that this was the place to start.

I didn't trust them, that was the last thing I would do right now, but looking at the humans by their sides I couldn't deny that they were all different. This wasn't some elaborate setup; one look at Rosemary confirmed that. Our people blended in well, but we couldn't fake the kind of humanity that she seemed to radiate and yet I *knew* that she was one of us.

I moved closer to Bethany as I wondered if feeding from her would have the same affect on me over the next couple of weeks, months; *years*. I strangely found myself hoping so, hoping for something to help thaw the ice I felt still encasing me. I could feed from her and it wouldn't injure her. My hands fisted as I inhaled the sweet scent of her and resisted the urge to take her from here and taste as much of her as I could right now.

Later, I told myself firmly. The most important thing was still her safety and keeping her alive. Leaving here now wouldn't get us anywhere on that front.

"Why do The Ancients only have children once every one hundred years?" Bethany asked.

"They want their children on this planet and they want them in positions of authority, but each couple only has one child alive at a time," I answered.

"Why?"

"Because their children are the only ones strong enough to pose any kind of threat to them. They need their children for their power, but they won't take any chance that they could possibly be outnumbered by them. Their children have an average lifespan of a hundred years or so, whereas the rest of us have a more human lifespan though we more often make it into our late eighties. When The Ancients children die, or are on the verge of death, they have another one," Rosemary answered.

"How much stronger?" Bethany asked as her amethyst eyes focused on me.

"Nothing that you haven't seen so far, only heightened," I assured her as I ran my fingers lightly over her arm. I didn't sense any anger in her as she learned about my family line but curiosity radiated from her. "We're faster and stronger than our own kind by almost double. It has been presumed that The Fountain of Youth not only granted The Ancients eternal life but that it also heightened their reflexes, speed and strength. Eternal life isn't passed onto us but the rest is.

Though we are superior even before our eighteenth birthday our abilities become even more enhanced then."

"Ok so where are the other three children?" Lloyd inquired.

"I am one," Jessica answered. "My parents are Agrona and Forseti."

"And yours are?" Bethany asked me.

Something close to annoyance twisted through me as I thought of the two most evil Ancients that had created me. They would be so unbelievably disappointed to see me in what they would consider a weakened state by loving a human. They would enjoy killing me for such a transgression, but that was ok, I wouldn't hesitate to kill them either. I felt nothing for them, other than a driving urge to see them dead, and Bethany safe.

"Mine are the two oldest Ancients, Isis and Osiris," I told her.

Her delicate forehead furrowed as she glanced between Jessica and me. "If you are both children of these Ancients than why would they choose to have you marry? Wouldn't your children also be powerful?"

"They would, but not in the way you're thinking. The speed and strength doesn't carry on into our progeny. It is only direct descendants that acquire any enhanced abilities. Our children would only be powerful because it had been set up for the two of *us* to be in positions of power."

"Where are the other two?" Bethany wanted to know.

"We don't know where they are," Rosemary answered. "There are about two hundred of us in this encampment, but that's just a drop in the bucket. There were thousands upon thousands of us on this planet and I would guess that the majority of them have never experienced what we have."

Lloyd moved away from the door as he finally approached the table. I eyed the gun in his hand but it was more loosely held than when we had first entered the building. It didn't matter though, I'd have it out of his hands and his neck snapped before he ever had a chance to fire it at Bethany or me.

"How do we stop them?" Lloyd inquired.

"There's only one way to do that," Rosemary answered. "We must take them down from the inside, which means that some of us would have to return to the main ship."

"The one that we were born on," Jessica said to me.

I had already assumed that much but it wasn't something I had ever intended to do. Rosemary walked over to the corner and gathered the rolls of papers lying on the floor. "We've been discussing ways to do this."

Unrolling the first one she laid it on the table. "The Ancients are smart and devious but they're also prideful and certain in their belief that *no* one could ever destroy them. For this reason, they're always together and that's their biggest vulnerability."

I stepped closer to the table but I kept my body in between Bethany and them. I was stronger than them, I would make sure to take them all down if they became a threat to her, but there were others out there, and there was Jessica. Her parents weren't as powerful as mine but she was still a great threat especially with so many Tintagelians present.

My gaze went to the woman I was supposed to have married. Looking at her I realized I never would have been able to pull off the marriage. I could barely stay away from Bethany and it only took one look from her, one smile, one touch to drive me near mad. Though she was pretty enough, I felt nothing for Jessica; something I knew would *never* change. Our charade of a marriage never would have been consummated which either would have resulted in my death, or her great happiness and relief at not having to deal with me either.

My attention shifted from Jessica to the drawings before me. My forehead furrowed as I realized exactly what they were. "How do you have a schematic of the ships?" I demanded.

"One ship," Jessica answered. "*Their* ship."

My eyes shifted to her as I bristled with tension and nudged Bethany back another step. She let me know her displeasure at being pushed aside by pinching my arm and elbowing her way forward again. Unwilling to make her unhappy, I relented but wrapped my hand around her forearm so that I would be able to pull her quickly out of the way if something were to happen.

I focused on Jessica. "How do you know what the inside of that ship looks like?"

"I've been on it," Jessica's voice was so subdued that I barely heard her.

A low hiss escaped me as I flattened my hand on the table. "You went up there and were able to look around *without* them knowing?"

"I've discovered a way to sneak on, one they never even thought of."

"How?"

"We may trust you more than you trust us, but for now that is for us to know."

"Why did you have to sneak on? I mean they're your own kind?" Lloyd asked.

"We may be the same species but they're not our kind, not anymore. Every one that enters the ships is carefully recorded and monitored once onboard. If we expect to learn anything, or do anything, we have to do so undercover," Rosemary answered.

Bishop frowned as he rubbed at his chin. "But they don't monitor you while you're down here?"

"No, upon entering the ship everyone is given a bracelet that locks onto the wrist and cannot be removed until they leave the ship. It records where you are at all times."

Bishop lifted his glasses and rubbed at his eyes. "So they know that something happens to some of you when you come to earth. They might even know that whatever happens to you has to do with you meeting certain humans and that is why they monitor you when you're on their ships."

"No they couldn't possibly..." Rosemary's voice trailed off as her mouth formed an O and her face went slack.

"They know," I muttered but my attention wasn't really on Bishop or Rosemary, it was focused on the plans before me.

"You really think so?" Jessica inquired.

"They never trusted anyone that stepped foot on those ships and it was more than them just being paranoid of everyone and everything. I had never thought about it until today, but Bishop's right, they know. It's why the Marshall's were killed. They knew something was wrong with me, but they had it wrong. They must have thought that if the Marshall's were dead I would go back to being like them."

"That doesn't happen," Rosemary said.

"No, I could never, *not* feel again," I agreed. "If I had been anyone else's child I'm sure they would have killed me outright, but all of their plans would have been ruined for the next century if they had done so."

I couldn't resist the urge to brush a strand of golden hair back from Bethany's face as she turned toward me. I would be devastated without her, but I knew I would never be as hollow as I had been before her. I could barely recall the emptiness that had been my life before her, the black hole that had been my inner workings before she had walked into my life, and I *never* wanted to experience it again, no matter how miserable my life would be without her.

A small smile spread across her full mouth, she turned her cheek into my hand. It took all I had to pull myself away from her and back to the plans before us. Another shock rolled down my spine as I noticed the name of a room in the bottom of the ship. "You made it into the *Hallowed* room?"

Jessica paled a little as she shook her head. "It's the one room that I couldn't get into, but I know where it is."

"What is the Hallowed room?" Bret asked.

"It's rumored that it's where the source of their life, perhaps even the Fountain of Youth itself or whatever constitutes The Fountain is located. *No* one, other than The Ancients, has ever gone into it," I answered.

Bishop's brow was furrowed over his glasses as he stared at me. "You think The Fountain may be more than water?"

"Perhaps, none of us have ever seen it. Our planet was largely made of water and it would make sense that The Fountain was water, but I think they also would have tried to throw everyone off of as to what The Fountain truly was."

"It's also rumored that if whatever is in that room is destroyed The Ancients will be destroyed too," Rosemary said.

The hush was so profound that I could hear the distant drip of water from outside and the faint laugh of children playing tag. "We need to get inside that room," I stated.

Jessica shook her head. "I'm not sure we can do that."

I leaned closer to her. "If you can get me on that ship, I'll get us in that room."

The abrupt intake of Bethany's breath sounded in my ear. I slid my arm around her waist and pulled her closer as I sought to comfort her, but I know it didn't do any good as she remained rigid against my side. "I can get you on the ship," Jessica vowed.

"Wait, why would you do that?" Leo demanded as he stepped forward. "We're safe here; we've found a place..."

"It's only temporary. They will search every corner of this world and they will hunt us all down. They may not plan to destroy every human, but we have no way of knowing what they will do to you after they've taken all that they came here for. What they will do to *all* of us. None of us will let you go without a fight and it's obvious that Rosemary has already undergone some changes. The exchanging of the souls and blood has kept the humans hidden, but at any moment they can release a new gas that also affects the people with type O blood and we'll lose even more of our fighting power. Something has to be done before that happens," I told him.

Bishop sat on the bed again, all the color drained from Jenna's face as Abby took a step closer to Aiden. Bethany's fingers dug into my back as she stepped closer. I could feel the tremor that raced through her muscles but I also saw the resolve that settled over her and caused her chin to jut out.

"They won't kill all humans, or at least I don't think they will, and if they don't, they will come back to this planet again. They will only get smarter and stronger while the human race will remain decimated. You will never again be as strong as you are now. Your numbers will only dwindle; your race will only grow weaker. This is a now or never situation," I pressed.

I turned to Jessica, unwilling to deal with Leo's protests anymore. "How many can you get on that ship?"

"Maybe ten, safely. Less than that would be better so we could stay more easily hidden, but more would be better to put up a stronger fight with."

It was a horribly unfair catch twenty two that I didn't have time to think about. "Who do you trust to go?"

"Anyone in this compound," Rosemary answered. "But there are some that are stronger than others."

"Gather the stronger ones so I can speak with them."

Greg held up his hand to halt Rosemary. "Hold on, this is moving *way* too fast. You can't just go back up there."

"You knew this was our ultimate goal and now that Cade is here we have even more power than we had ever hoped for. It's something we have to do. Jessica, go outside and gather Betty, Steve, Cory, and Craig. We'll start with those four for now."

"Wait!" Leo commanded. "If you're going up there than I am going with you."

"Leo..." Jessica started.

"No, he's right," Bethany interrupted. I saw the fire in her eyes as they slid to me. "You can't just leave us here. You did this to us; you changed us and made us different. You made *me* different. You can't just expect to get up and leave us here with no way of knowing what is going on."

"No one is going anywhere right now," I assured her. "There are things to discuss first."

"Jessica, please go get the others," Rosemary said.

Jessica nodded and took hold of Leo's hand. "Come with me."

I barely paid them any attention as they disappeared out the door. "Bishop come and take a look at this."

Bishop took a deep breath and straightened his shoulders as he rose to his feet. I pushed the drawing more firmly down and pointed toward the Hallowed room. The hesitation faded from Bishop's face as his curiosity was snagged by the drawing.

"If I can get in there and destroy this room there is a good possibility we can end this," I told him. "Without The Ancients the others would be lost, they may continue to put up somewhat of a fight, but I think it is more likely that they would flee in panic. Also, The Ancients are the ones that control the gas; the others wouldn't be able to make a new batch without them. The rest of you would be safe."

"What if we try giving all of the type O people my blood or the blood of one of the others like me? It hasn't been done yet and maybe our diluted blood would be able to keep them safe from the gas, but not kill them. Unless you have tried it already?" Bethany asked Rosemary.

I lifted my head to look at Rosemary. "There are humans here that have no ties to any of us. They decided to stay with us after we freed them from being prisoners but we haven't experimented on any of them, we wouldn't do that. There's no way to know what her blood, or any of the others like her, would do to them."

"I've seen what his cells have done to your blood Bethany, they're aggressive and your cells may likely be the same way now. Would we have any notice if they release a new gas?" Bishop asked.

"Not much. *We* will know because we'll be able to smell it, but it's odorless to humans. We won't have more than a day's notice at best, maybe even less," I told him.

"What if you do that whole soul exchanging thing with us?" Molly inquired.

Bethany's fingers dug further into my skin and I couldn't help but feel pleased that such a thought irritated her. "No. There would be no exchange between us; we would take until there was nothing left of you," Rosemary answered.

"Ok so the soul sucking thing is out," Jenna confirmed.

"I gotta say I'm kind of relieved about that one," Bret admitted.

"If I can find some supplies I will take a look at your blood again," Bishop said. "It's worth a shot, especially if they release a new gas. I'd rather die from your blood than turn into one of The Frozen anyway."

"I have to agree," Lloyd said.

"Fine, that's all well and good," I told them. I turned toward Rosemary. "I need to know what you have for supplies that will help us when we get on that ship."

She frowned as she tapped her foot. "Not much. Most of our supplies were used to take over the encampment. We have some ammo left, a couple of bullet proof vests, and four flash grenades but that's about all."

I wasn't entirely sure I believed her but then I wouldn't divulge all of my secrets and supplies to her either. "Bishop, with the supplies we have on hand, can you make me something that if I get into this room, would be able to render whatever is inside of it unusable?" I inquired. "I don't care if it's a gas or a pill, or whatever, I just need something that could ruin a water supply and anything else that may be in that room."

Bishop frowned as he shook his head and opened and closed his mouth. "I've got something that will blow it to smithereens," Lloyd informed me.

I glanced at him. "I'll need that too, but I'd like something a little less 'here I am' also."

Bishop's frown cleared as his mouth parted and a sparkle lit his gray eyes. "I do, or I should be able to find supplies to make something like that. It may take me a couple of days, maybe even a week but I can do it."

Relief filled me as I nodded at the young doctor. "Good."

I turned as the door opened again and Jessica stepped through it with Leo and four other Tintagelians. In her arms was the little girl Jenna had waved to earlier. Her chubby fist was shoved into her mouth and her chocolate hair had been pulled into two pigtails that curled at the ends. I frowned at the child, unable to place what she was as her scent completely threw me off. It wasn't human or perhaps it was as she tilted her head and examined me from deep brown eyes.

"She wouldn't stay away any longer," Jessica said.

Rosemary was smiling from ear to ear as she moved around the table and held her arms out for the girl. I heard the increased beat of Bethany's heart as she grabbed hold of my arm with both hands. "Cade." My name was a bare whisper on her lips as Rosemary took the child from Jessica's arms and hugged her close.

I frowned as I watched the two of them. The child wrapped her arms around Rosemary's neck as she turned to face us again. "She's yours," I stated.

"She's *ours*," Rosemary said with a nod toward Greg.

"She's fine?" Bethany asked in a choked voice.

"She's fine," Rosemary confirmed with a smile.

"But then why didn't they want you to have children if you had married Greg with their knowledge?"

Rosemary's upper lip curled. "We couldn't be allowed to weaken our DNA by mingling it with the humans. They would have destroyed any child that we created."

"Amazing," Bethany whispered.

I felt my own heartbeat pick up as my gaze slid to Bethany. There were tears in her eyes as they met mine with a hope and joy I'd never seen in her gaze before. I wanted to pull her against me and kiss her with everything I had, but that hope in her eyes terrified me. Offspring would have been expected from Jessica and me, but I'd never even considered the thought of allowing Bethany to have my child.

Now she was looking at me like I'd just handed her the moon and Rosemary was holding living proof that a child hadn't destroyed her, or at least it hadn't destroyed an *alien* carrier. "You are not human though," I said.

I felt like the worst form of life when Bethany's shoulders slumped and her grip on my arm slackened. Rosemary's smile only widened as she adjusted the young child in her arms. "There are two human women here who have survived the birthing process."

Her breath was warm against my neck as Bethany stepped even closer to me. Through the fabric of our clothes I could feel the heat of her skin. The missing piece, that's what she was to me, the piece of myself I'd never even known was missing until she walked into my life. She was the only thing that could make me feel as scared and excited as I felt right now.

She could have *my* child. If I survived what we proposed to do, she could become the mother of my children. Our child, excitement trickled through me at the astonishing prospect of such a thing.

Our child.

Bret stepped closer, his gaze slid toward me but I didn't acknowledge the condemnation I saw in his eyes. He'd moved on from her, I knew that, but he still cared for her and didn't want to see anything bad to happen to her, but this was none of his business.

I kissed Bethany's temple as I nuzzled her hair. There was so much hope out there for our future. I just had to make sure we survived to see it.

CHAPTER 16

Bethany,

I remained silent as the last of our group filtered out of the massive gates to rejoin the others. "I wish you would rethink your decision," Rosemary said.

"We have to speak with the others, it needs to be their decision too, and we can't leave them out here. We'll talk again in the morning," Cade assured her.

"We'll leave the gates partly open. If anything comes you must get inside them quickly or our cover could be blown."

"We will."

"Cade." He held me up as he turned back to face Rosemary. Lloyd stopped beside me and though he was still looking at me as if he was tempted to shoot me he had loosened up a little. "We *are* your allies in this. We only want the same thing as you."

"And what is that?"

"To ensure the continuance of the human race and put an end to the tyranny of ours."

Cade's hand tightened on my waist. "I can agree with that," he said quietly.

Rosemary bowed her head before slipping back inside the gates. Darnell was eyeing us both like bugs he wouldn't mind stomping as he approached with caution. "What happened?"

"I'm not entirely sure," Lloyd muttered as he ran a hand through his hair and stared at the gates.

"Are we leaving here?"

"No," Bishop answered. "No we're not."

"Is it safe?"

"Is anything?" I elbowed Cade in his ribs for that response. The scowl slid from his face as he rubbed at his ribs and took a deep breath. "It's safer than anywhere else we've been in awhile. It won't hurt us to stick around for a bit and for you to hear what they have to say. We can go inside tonight if you would like but I thought you'd prefer to talk first."

Darnell's scowl deepened as he rubbed thoughtfully at his chin and focused on Bishop and Lloyd. "You agree with this?"

"I don't agree with any of this, it goes against everything in me to work with them, but I think this may be our best chance and I really think they want what's best for their... what would you call them? Your people?" His blue eyes focused on me as he asked this question.

"No, that is *not* what I would call it," I informed him.

"Apparently not," Cade replied. I frowned as I looked back up at him. *He's starting to get a sense of humor,* I realized. I didn't know if it was because of what we had exchanged or if because for the first time there wasn't as much pressure on him anymore. He could finally give into the urges that he had been fighting for so long with no fear of what would happen to me.

"Perhaps it's the closest thing to an actual soul mate any of us will ever see," Bishop said as he rubbed at his chin. "Perhaps this alien-human connection is what spawned that term in the first place." I felt my eyebrow quirk as I glanced at Cade and wondered if Bishop was right. "It may actually be her soul you see."

"Well it sounds like I have a lot to learn." Darnell lowered his gun to his side. I couldn't meet his gaze as he continued to stare at me as if he didn't know me. It would be a long time, if ever, before they forgave me or at least started to trust me again. "And I'd like to start hearing it."

Cade nodded his agreement as the others gathered around us. "Away from the gates would be preferable."

Darnell nodded and fell back as Cade led the way toward the edge of the forest. They gathered in a circle around us while Cade, Bishop and Lloyd began to fill them in on the details. I settled onto the ground and pulled my knees against my chest as Abby sat beside me. "You could have told me," she whispered.

I couldn't bring myself to look at her as I shook my head. The firelight played over Cade's skin, highlighting the contours of his face and the shadowy hue of his eyes. Though he didn't seem to radiate the warmth of Rosemary, there was something different about him as he actually conversed with the others instead of remaining distant and cold.

A child, we could have a child. My heart soared like a bird just freed from its cage as dreams I had thought impossible unfurled before me. There were many things I had thought impossible now but to have this one thing back was one of the greatest gifts I'd ever been given. To bring a child into this world wasn't something that I wanted to do, but if we won, if we managed to somehow beat them back we could have a child, a *family*. It was one of the best things I'd heard since this entire mess had started.

"No, I couldn't have. It wasn't my secret to tell." The look of betrayal in Abby's eyes was a knife to the chest but there was little I could do to ease that. "I'm sorry, I really am. But just as I'll always protect you, I'll also protect him."

"You don't need to protect him from me though."

"No, but I had to protect you. It was a big secret Abby, one that you shouldn't have been burdened with. You have enough on your plate right now."

"I'm not a child anymore."

I took her fingers within mine. "I know, but I would like it if you could be for just a little while longer."

Some of her anger with me seemed to ease as she leaned against my shoulder and rested her head against mine. "Are you going to be ok Bethany?"

"Of course."

"The side effects that you've been experiencing..."

"I'll be fine Abby, they're not so bad. At least I don't walk into everything anymore and I don't trip over my own feet.

You heard Rosemary, I'll be fine," I assured her with a smile.

Her breath was warm against my chilled cheek as she chuckled. "True. That little girl was cute."

"She was," I agreed.

I closed my eyes and inhaled the smoky scent of her hair. I didn't realize I'd drifted off until I felt the solid strength of Cade's arms wrapping around me. Sliding my arms around his neck, I buried my face in the hollow of his throat and sighed contentedly. "Do they forgive us?" I whispered.

"That will come in time."

I shivered as he pressed his lips against my temple. My toes curled as I felt the increase of his pulse beating against my lips when I pressed my mouth to his neck; I wasn't sure if it was passion for him though, or the spark of hunger that shot through me at the smell of his blood that caused the heightened beat of his heart. His hand tensed on my thigh as his heated mouth brushed over my forehead.

"Bethany," he whispered against my skin.

I reluctantly forced myself away from him. My eyes fell to my hands as they lay curled within my lap. He stepped around a large oak and settled the two of us onto the ground. I found myself unable to meet his gaze as he seized hold of my chin and turned my head toward him. There was a gleam in his eyes that made my stomach feel as if there were thousands of butterflies fluttering within it.

I could see the flicker of the torches from the compound as they sparked and danced amongst the trees. They were a reminder that we weren't alone out here but when he was looking at me like that I felt as if we were the only two people in the world.

He brushed the hair back from my face. "Why didn't you tell me about the side effects?"

His thumb rubbed over my cheek as his lips brushed over mine. I didn't know if he expected an answer, but when he was kissing me like that there was no way I could think of a reply. My fingers curled into his shirt, a small mewl of protest escaped me as he pulled away. My gaze focused on his full mouth as I trailed my finger over his bottom lip.

"Because I didn't want to burden you," I finally lifted my gaze to his. "And because I didn't want to acknowledge them either."

His hands clasped hold of my cheeks as he pulled me away from him. There was a fever in his eyes that I'd never seen before as anguish caused his mouth to purse. "I didn't... I never meant..." his voice broke off as he kissed me with an intensity that robbed me of my breath. "I never meant to burden you with this. I never meant for you to know what it was that I lived with."

"Don't," I managed to gasp out. "This is why I didn't tell you. Don't blame yourself, there's nothing else you could have done."

"Apparently I could have given in and tasted you," he whispered. His mouth tickled against mine as he spoke. "You wouldn't have to be going through this right now."

I clasped his hand against my face and turned my mouth into his palm. "You couldn't have known," I assured him. "You did everything you could to keep me alive, and I'm *here*. I can live with a little craving for raw meat as long as I have you."

His eyes glimmered in the torchlight before he bent to kiss me again. Yes, I could definitely deal with a little craving for blood as long as he was holding me and kissing me with such reverence that the world slipped away and I forgot about everything else. His heated breath filled my mouth when his tongue slipped in to temptingly tangle with mine.

My fingers slid through his thick hair, I felt something within him rising up to enter into me. I pressed closer against him as the part of him that sought my soul coursed into my body with the flowing ease of a melody from a songbird. I felt when it latched onto a piece of me, and when something inside of me reached out and latched onto him in return.

A subtle growl escaped him and he pulled me more firmly against him. Before he'd been almost hesitant with me but after today he seemed to have realized that I wouldn't break. That he could take from me as much as he needed and I would still be here and I would still be *me*. I felt my soul being pulled from me in forceful tugs that made my knees go weak and my bones turn to liquid.

I could feel pieces of his soul entering me and moving throughout my body. Heat pooled through my extremities, my body went limp as he blended and moved effortlessly through me. He invaded me completely as I brought him deeper into me, joining with him in an intimate way that went beyond sex, beyond anything I ever could have imagined as I felt him entwining with my soul.

He was panting as he broke away from me and his mouth fell to my neck. I clung to him as my body continued to float in a haze of bliss the likes of which I never could have imagined. "Dangerous," he murmured against my skin as his lips traveled over me.

"No," I assured him as I gently took hold of his hand and pressed it against the place where my heart beat so fiercely. "I can feel you here, inside me. It's where you belong Cade, where you've always belonged."

His striking eyes searched my face as his hand slid around my back and he slipped the knife at my waistband free. "There's something more you want though."

I didn't want to admit it, didn't want to look but a tingle of anticipation gripped me as he lifted the knife between us. His eyes never left mine as he unfolded the blade and drew it across the inside of his wrist. The smell of his blood was potent in the crisp air as he lifted it to me. I tried to pull away but his hand in the small of my back held me steady.

"Denying it will only make it worse and you more volatile. Drink from me tonight Bethany and tomorrow I'll take you into the woods and teach you how to hunt so that you'll be able to feed yourself if the situation becomes desperate."

His unspoken words caused my throat to clog. *In case he didn't return from the ship. In case he died.* I couldn't think about that now though I wasn't sure I'd be able to function if I did.

The blood glistened on his wrist as he held it out to me. Something inside of me screamed to take it and drink it as saliva rushed into my mouth. The part of me that was still human, and repulsed by the notion cringed at the idea of doing such a thing. He lowered his head to look up at me before biting into his bottom lip. A low groan escaped me as a bead of blood swelled onto his lip.

I didn't have time to protest as he pulled me against him and captured my mouth once more. My hands pressed against his chest as his tongue swirled into my mouth, along with his blood. Whatever fight I'd had in me vanished as I slumped against him. A low moan escaped me; I grasped hold of his biceps in an attempt to keep myself grounded. His blood was the most delicious thing I'd ever tasted as I nibbled at his lip.

Pleasure raged through my long denied body as his blood coalesced with mine. A small sound of discomfort escaped him when I bit down harder than I'd meant to on his lip. I recoiled, horrified that I'd hurt him and would continue to do so if it meant getting more of what I yearned for.

He didn't give me a chance to get far though as he grabbed me and pulled me back against him. "Don't fight it Bethany, as much as you wanted to do this for *me*, I want to do it for *you*. Don't fight me, please."

It was the burning look in his eyes that made me cave to his wishes. "Cade..."

Before I could finish speaking he was kissing me again and then I just didn't care, not anymore. I lost myself to the taste and feel of him as he broke away to offer me his wrist again. I brought his wrist to my mouth as his lips traveled over my neck and down to my collarbone. Even the distant flicker of firelight faded away as my entire world became focused on him and the pleasure that he so willingly gave.

CHAPTER 17

Cade pressed his finger against his mouth and gestured toward the mountain lion that had roamed into our path. Apprehension trickled through me at the same time that the electrical pulses in my brain fired with excitement and disbelief. He couldn't possibly be planning to go after *that* animal; it weighed almost as much as he did. Not only that, its claws alone could carve a man open with just one swipe. It was a lot different from the deer he'd shown me how to catch and take down an hour ago before allowing it to go free.

'Stay,' he mouthed to me before slipping into the woods. The movement of the red and orange leaves was the only indication that he'd been there at all. No matter how many years I knew him, I knew I would never get over how fast and soundlessly he could move. I was just turning away from the place where he'd been when he launched himself from the woods and onto the animal.

The lion let out a guttural cry as Cade wrapped his arms around its neck and wrestled it to the ground as if it weighed no more than a house cat. He straddled the animal as he pressed its neck into the ground and sat on its shoulders. "You can come out," he called to me.

He was stroking the creature's neck and talking reassuringly to it as I hesitatingly approached from the forest. I watched in amazement as the large animal's legs stopped kicking and it began to relax beneath him. "What? Are you the lion whisperer now?" I asked in a hushed voice.

A small smile curved his full mouth as his eyes twinkled in the sunlight streaming through the trees. "We're just predators that have a mutual understanding of each other."

Predator, that's what I was now, but then I supposed that's what I'd been all along, I'd just never had to hunt for my food before. "Don't be afraid," Cade urged.

How could I not be a little afraid, he was sitting on a hundred and fifty pounds of pure muscle? The cat's eyes rolled toward me but it remained calm beneath Cade. "Come," he said with a wave of his hand.

Despite my trepidation I was irresistibly drawn forth by him. He took hold of my hand and moved me away from the massive claws extended from a paw that was bigger than my hand. "It's beautiful," I whispered as he pulled me close to its side.

Its nostrils flared and its eyes rolled toward me. My muscles quivered, I waited for it to knock Cade free and pounce on me. It remained relatively calm beneath him though as he placed a hand against its neck and began to rub it. "How are you doing that?" I asked.

"Years of practice," he answered flippantly.

"Cade..."

"It's not mind control or anything like that. We simply have a way of calming things, it helps when we are hunting our prey. Perhaps it is our touch or maybe our voices that they enjoy so much." I could see that, as both his touch and voice had a way of making me do things too. I was certain the massive animal wasn't going to be as enthralled by my voice or touch though.

He took hold of my hand and pressed it to the corded muscles of the animal's neck. Admiration filled me as I stroked the lion's coarse coat and thick muscles. Its upper lip curled back to reveal canine's that I was certain would have made a sabre tooth proud. A loud snort escaped it as its snarl fell away and its eyes closed briefly.

I couldn't get enough of the animal as my hands roamed over its body. A smile spread across my lips as I lifted my head to look at Cade. The smile that curved his mouth wasn't as rare as it had once been, but it still melted my heart.

The cat snorted beneath him and my attention was drawn back to it as it yawned loudly and kicked one of its legs. "I'm going to let it up, do you think you can do what I did?"

My eyes flew to his; I inhaled sharply as I took in the massive animal. "I'm not strong enough..."

"You don't know that, not yet, and we have to learn just what it is that you might be capable of Bethany. I'll be right here and I won't let it attack you."

I believed him, but even so the thought of trying to wrestle down the massive animal was enough to make my bladder tighten and my head spin, but I was also curious to find out if I could do it and surprised by the fact that the curiosity appeared to be winning. This was a lot different than a deer; this animal could get me before I even had a chance to blink.

"Are you ready?" he inquired.

I studied the animal before finally forcing myself to nod. "I'm ready."

I wasn't but if I thought about it, I wouldn't do it at all. Cade hesitated before releasing the animal's powerful neck and launching himself to his feet. The cat was almost as quick as Cade was as corded muscles hunched and it shoved itself to its feet in one mighty push.

There is no place for fear here, I told myself. I became completely still as I allowed my mind and body to focus inward in search of the power that flowed through me like Cade had instructed me to. The world around me became completely still, the sounds of the birds and the insects within the woods faded away to nothing as an almost complete deafness took me over.

It was strange and a little unnerving to have the sudden calm of Cade's DNA asserting itself over my body. Maybe it was because he had given me more of his blood last night, but I found it far easier to focus on that part of myself than I had anticipated. My fingers tingled as something within me, something that he had given to me, came to life.

I could hear the animal's heartbeat and feel the air particles as they drifted around me in the hushed world. The animal shook its head as I raced forward and grabbed hold of it. I felt the shudder that rocked the lion as I wrapped my arms around its thick neck and flung myself to the side as Cade had.

The formidable animal rolled with me but I knew immediately that I wasn't going to win as thick muscles bunched beneath my hand and my grip was effortlessly torn free of it. I barely dodged the massive paw that swiped at my face as I bounced across the ground. A startled cry escaped me as teeth filled my vision and the mountain lion came at me with every intention of ripping me open and feasting on my insides.

I was certain I was about to die when Cade threw himself in front of me and caught the animal in mid leap. Struggling to my feet, I braced myself to help him, but he already had the wild creature shoved away from him and his arms open as he stood before me.

The massive cat's tail twitched in annoyance as it licked its lips, but it didn't come at me again. Obviously while I looked like an easy, tasty treat, Cade was a lot more off putting as the creature
slinked back into the woods. Cade waited a moment, his head turned as he followed the cat's progress through the woods.

He glanced at me over his shoulder. "Are you ok?"

I wiped at the dirt smeared across my ass as I took stock of my body. I was a little sore but all my insides were still intact and I was standing so that was a good thing. "Pride's a little bruised, but otherwise I'm fine."

There it was again, that smile that used to be so rare but could light up a room and melt my heart. I couldn't help but return it as he lowered his arms to his sides and turned to face me. "We'll stick to deer from now on," he assured me.

I didn't exactly relish the idea of taking down Bambi on a consistent basis, but it was far more preferable than trying to take down a mountain lion again. Something I wasn't about to try a second time. "I may be different, but I'm not as strong or as quick as you."

"No, you're not" he agreed.

"That means that maybe my blood could be used to help others."

He groaned as he slid his hand into mine. "We'll see what Bishop has to say on it and if there's any way he can take a look at your blood again."

With unerring ease he led the way through the woods. "Where are we going?" I asked.

"To find Bishop and the others."

"How do you know they're this way?"

He flashed a grin at me as he touched his nose. "I can smell them."

"Well that's an interesting little talent."

He pulled me against his side and kissed the top of my head. "You have much to learn little grasshopper."

I couldn't help but laugh as I wrapped my arms around his waist. I could feel the solid ridges of his abdomen as it flexed and bunched with each step that he took. Reaching out, he pushed aside a tree branch to reveal the backyards of a neighborhood I hadn't known was there. "What are they doing here?" I asked.

"Bishop's looking for something that he can make to use on the ship."

"Cade, do you really intend to go on that ship?"

He stopped walking and turned to face me. "If it means keeping you alive than yes, I do."

"And what about you?" I asked in a choked voice.

"I'll be fine."

He went to turn away but I grabbed hold of his shirt and pulled him back. "I'm going with you."

The old Cade returned in an instant as his face became as hard as granite. "No."

He may be acting a little more human but he had no idea how infuriating he could be when that alien side took over again. "I'm stronger now Cade, faster..."

"And you're still human. No matter the changes Bethany I can still smell the humanity on you and they'll be able to also. The second you step foot on that ship they'll know you're there, they will find us and they *will* destroy us."

My breath rushed out of me as my protest died on my lips. I longed to ask what I would do without him, how I would possibly survive if he was gone, again, but I remained silent. There was a haunted look in his eyes that made it impossible for me to lay such a guilt trip on him. It didn't have to be him that went, but even as I thought that I knew it *did* have to be him.

"You would have been one of the leaders of your people, here on earth?" I asked.

His shoulders slumped in relief as he realized I wasn't going to pursue my plea to have him stay here, with me. "That was what was intended, yes. My parents are the most powerful and therefore I would have been looked to as our representative here on earth if they hadn't returned in our lifetime."

"They'll still look to you as their leader?"

"Yes." He pulled me against his chest and wrapped me in a firm embrace. "I'll keep you safe, always."

"I want *you* to be safe," I whispered.

His lips curled into a cocky grin as he pulled back to look at me. "There's no stopping me."

"Har har," I muttered as I leaned forward to press a kiss against the bottom of his chin.

We both knew if he was discovered on that ship he was as good as dead. "It may not even be a definite thing yet. There is still a lot to discuss. Come on let's find the others."

He took hold of my hand again and led me through some of the backyards before we came across Bishop, Aiden, Lloyd and Jenna in a small backyard. Bishop and Jenna were filling a pillowcase full of the little red berries from a yew; Aiden was cutting snips from the bush while Lloyd stood guard by the back gate. Lloyd's gun turned toward us as Cade stepped through the open gate but he quickly brought it back to his side.

"I almost shot you," Lloyd muttered.

"You could have tried, but you would have failed," Cade told him.

Even my eyebrows shot up at that one as the others stopped in the act of filling their cases. Cade didn't seem to notice their astonishment though as he strode toward Bishop. "What are you doing?" he inquired.

Bishop managed to close his mouth as he stepped away from the bush. "Yews are poisonous, especially the seeds of the berries."

Cade frowned as he stared at the bushes. "I don't know if that would be enough or if it would even affect us."

"I thought of that." Bishop stepped away from the bush and walked over to a set of trashcans sitting next to the back gate. "There are some wisteria clippings and seedpods that I'm hoping have some seeds left as they're highly poisonous. We've also gathered some Rhododendron and Azalea clippings. I've found a few hydrangea flowers and I'm going to try and locate some deadly nightshade next. It should still be alive this time of year but it might be tricky to uncover. By the time I'm done this is going to be the most lethal combination of poisonous plants we've ever come across. Each plant will have a different effect so if one plant doesn't work hopefully the next one will. But just to be on the safe side we've also gathered some rat poison from a few of the homes."

Cade nodded as he looked over the assortment of pillowcases. "That kind of combination should work."

"Want to be the guinea pig?" Lloyd asked.

I shot him a ferocious look but Cade simply chuckled, "Not today."

Aiden offered me another pillowcase and a pair of scissors. "Give me a hand with this, Killer," he added from the corner of his mouth.

"You're funny," I muttered as he began to fill my bag and Cade retreated to keep watch with Lloyd.

"He'll be fine," Aiden assured me.

"Will he? He plans to go on that ship."

Aiden turned to survey them. "I know, but he'll come back. That alien has nine lives."

"Aiden..."

He squeezed my hand and dropped another handful of yew branches into the bag. "He'll come back."

I could only pray that he was right as I held my bag open for the next handful of clippings. My heart swelled as I looked over at Cade, but no matter what I would stay strong. I wouldn't make him feel bad for going; I wouldn't cry and beg for him to stay even if it was the *only* thing I wanted to do. There was no reason to make him feel bad for something he was going to do no matter what.

CHAPTER 18

Cade,

"So if you can get us on through here, we could make it to the Hallowed room within an hour."

Jessica lifted her head to look at me. Her brown eyes shimmered in the dim light of the lanterns as she gave a brisk nod. The subtle aroma of our species wafted from her. There was nothing on earth that our scent quite compared to but I supposed the closest thing would be the scent of a fresh spring rain. The many rivers that had once flowed through our planet seemed to still be engrained within our essence somehow.

"If all goes well," she confirmed.

I leaned back to survey the people in the room. Rosemary stood at the head of the table with the lamp to the right of her. Greg's face was pale and drawn as he glanced between the plans and Rosemary. "We should be allowed to come," he asserted.

"You'd be discovered in a heartbeat, but don't worry because Rosemary's not going either," I informed him bluntly.

Rosemary did a double take. "What!? Why!? I can be of use."

"You could have been," I admitted. "But there are too many changes in you, I can see them, even the humans can see them. There's too much of a risk that you could alert The Ancients to our presence on that ship."

She looked about to protest further but then her face fell and she looked helplessly toward Greg who couldn't contain the smile that curved his mouth. "What about you? Won't they be able to pick up on changes in you too?" Bethany demanded.

I'd been avoiding her gaze. I couldn't stand the sadness I knew would be reflected back at me in her amethyst eyes.

"There are fewer changes in us." *And even less in me*, I added silently.

Bethany's face remained immobile but I could sense the thoughts rapidly running through her mind. She gave a subtle shake of her head and dropped her eyes to the floor. I wanted to go to her, but I remained where I was as, Cory, one of the Tintagelians Rosemary had brought in to help, took a step forward. Despite his Tintagelian heritage, Cory's hair was so light that it was nearly blond and his eyes were almost honey in hue. I'd heard that there were a few fairer ones amongst us now that had exhibited signs of their DNA already beginning to adjust to life away from the three suns of our planet, but Cory was the first one I'd ever seen.

"There is far less in us," Cory agreed. "We should be able to fly under the radar, but not you Rosemary. Maybe one day we'll be where you are as we're all steadily becoming more human in some ways, but we're not there yet."

My gaze ran over Betty, Craig and Steve, the other three Tintagelians that Rosemary had thought would be best to go with us. I had to agree with her choices. Over the past week I'd met everyone within the camp and though Rosemary had been highly affected by Greg's soul, there were others that had been even more so. These were the four least affected and most powerful within the camp.

"We can take more," Jessica suggested.

I was greatly tempted too but more of us on that ship just felt like begging to be caught. "No, I think six of us will be enough."

I felt my gaze slide to Bethany. She remained immobile, her shoulders thrust back and her gaze focused on the wall behind me. I'd never known fear before I'd met her. Never known what it was like to worry for someone or care about them. I'd never known anything except for an emptiness so complete that it had been like a black hole within my body. I don't know if this was the way that all of my kind felt, or if it was only those of us that had someone out there waiting for them that felt as if there was absolutely nothing within ourselves before we found them.

Then I'd seen her standing there all those years ago with her freckles, skinned knees and pigtails and I'd known fear, almost instantaneously. I'd also known a hunger the likes of which I'd never experienced before and that hadn't even come close to being sated until I'd finally tasted *her* soul. And what a soul it was, even now I could see the golden edges of it surrounding her and tempting me as it called to me in the way that only she could.

I could still taste the sweetness of it, still feel it filling me, seeping within my body and warming me in a way that no deer, bear, cougar or other human could. I'd loved her and been troubled about her from the second I'd first seen her, but now, I found myself beginning to like Aiden, Abby, Bishop and the others too. And not only because Bethany loved them but because I found myself beginning to care and worry for them too. I was even beginning to be able to stand Bret better now, though I couldn't acknowledge the fact that he had once hugged and kissed her too. I'd driven her into that relationship, I'd done nothing to stop it from forming, but then there was nothing I could have done without risking her life.

No, I'd never known fear before her, but it had been a constant part of me since I'd first laid eyes on her. I'd been convinced she would reject me for what I was, that she would hate me, but I'd been even more afraid that she wouldn't. That she would love me as much as I loved her and her life would be a never ending battle of misery and death.

I'd had a choice before, to let her live her life, a normal *human* life, but that choice had been taken from me when my kind had decided that it was time to invade. Now the only concern I had was what would become of her if I didn't return.

I'd put her in this highly perilous position and I'd do everything I could to make sure she remained safe, even if it meant I never came back from that ship. She'd survive, I knew that. I'd break her heart again, I'd leave her in a precarious world, but she'd survive her broken heart, and her loved ones would be there for her. Including Lloyd, who still grumbled about aliens and watched me like a hawk, but I'd given him more than a few chances to attack me and he hadn't taken them. He wouldn't have succeeded but at least I knew where he stood, and if he did go after Bethany I was certain she would be able to take him down with much more ease than she'd shown with that cougar.

I'd do whatever it took to keep her safe and the only way to ensure her safety was to get on that ship and destroy the Tintagelians that had driven us into this remote corner of the state, and to each other. I still didn't entirely trust the Tintagelians in the room with me, but I saw the love between them and the ones they loved. If they had one ounce of the same amount of love for their Souls as I had for Bethany then they would also sacrifice everything in order to ensure that they stayed alive.

My gaze slid back to Bethany as Bret bent to whisper something in her ear. Jealousy slithered down my spine, not that they would get back together as I knew that wasn't a possibility, but that he would get to see her when all of this was over. That he would continue to be in her life when I highly doubted that I would be. It wasn't a suicide mission exactly, but it was on the borderline.

"When would you like to go?" Jessica asked.

I forced myself not to glance at Bishop who had assured me his concoction of every deadly thing he could get his hands on would be ready to go tomorrow. It wasn't nearly as much time as I wanted with her but the longer we waited the more likely the chance we would be discovered here.

"Tomorrow night."

I didn't miss the sudden, harsh inhalation of Bethany's breath or the flutter of her eyes as they darted past me to the window beyond. Less than a day, it was all we had left together. I wasn't willing to spend one more second standing here amongst this group. Striding over to Bethany, Bret took a step back as I slid my hand into hers and clasped it before me.

"We'll leave at sunset," I added.

I didn't look back as I led Bethany out of the small cabin and down the steps. Avoiding the main gate of the encampment, I led her through the deeper shadows, passed the shanties crudely assembled from tin, plywood, and even some tires. She didn't labor to keep up with my pace anymore, but walked at my side with her gaze focused straight ahead. This new woman beside me was fascinating to watch grow and learn new things about herself, but I'd also loved the girl who had stumbled over her own feet and sat in gum at lunch.

I stopped at the back fence and pulled aside the hole I had discovered in it days ago. Bethany slipped through it with me close on her heels. Though the others would stay within the camp, or outside the main gate, we were going to stay in the small shack on the outskirt of the fence that had been established as an outpost for the encampment.

Arriving at the door of the hut I released her hand and opened it cautiously. I poked my head inside but I smelled nothing off within and I didn't hear the pulse of any heartbeats. Taking hold of her hand I led her inside and lit the small lamp sitting beside the bed. There was so much to say and yet there were no words that I could give her, no promises that I could make.

She seemed to understand this as instead of trying to talk me out of it, instead of trying to convince me to take her with me she simply came to me and wrapped her arms around my waist. A contented sigh escaped me as I embraced her against my chest. I hadn't expected tears; I knew she wouldn't cry, not in front of me, she would save her tears for when I was gone.

I inhaled her sweet scent as I buried my face in her hair. In school she'd smelled of strawberries or apples, depending on which shampoo she was using at the time. Now she smelled of woods and earth and a scent that was inherently *her*. Something sweet and magnificent that made my blood race and my breath quicken as her hands slid up the back of my shirt and around to the front of it.

I had planned to talk and kiss and hold her as I savored every second of the time we had left together, but as her fingers slid down to the waistband of my jeans I knew that what I wanted more than anything was to lose myself in her. To bury myself in the taste and feel of her, to become consumed by the pleasure that only she could give me.

Too fast, it was far faster than I had anticipate for it to be, but she didn't protest as I lifted her up and deposited her on the small bed within the room. It was too out of control but as I lost myself within her body and soul I knew there was nothing controllable about what was between us.

***

"Cade?"

"Hmm?" I inquired as I traced the contours of her slender, pale back.

"Do you still have your crystal?"

I frowned as my hand stopped moving. "No."

She turned her head and rested it on her folded arms as she looked up at me. "You got rid of the crystal that allowed you to see your homeland?"

"The day I met you."

I brushed the hair back from her face as her mouth parted. I couldn't tear my eyes away from her as I memorized every minute detail of her, right down to the different shapes of her freckles. She wasn't beautiful, not like Jenna's refined and delicate perfection. No, Bethany's beauty was far more understated but her soul was nearly tangible as it radiated from her like the sun and lit her from the inside out.

"That was the only piece of your home you had," she whispered.

"You're my home Bethany; I've known it since the day we met."

Tears filled her eyes as she moved closer to me and buried her face in my neck. I enveloped her within my arms and held her against me. The press of her body against mine was the only thing that could ease the ache within my heart. This could be the biggest mistake of my life, leaving her like this, but I didn't know how else to protect her. I didn't know how else to give her a chance to survive in this world.

I wasn't leaving an unruly and precarious creature behind that couldn't defend herself. She could control her appetite and knew how to feed on prey that wasn't human in order to ensure her survival if the meat supply ran low. She was better able to defend herself than I ever would have imagined six months ago and not because she was stronger and faster than most humans now, but also because she had struggled to survive with the others. She hadn't spent the past few months hiding from the monsters but rather she'd spent that time learning how to fight them. It would be difficult for her without me, but she'd live, I *knew* that.

"No matter what happens Bethany, to me or to you, I need you to know that I love you."

"And I love you," she whispered. "But you'll come back, I know you will."

"I'm going to do everything in my power to come back to you."

I couldn't bring myself to issue promises to her that I would definitely come back. There was a good possibility that I wouldn't be back, and I refused to lie to her. I wiped away the tears that slid from her eyes.

"I'll be here," she promised. "I'll *always* be here for you."

She was finally beginning to realize what I'd known all along, she was stronger than she'd ever given herself credit for. Even after her father's death, when she'd been so broken and lost, she'd had a rod of strength within her that few humans possessed. She had her weaknesses, but they no longer crippled her, she faced them head on and dealt with them as they came at her. She would face my loss with the same stalwart determination she used to face everything else in her life.

"They have a child Cade."

I smiled as I wrapped a strand of her hair around my finger. It was nearly as golden as the aura she radiated. "They do."

Hope radiated within her eyes as her hand fell upon my arm. "We could too, if you come back?"

Dreams I'd never had unfurled before me and I knew there was nothing I wanted more than to come back here and have a child with her. Nothing I wanted more than to start a family with her, to call her mine for the rest of our lives and to be able to love her freely.

"If I come back we *will* have a child," I promised her.

I couldn't resist kissing her again. Pulling her against me, I slid my hands through her hair as her mouth opened to my invasion. She was always so warm, so willing and giving. I'd never met anyone like her; I doubted they even existed as she gave her heart, body and soul freely to me with an eager acceptance that left me desperate for even more of her.

I felt the edges of her soul tickling against mine and the driving urge to grasp hold of it seized me. I fought the urge though as my hands slid over her silken skin. Though I was hungry, I couldn't take anymore from her, I'd seen the changes it had rendered in Rosemary and I couldn't take the chance that consuming more of her would have such an effect on me before I made it onto that ship.

She'd already made me more human by loving me, the beauty and strength of her soul was only going to continue that process.

Then she latched onto something within me. The breath left my chest as she began to taste me in pulling waves that shook me. My hands clenched in her hair, instinctively I wanted to pull away from the feeling of vulnerability the action aroused in me, but then pleasure swamped me as I gave myself over to her quest for more.

My heart raced as her fingers curled into my arms and she held onto me. Her breath was subtle against my lips as she opened even further to me. She was the most magnificent thing I'd ever experienced and I simply couldn't get enough of her. There was no doubt within me that I would gladly hand over my own life for hers.

CHAPTER 19

Bishop slipped the leather pouch with the ten vials of poison he'd created safely into a pocket sewn on the inside of the shirt he held. "One drop of this stuff would kill a human but I have no idea what it would do to an alien without testing it on one of you first."

"Well let's just hope that it will be effective against them," I said.

"There's a syringe in here too, if you're able to get close enough to inject someone with it they should drop like a drunken sailor on leave." Bishop's gray eyes appeared even larger behind his glasses as he lifted his head to look at me. His ingrained curiosity was evident as he studied me. "I plan to try and find some more medical equipment to study Bethany's blood if I can."

Everything in me protested the statement, but there was nothing to hide anymore. "Ok," I said.

My gaze slid to her as she stood surrounded by Abby and Aiden. Bret stood slightly to the side with his arms folded over his chest. Jenna stood beside him, and though they weren't showing it around anyone yet, I'd noticed a subtle change in their scents when they were around each other now. A spike in their hormone levels that no human would have been able to detect but I knew it indicated that they had resumed their old relationship.

"There could be something in her blood that could help us, maybe," Bishop said.

I turned my attention back to the doctor. I trusted these people with the most important thing in my life, it was something I'd never done before, but as Bishop held my gaze I knew I was doing the right thing. They would all do what it took to keep each other safe. Even Lloyd, who was still sullen and resentful toward Bethany and me, was standing protectively behind the others with his rifle pressed against his chest.

I nodded as Darnell stepped beside Lloyd and they spoke softly. Darnell took hold of Lloyd's rifle before he came toward me. "I told you I'd give you something that could cause some damage to that monstrosity." Lloyd dug into his pocket and pulled out a grenade. "It's our last one so put it to good use by blowing those assholes out of the sky."

"I will," I assured him as I took it from him and slipped it into my pocket.

"Do you know how to use it?"

"I've got a pretty good idea."

"I've also got these for you." Lloyd pulled a small pack forward and pulled out an oilskin cloth from a pouch within it. He rolled the oilskin open to reveal a small pipe with a single fuse sticking out the end of it.

"You're going to have to be really careful with these," Lloyd told me. "I'm good with explosives but these certainly do *not* contain military grade materials. They contain a hodgepodge collection of whatever I could find in the nearby homes that could be used as an explosive. Too much jostling and these things could blow. I would suggest ditching them if you have even a little doubt that they'll be able to make it through."

He handed me a Zippo lighter and a small pair of scissors. "You've got about five seconds after you light it before it explodes. I normally would never make it so short but you guys are so fast that five seconds may be too long even. If you feel you need less time cut it shorter before lighting it."

I studied the deceptively innocent looking soldier as he folded the oilcloth and tucked it into another pouch that had been sewn into the inside of the shirt. He'd been resentful after learning the truth but as he handed me the shirt I realized that he hoped for my return. It was a strange realization as I thought Bethany was the only one that had any real concern for me, but as I looked at the group I saw the strain on all of their faces. Abby and Jenna even had tears in their eyes. Perhaps, if I somehow made it back, these people could become my friends. Or perhaps they already considered themselves my friends and I had never realized it. Either way it wouldn't matter unless I returned.

"Good luck and don't blow yourself up first," Lloyd said to me.

I forced a smile to my face, I didn't feel as distant and cold as I had before tasting Bethany's soul, but I wasn't entirely sure what was changing within me yet either. "I'll try not to." I assured him before turning away from him. I slid a t-shirt over my head and turned as Bishop held out the black button up shirt to me. I could feel the weight of the pouches against my chest but the baggy black shirt hid them well as I slid the buttons into place.

Bishop nodded his approval. "You can't even tell they're there."

"Good."

Taking a deep breath, I turned to Bethany. This was going to be the worst part. Bethany forced a smile as I walked over and took hold of her hands. "I promise as long as I draw a breath I will try and come back to you."

Tears shimmered in her eyes, but she kept the smile on her face as her hands clenched around mine. "I'll be here."

I clasped hold of her cheeks as I bent and kissed her forehead. "I love you," I whispered in her ear.

Her hands clenched on my arms. "I'll always love you, always."

I reluctantly released my hold on her but her fingers dug into my flesh. "Bethany..."

Her eyes were closed as her hands slid away from me. "Be careful, don't do anything to get yourself killed, if you can't succeed then come back and we'll figure out another way," she gushed out.

There was no other way; this was the only chance we would have to defeat them, if we failed in this than all hope for humanity would be lost. I didn't say this to her though, I couldn't take away this bit of hope she had. Unable to resist, I kissed her quickly again before tearing myself away from her.

"Stay safe Bethany, don't do anything crazy."

"Never," she replied with a fleeting smile.

I didn't look back as I turned and walked away, but I caught the scent of her tears as I made my way out of the small clearing. It took everything I had to keep walking, to keep putting one foot in front of the other instead of turning back and refusing to let her go again. Darnell fell into step beside me and Bret appeared on my other side as we moved further into the woods.

"Are you sure about this?" Bret asked.

"Can you think of another way?" I inquired.

"I mean are you sure about leaving her? With the way that she is now and the changes she's gone through?"

I stopped walking and turned to face him. Bret almost walked into me but managed to catch himself in time. "She's the same girl you've always known; she's just stronger and faster."

"With a taste for blood."

"She's controlling it and she will continue to do so. Do you think Bethany would ever purposely hurt someone?"

Bret's eyes flickered behind me and his shoulders slumped. "No but she's so different and without you to lean on..."

"Bethany is far stronger than she, or you, ever gave her credit for. It's time you started to realize that because she's going to need all of her loved ones in the coming days."

Bret's eyes widened as realization set in. "You don't plan on coming back."

"I have every intention of trying to make it back here."

"But you don't think it's possible?"

"No, I don't."

Bret's gaze went back to where we had left the others. "It almost destroyed her when she thought you were dead the last time."

"She knows what my leaving means this time." Bret swallowed heavily as he turned back to me. "It's the only way I can give her a chance to live, the only way to give her the life she deserves. It will be a difficult one but she'll at least be *alive*. It's all I've ever wanted for her."

Bret stared at me as if he were seeing me for the first time. "You're not who I thought you were."

"I've never been who you thought I was."

Bret released a snort of laughter. "Very true."

"We should go," Darnell interjected.

I glanced up at the setting sun and nodded my agreement. Most of the others from the group we had left the tunnels with had moved inside the gated compound, but others, like Arlene, were still wary and remained sleeping outside of the gates at night. Arlene was now standing by the group that had been gathered within the gates to make the journey. Her head tilted toward us as we approached but she didn't speak and the firm set of her mouth told me she still wasn't pleased with our decision.

"Are you sure there is no way they can trace you back to this location?" she inquired.

"We wouldn't be going if there was," Jessica assured her as she slid a knife into her belt and took the other knife that Leo offered her. I recognized the look in Leo's eyes and had to force myself not to glance back toward where I'd left Bethany. I wouldn't be able to see her from here anyway and looking back was something I wasn't going to do.

"That doesn't mean they couldn't find us at any time," Rosemary told her.

Rosemary stepped forward and handed another knife to Betty, a small brunette girl with a compact body that would have been better suited for a twelve year old boy. She was quick though and far more agile than what I'd expected upon first seeing her. She slipped the knife into the holder at her side and turned toward Art, the man hovering anxiously beside her. I turned away from their goodbye and stepped beside Jessica as Leo turned away.

Craig, a large man with hair even darker than mine and skin nearly as dark, bent low to kiss the small blond woman, Jodie, standing at his side. Craig appeared to be nearly thirty and I assumed Jodie was about the same age, but her small stature made her appear much younger. Steve, a small Mediterranean looking Tintagelian was hugging Leighann as they exchanged their goodbyes.

Jessica handed me a large plastic bag. "You'll need it later." I took it from her and shoved it into my back pocket. "Does Bethany know?"

"Know what?"

"That we most likely won't be coming back."

"She knows. Does Leo?"

Jessica's eyes traveled to the young man gathered with the others. "He does."

The first splash of color began to streak across the sky as the sun started to set. The filling station that Jessica had shown us on our test run three days ago was almost a hundred miles away. It would take us less than an hour to make it there but I was eager to get this over with. I remained immobile though as I hid my impatience and waited for the others to say their goodbyes.

The last streaks of pink were fading from the sky when we finally made our way into the woods. It was freeing to run again, to move, to do something other than think because all of my thoughts only brought me back to one realization. I'd just left behind the only person I'd ever loved.

If I thought too much I would go back to her. I didn't fear death; it was simply a fact that it would happen one day and it wasn't something that I thought about often. The imminent threat of death didn't make me want to turn back, but even now I could feel the pull of Bethany trying to lure me into returning to where I belonged. I could sense it in the others too as they didn't slow, but there seemed to be a heavier weight upon them as their shoulders slouched and their mouths became more pinched with every step they took.

It was refreshing to feel the wind whipping past me as I concentrated on avoiding the obstacles in my way. My heart raced as we rounded the top of a hill and the filling station came into view. Unlike the encampment we had just left behind there were no humans here but only a simple train station looking platform that was a good ten feet off the ground. The tangy smell of blood wafted up from the valley the station was nestled in below.

I'd seen it before but even so I felt the hunger within me stirring to life. It wasn't a part of myself I was proud of, but I wasn't ashamed of it either. It was who I was, a predator, one that ranked even higher on the food chain than the humans that had mistakenly thought themselves at the top of it.

I slid over top of the hill and behind an outcropping of rocks. Settling behind a large boulder I rested my hands on it as I rose to look into the valley. Jessica's shoulder pressed against mine as she stood up beside me. From our vantage point we could see some of our kind walking a patrol around the ten foot high fence surrounding a few acres of the land below us. Actual buildings had been erected; they weren't hastily assembled shacks but rather they were elaborate creations with roofs that wouldn't leak and floors that weren't dirt.

"Are you going to tell me how we get on the ship now?" I asked.

She'd kept her secret to herself until now, but I didn't doubt she had a way onto the ship just as I didn't believe she would betray me. I'd seen her love for Leo and I knew that what was driving her to get on that ship was the same thing that was driving me.

"It's not fun, even for our kind," she answered.

I didn't like the sound of those words but I'd never expected this to be fun. She gave me a secretive smile and nodded to the left. Creeping out from behind the boulder we carefully made our way through the woods and around to the side of the platform. Jessica put her hand up to halt us. I knelt down as I surveyed the fence and the land sprawling out beneath us.

The ground shook as a Seeker full of blood approached the platform on its spiderlike legs. From its lower midsection a single, its main spindly tentacle slid out like a worm from the earth and into a metal tube. Like a person pumping gas, the blood pumped out of the creature and into the waiting canisters that would be transported back to the ship.

As the blood left the Seeker, it began to dwindle from the size of a school bus to that of a midsize sedan. The tentacle retreated from the pipe on top of the canister and pulled back within the creature that had returned to its natural opalescent hue now that it was empty. The three silver canisters that had been filled moved forward on a long conveyer belt that aligned it behind four other full canisters set out on the platform.

"That's how we get on," Jessica whispered in my ear.

"In the containers?" Cory blurted.

"Yes. They'll keep filling them until morning when one of the smaller ships will arrive to pick them up," Jessica explained.

"How do we know they'll go to the main ship?" Steve inquired.

"All the blood supplies originally go to the main ship. It's decided where else they go from there," Jess explained.

"And we come back in those things?" Craig inquired.

"Yes."

"They don't notice the weight difference?" I asked.

She shook her head. "It's all robotic arms that lift them in and out of the ships. I don't think they put a weight system into effect because they never expected anyone to try and sneak on or off the ships in the containers. They would *never* expect anyone to disobey them."

"How did you know that before you went on there last time?" I demanded.

She shook her head. "I didn't."

"And you went anyway?" Betty inquired.

Jessica looked at the others before meeting my gaze. "I met Leo before this happened, before I even knew that The Freezing was going to occur for certain, before we graduated from high school. I knew that you and I were supposed to meet our freshman year in college, but I simply... I just couldn't," she whispered. "They had another station like this on an island off the coast of Maine. I only knew about it because the family I'd been placed with was Tintagelian too and I overheard them discussing the island. The island was set up as a test run for The Seekers and the ships, along with other places where I'm sure that the missing populace wouldn't be overly noticed.

"I went onto that ship with the hope of finding a way to end all of this before it even started. In the hopes that I could free myself from the destiny they had set out for us, and instead I discovered that The Freezing was going to occur before the summer ended. The Freezing wasn't the escape I'd been looking for, but it was a way for Leo and me to get away all the same. I took a chance going up there, I didn't know if I would be able to make it back to him, but I was going to lose him no matter what and I wasn't willing to do that without a fight. It may have been stupid and rash..."

"I understand," I interrupted as she continued to try and justify herself. I may not have boarded a ship, but I'd risked Bethany's life with my own stupid and rash decision. I could only hope The Ancients arrogance in believing that no one would dare cross them, or outsmart them, would be their ultimate downfall after this day.

I leaned back on my heels as I studied the containers. She was right, even for one of our kind I wasn't exactly thrilled at the prospect of using them to enter the ship. "We have to go now," Jessica urged. "The last time I was here there was only one hour between each one of those things arriving. I doubt it's happening as quickly now as they have to be running out of people, but I don't want to take the chance that it's not any different."

"Let's go then," I said as I slipped away from the tree.

We descended the hill rapidly and perched at the corner of where the fences joined. From here I could see the patrol making their rounds on the other side of the compound near another platform. Jessica broke out a set of wire cutters and began to snip at the metal wiring. The metal was cool beneath my hand as I helped to roll it out of the way for her. Pinning the makeshift gate back we moved quickly through the hole and kept to the shadows as we hurried toward the elevated platform.

Reaching the platform, I cupped my hands together before me and helped to boost Jessica up. She grabbed hold of the platform and lifted herself onto the landing. Craig helped push Betty up as Steve boosted Cory upward. I could hear the three of them moving around above us, but from this angle I couldn't see them up there. "Lowering one down," Jessica whispered.

Raising my hands above me I braced them to grab hold of the bottom of the canister. My knees bent beneath the weight of it but I brought it down and placed it on the ground beside me. Jessica disappeared briefly before reappearing with another one. I lifted it down as she jumped off the platform with Cory and Betty at her side.

I didn't know how much time had passed but I could hear the steady click of the clock winding down as I lifted one of the canisters onto my shoulder and scrambled back through the fence and up the hill with it. Jessica and I, faster than the others, made it to the top of the hill first.

"This should be good," she panted.

Grabbing hold of the edge of the canister, I yanked the top free. The blood was the color of coal in the dim moonlight but the scent of it assailed me. Inhaling deeply, I had to fight the urge to dip my hand in and savor in the warm life pooled within. I forced my head up and wasn't surprised to see the darkness that resided within us, and that was ruled by our hunger and rage, creeping across Steve and Cory's faces. There was no name for it, it was simply who we were, who we had always been, and what resided within us, but I believed it was what had caused the humans to come up with the legends of demons.

Though their desire was evident, Steve and Cory tipped the canisters onto their sides and poured the blood onto the forest floor. I placed the canister upright again and gathered leaves and pine needles to cover the massive puddles seeping into the earth. I knew there was no way to cover it all but I was hoping that between what we did now, the location, and the trees they wouldn't be able to spot the blood from above.

"Leo helped you do this the first time," I said to Jessica as we started back to the platform with our much lighter stowaway containers. Her head tilted as she studied me. "This isn't a one person job," I answered her unspoken question.

She took a deep breath and shook her head. "No, I never told Leo I was going to do this until after I was back."

"Who helped you then?"

"Rosemary."

She turned to face me when I stopped walking. "How long have you known Rosemary?"

"She was a teacher at my high school; I think she had been placed there with the sole purpose of watching over me." I didn't doubt it. The Tintagelian that had watched and reported on me was the adoption agent that had originally placed me with the Marshall's and moved me about over the years. He had also been the one to decide that the Marshall's had to go.

"Rosemary saw the difference in me after I met Leo; she knew what was happening to me even when I didn't. I don't know what I would have done without her there to guide me; I don't know how you or any of the others managed to navigate those waters alone. It must have been horrible."

It had been but I wasn't about to admit that. "She let you go alone?"

Jessica flashed a wild grin. "She didn't have a choice. Our breeding has ensured that we are the stronger ones after all. I don't pull that card often but in this case it helped me to get my way."

I couldn't help but smile back at her as I nodded. "I understand."

It only took a few minutes for all of us to help each other onto the platform. We were just beginning to get organized when I began to feel the solid thump of one of the larger Seeker's approaching the station again. Placing the empty canister down I lifted my head to see if I could locate it. The solid wall behind the platform made it impossible to see what was coming our way though.

"It's too soon," Jessica whispered.

Betty bent over the canister still situated in the middle of the wall between where the full ones slid through and where the empty ones remained. She stood immobile for a full minute before turning back to us. "There's one coming!"

I jumped forward to help shove the empty canisters back into the places we had removed them from. "We have to go," Steve, who had taken over Betty's position, declared.

Grabbing hold of Jessica's elbow, I pulled her toward the edge of the platform as the others leapt off. I landed smoothly on the ground and took a swift step back so that we were underneath the edge of the platform. The wall behind us should keep us blocked from the Seeker but even still I bent low as I crept toward the edge of the platform and rested my hand upon the ground. Drawing within myself, like I had taught Bethany to do, I searched the world outside of myself. My ears became more attuned to the subtle sounds of the earthworms moving through the dirt, the mice within the forest, but I mainly focused upon the creature less than twenty feet away from us.

I could hear the pulse of blood exiting the creature as it filled the next canister in line. The sounds of it withdrawing from the canister reached me as the line of containers was shoved forward. Another click indicated that another full canister was moving forward but from the less forceful pumps of the Seeker I realized that the creature was starting to empty out. Jessica knelt by my side as another canister slid into place. More blood rushed out, but the next container wasn't completely filled as it didn't slide forward.

Dull thuds resonated as the creature retreated from the platform. "We might as well take our clothes off now," Jessica suggested in a low voice when the ground stopped trembling from the Seeker's retreating weight.

I glanced at her and then back at the others. "Why do we need to take our clothes off?" Betty inquired.

"The minute we climb into those canisters we're going to be coated with blood. We can't walk around the ship like that."

I nodded as I pulled the folded up plastic bag from my back pocket and began to hastily unbutton my shirt. I didn't look at the others as I carefully folded the shirt and wrapped it within my other clothes to keep the explosives as protected as possible. I barely noticed their naked bodies as I pushed my sneakers and socks inside and knotted the bag.

Their eyes didn't flicker away from mine when I looked at them again, I didn't try to shield myself from them nor did they attempt to cover themselves either. I assumed the sight of my naked flesh had the same affect on them as theirs did on me, nothing. I didn't feel curiosity, didn't feel a stirring of lust or attraction or even a morsel of embarrassment at being naked before them.

The air was cool against my skin as we stepped back out from under the platform but I barely felt it as we maneuvered ourselves back onto the platform. I made sure the others were in containers before settling into one with the bag on my lap. I met Jessica's gaze across the platform before I pulled the lid into place and tugged it down until I heard the click of the locks sliding into place. The blood still lining the container was warm against my flesh but I fought the impulse to taste it as I impatiently waited for the smaller ship to come and pick us up.

CHAPTER 20

The ride was far less jostling than I'd expected it to be, a fact I was extremely grateful for with Lloyd's makeshift bombs in my lap. I wasn't sure how much time had elapsed though before the container was finally settled into position somewhere aboard what I assumed was the main ship. I remained where I was, curled up amongst the blood and over my bag of clothes. I was about to lift the top off the container when a small tap on the side sounded near my ear.

Dim illumination flooded in as I pushed the top off with a soft pop of air. I inhaled the fresh air as I rose to my feet and stretched out my cramped legs. Grabbing my bag of clothes I climbed from the container. The others were streaked with blood that smudged their cheeks and foreheads, and coated their backsides. I knew I wasn't much better though as I could feel it sticking and cracking against me with every step I took.

As I worked the cramps out my legs I got my first good look at the ship I'd spent the first two years of my life on. I didn't remember those days, but then I had no aspiration to either. Especially not as I looked around the football field sized room that contained canisters for as far as I could see. I'd never imagined anything like this could exist and though I'd never been ashamed of what I was before, I was suddenly disgusted by the more twisted ones amongst us that thrived on such atrocities.

"Oh," Betty breathed and lifted her hand to her mouth. She winced and instantly jerked her hand away to reveal the blood print it had left on her mouth. "This is awful."

I met her stricken gaze. "If we're successful it will end today."

Tears briefly swam in her eyes before she nodded. "Art will never know this atrocity, he'll never experience this. I don't care what I have to do to make sure of that."

I knew exactly how she felt as I began to move through the endless rows of blood and human life that cluttered the room. It wasn't until we were halfway through the room that I realized it was even more massive than I'd originally thought. At least three football fields could fit within this part of the ship, and at least two of them were full of containers. The other one was stacked full of people that remained frozen within their bodies.

I stopped walking, and so did the others, as we spotted the humans packed like sardines into the other third of the ship. "What is this room?" I asked Jessica.

"It's the lower level of the ship. There were only a few canisters the last time I was here, I wasn't... I didn't expect this," she choked out.

Though the room appeared cavernous and never ending, our voices didn't echo amongst the nearly black walls that had an almost reflective quality to them. I tilted my head back to take in the recessed lights burning down from the ceiling. *It's like some kind of crazy ass greenhouse except they aren't growing plants, they're cultivating humans,* I realized.

I half expected twigs and vines, or perhaps even a flower, to be sprouting out of the human's heads but they remained immobile and completely human in appearance. "Let's get out of here," Betty whispered.

"There's a shower station at the other end," Jessica said.

"Why..." Craig's question faded away as he took in the people. "They *bathe* them when they bring them up?"

"They're unclean," Cory said in a hushed voice.

"Thank you Jodie," Craig muttered the name of the human woman that had stood by his side all week. The woman that had given him a new perspective on human life, and his own.

I couldn't help but share the sentiment. It was difficult to imagine that at one point I would have stood within this room and felt nothing but excitement at the spectacle spread out before me. I'd always been glad that Bethany had appeared in my life, but now I was so unbelievably thankful for it that I could barely breathe.

She'd saved me from a lifetime of nothing. She'd given me a gift and even if my life ended today, that gift made it completely worthwhile.

"This way," Jessica said.

She led the way through the barrels to the human side of the ship. The thought of touching them made my skin crawl but they were impossible to avoid as we wound through the thousands upon thousands of bodies crammed within the room. I was repulsed by the feel of them and though I knew they were unaware of us, I could almost hear their voiceless pleas to be free of their arctic state.

Relief filled me, and I was finally able to inhale deeply again, when we finally found the end of the people. Jessica moved to the right and a doorway that almost blended in with the rest of the room. The only distinguishing difference between the door and the wall was the simple gold square in the center of the door. Jessica slipped her index and middle finger into the center and pulled the rectangle handle up.

The door slid silently to the side to reveal a dull gray shower room within. There were ten nozzles lining the walls but only one drain. "Won't they hear the water?" Steve asked.

"They didn't last time and honestly it doesn't matter, we can't go out there with blood all over us," Jessica answered.

"We can't leave a wet trail everywhere we go either," Betty said.

"We have to stay in here for a bit after," Jessica informed her. "It sucks, but it doesn't take as much time as you would think to dry off in that main room."

The last thing I wanted was to sit around here with the greenhouse humans for any longer than we had to, but I wasn't willing to do anything to jeopardize our secrecy upon this ship. Stepping into the room, I twisted the knob at the end until a clear stream shot out. The spray was room temperature and unlike earth water there was the subtle taste of fruit and an almost coppery blood tang to it. The taste brought back memories of my infancy and a memory of being bathed in the sweet water tickled at the edges of my mind. I recalled the name of the fruit that had given the water this taste, the olinade. It grew within the water and added its flavor to the supply that was recycled throughout the ship.

My head bowed as the water rushed over me and I tried to shut out the memory. I didn't want to remember anything about this place, it wasn't a part of me but even as I thought that I knew that it was. This place was as much a part of me as Bethany was. It was engrained into the fabric of my being; I had been conceived on this ship and kept alive here for the first two years of my life. This was my beginning and I was willing to destroy my beginning to ensure *her* future.

I wondered what she was doing now, how she was. Yesterday had been amazing, the only day we'd ever gotten to share with just the two of us; I would have given anything for just one more of those days. I closed my eyes as the water poured over me and I rested my hands against the wall before me. I could almost taste her again, so much sweeter than the water.

My fingers curled into fists as I tilted my head back so that the water was hitting me full in the face. The needlelike spray helped to turn my thoughts off of Bethany and back to where it belonged, on the mission now facing us. The water swirling down the drain became entirely red before it began to finally run clear.

I tried to ignore the thousands upon thousands of frozen humans surrounding us as I stepped from the shower room. My foot tapped and my gaze ran constantly around the room as I waited for the water to stop dripping from my hair and body onto the floor. The heat of the room was helping the drying process but it was nowhere near fast enough as far as I was concerned.

My hair was still damp but the rest of me was dry when I bent down and began to pull the clothes from my bag. The girl's hair was still wet but I didn't have the patience to wait for that right now. I shrugged the shirt back on and slid the buttons into place. "Everyone ready?" Jessica asked as she stepped in front of the door next to the shower room.

"What if someone is out there?" Betty asked.

"We take them out," Jessica answered. "If we can," she added in a muttered aside I was certain only I heard.

I shifted back on my heels as I braced myself for what was on the other side of that door. If anything was out there I was going to destroy it. The door slid back as soundlessly as the shower door had. I spotted the male on the other side of it before it was even completely open. His hand went to the weapon at his side but his posture relaxed when he recognized his own kind emerging.

It was that relaxation that was his downfall as I leapt forward, grabbed hold of his head and snapped his neck before he could put up any kind of a defense. From the corner of my eye I saw Jessica and Steve rushing to take down the other Tintagelian that had been in the hall. Jessica dodged the shards of ice that noiselessly burst from his weapon in a blue cloud, but Cory wasn't as fast.

Lifted off his feet, Cory was thrown back a good ten feet by the impact of the shards. I ducked his body as it soared over my head and crashed into the wall behind me. I didn't have to look; I knew he was dead before his body hit the wall. No one survived a direct hit from a frost gun. Jessica slammed the guard's arm down with her fist before he could fire off another round and drove her fist into his nose. She twisted the man's hands around, pressed the gun against his chest and pulled the trigger.

The force of it was hard enough to thrust the guard back, but Jessica had kept hold of his hands and jerked him down before he could hit the wall. His body slumped to the floor when she released him. I stayed low as I studied the hall and waited for more of them to emerge, but it remained still and I sensed no one else out there.

When I was certain it was safe, I lifted Cory's prone body over my shoulder and placed him back into the storage room we had just exited. It may not be possible, but if we were able to escape this place I was going to make sure he made it back to earth where the human he loved, Blanche, could have some sort of goodbye.

Craig and Steve dropped the bodies of the Tintagelians unceremoniously into the room and closed the door. I knew it wouldn't be long before someone came to look for them or to relieve them. "Why are there guards posted?" Steve asked.

"I don't know," Jessica said. "No one was here last time but there was nowhere near as much blood and no humans inside before."

"We don't have much time, let's go," I said crisply and hurried to the door at the end of the hall. I pulled the small rectangle handle down to open the door.

I frowned as I stared at the ground before me and then at the wall across from me. "What the...."

"You have to step forward," Jessica said. "I was stuck here for a good ten minutes before I figured that out. It's going to take you for a ride and a pretty amazing one, but it will be fine. Or at least it was last time. Just stay on the same pathway."

Those weren't the most comforting words after the events that had just transpired, but I didn't see any other choice as I studied the polished white floor before me. Taking a step forward I watched in amazement as a step molded itself out of the floor and around my feet before me. It was like an escalator but unlike an escalator it was only one stair that rose up a good ten feet before it began to slide forward.

There wasn't anything holding me to the step but I felt secure on the single two by two piece I was standing upon. I could hear the faint clicking of the mechanics running the "escalator" and as it began to move forward I could clearly see the gold encrusted rail running beneath it that drove it onward.

The walls around me gave way and when I looked back I could see Betty on a stair behind me. I kept my face impassive as I began to move into a wide open room. Other Tintagelians began to appear on steps above and below me as they slid across the cavernous room. There were a few Tintagelians that were moving parallel and even perpendicular to me. The rails running the system were so faintly hued that it almost appeared as if some of the steps were floating through the air.

Massive white crystals reflected the light filling the room as they flipped through pictures of a planet that none of us had ever seen, and that had ceased to exist centuries ago. Even so I found the rolling hills and shimmering water displayed within those crystals captivating as they played through the stones like a movie of a time long forgotten.

Despite my best intentions I found myself more than a little amazed by the world surrounding me. I didn't understand how a species that could create such wonder could commit such atrocious acts. Even as this thought was crossing my mind the stairs began to move over what I assumed was the center gathering area within the massive room.

Royal purple vines twisted over railings that marked what appeared to be a large dining area beneath us. Large sage and orange flowers bloomed from the vines and I dimly recalled that they were the flower of the Tintagelians, the lalitus. Through the center of the massive room ran the clear blue river that provided water to the entire ship. Drifting along the top of the water were dozens of the large red olinade fruits. Looking at them now I recalled that biting into them brought a surge of juice into the mouth. Juice that had a coppery tang to it, much like the blood that pulsed through the prey we all sought in one form or another. It was the only fruit my species ate, perhaps the *only* other thing, besides blood and souls that they consumed while aboard the ships.

This part of the ship didn't have black walls like the holding area; they were a blue so clear that it made me think of the pictures I'd seen of the Caribbean Sea. It almost seemed as if I could dive right into those walls. The ceiling was ablaze in a yellowish orange glow that reminded me of the sun and as I turned in the other direction I spotted the receding night. It took me a moment to realize that from within the ship the top of it was a massive dome that revealed the open sky, instead of an impenetrable wall like we saw of the ship from the ground.

Beneath me Tintagelians went about their day as normally as any human would have. They greeted one another but where there may have been laughter and loud calls between humans, these were simply nods and quiet exchanges between the Tintagelians. No smiles were exchanged as heads bowed and they moved by one another.

A bell in the distance brought my attention back to the room beneath me. Though no one spoke, excitement rippled through the crowd as they all moved toward the river. I kept my head up as I tried to appear indifferent, but my eyes kept drifting to the spectacle beneath me as they all lined up at the edge of the river.

Another bell went off and from somewhere in the ship I heard a low rumble. I didn't know what had happened but the water in the river began to go down like someone had just pulled the plug from a bathtub. The olinade swirled down to the concrete looking bottom of the river bed and fell onto their rounded sides.

From somewhere within the ship, the sound of something opening reverberated throughout and a small rumble began to shake the step beneath my feet. In a torrent of red, a wave of blood rushed through the empty basin beneath me. Like a fishing bobber, the fruit popped back up to the top as the blood followed the route of the river throughout the ship.

Saliva filled my mouth; my stomach rumbled as the Tintagelians dipped large goblets into the blood and lifted them to their mouths. The olinade danced and swirled throughout and a light bulb went off in my head as to how the fruit had acquired its sweet, coppery taste. Revulsion swirled through me but I couldn't shake the pulsing hunger that the scene beneath me awakened.

This level of greed and gluttony was what I had expected all along as they gulped down their goblets and went back for more. Some dipped down and took hold of the softball sized olinade with both hands. They wiped away the pink juice that trickled from the corners of their mouths as they eagerly ate it.

After the initial rush of blood the viscous liquid settled down to a few inches off the bottom of the basin, a few inches that was quickly consumed by the thousands lining it like pigs lining a trough. With the fourth goblet load by each Tintagelian the blood was nothing more than streaks along the side of the trench beneath me.

The faint grinding of gears reverberated through the ship again and fresh water flowed forth. Water that served as nothing more than a device to wash away the blood, and as a reminder of the once fertile land that The Ancients had ravaged.

I lifted my eyes from the room beneath me as they all resumed their day again and the walls surrounded me once more. Relief filled me as the step came to a halt at the beginning of a hallway. I stepped off and searched up and down for any enemies, but there was no one about.

"It was very calm from here on out," Jessica said in a strained voice. I knew how she felt. My body fairly vibrated with the need to feed that being in the container had awakened, but the river of blood had fanned the flames of hunger to nearly uncontrollable levels. I felt sorry for anyone that got in our way between here and the Hallowed room. "This way."

I stayed close on her heels as she turned to the right and led the way down the hall. We slipped around another corner and doors began to roll out before us in an endless aisle that reminded me of the cabins I'd seen on cruise ships. There were even more rooms here though and I didn't think anyone would make it off alive when this ship went down.

Our footsteps were muffled by the floor beneath us as we moved forward. It wasn't carpet underfoot, but the material the floor was made out of was almost spongy beneath my feet as it gave way a little with each step. The doors on either side of me were a white crystalline color that resembled the crystals in the main room and the one that I had thrown away all those years ago. The more I studied the doors though, the more I realized that they were made up of a different type of stone as they gradually began to change color to a deeper pink. By the time we made it to the end of the hall they were all a deep orange and becoming steadily redder.

At the end of the hall was another wall with stairs that curled upward. "How much time did you spend up here before?" I asked Jessica as she bypassed the stairs and moved down another hall.

"It took me two days to find the Hallowed room and a whole lot of wrong turns."

I imagined that it had as she stopped before a different alcove. She took a deep breath, set her shoulders and took a step forward. I watched as the step appeared but instead of going up or forward, it began a steady descent straight down. For the first ten feet I could see her head and then the floor reformed beneath me. Walls enveloped me as I stepped onto the stair behind her and began my descent into the bowels of the ship once more.

After what we had seen in the last basement area, I wasn't looking forward to this, but as the stair reached the bottom I discovered we were only in another hall. Jessica waited till everyone had arrived before nodding toward the right and creeping forward. Following behind, I kept my breathing as silent as possible as we moved onward.

We rounded a corner and a massive, arched door came into view at the end of the hall. It was made of the same crystal as the other doors but it was a lot larger and an angry, mottled red. Jessica stopped before the door and pointed to the pad next to it. I recognized instantly that a sample of our DNA would be needed to get the doors to open. Only it wasn't *our* DNA that this pad would accept. My hands fell to the bombs tucked within my shirt as I studied the formidable door before us. I wasn't sure they would be enough to get us through the layer of rock currently blocking our path.

"Are you sure this is it?" Betty asked.

"The only other area of the ship that I was never able to gain access to was the corridor that The Ancients slept in. However I don't think they would keep The Fountain in the same area as their sleeping quarters. I don't know where else the Hallowed room would be, and judging by the size of this crystal I would assume there's something important being protected by it," Jessica answered.

"This is the only chance we have, if we use one of those bombs it's all over for us. They'll know we're here," Craig said.

"We always knew it was likely that we weren't getting off of this ship," I said as I pulled a bomb out.

"Better make it two," Steve said.

"That could bring the ceiling down on us."

He glanced at the walls above us and nodded. "You're right, let's just hope one will be enough."

I was thinking the same thing as they retreated around the corner and I pulled the lighter from my pocket. I took a deep breath, lit the fuse and placed it firmly against the crystal wall. Turning, I sped down the hall and around the corner where I braced myself for the explosion. The force of the blast caused the ship to lurch beneath my feet. I was thrown against the wall but managed to catch my balance before I fell over completely.

Sirens began to blare and orange strobe lights flashed over the walls and floor in a dizzying pattern. If the bomb hadn't alerted everyone to our presence on board, there was definitely no hiding it now. Pushing off the wall, I braced myself before stepping around the corner. The bomb hadn't completely destroyed the crystal, but it had knocked a good four foot round hole into the base of it.

"Let's go," I said as I hurried toward a room I was certain no one other than The Ancients had ever entered into.

CHAPTER 21

Bethany,

"Bethany." Bishop stuck the cotton ball against my arm as Aiden appeared in the doorway of the small house we had chosen to use as a makeshift research facility. Bishop had uncovered a small microscope and a couple of slides in a teenager's room. He'd found some needles in a medicine cabinet beside some insulin. It wasn't much, but he had chosen today to return to examining my blood. I wasn't enjoying being stuck again, but I was actually grateful for the distraction from thoughts of Cade that he was providing. The look in Aiden's eyes caused me to jump off the chair I had been perched upon though.

"What is it?" I demanded.

"The ship."

A sick feeling settled in the pit of my stomach as I grabbed my gun from the table and hurried toward the doorway. The ship hovering in the distance appeared perfectly normal except for the small puff of smoke that was now trailing from the side of it. My heart plummeted into my feet; it took me a minute to catch my breath as terror constricted my chest and tears clogged my throat.

I would have much preferred to have been on that ship, to know what was going on, what he was doing and if he was ok. I understood that I couldn't be there, but as I watched the last of the smoke drift away I would have given anything to be with him.

"Cade," I breathed.

Lloyd looked at me over his shoulder as Bret squeezed my arm. "I'm sure he's fine," Bret assured me.

I nodded but I didn't believe him. Molly stepped forward and took both of Aiden's hands within hers as I waited breathlessly for something more to happen. I didn't know how much time passed but it felt like hours as my muscles became rigid and my neck was so stiff I could barely move it. The sound of Bishop's steps on the porch finally tore my attention away from the ship. "I have something to show you."

I frowned at Bret and Aiden as the doctor retreated into the house again. Forcing one foot in front of the other I followed Bishop into the house. I felt as if I'd just downed twenty sodas as my hands wouldn't stop fidgeting and jumping everywhere as I hovered behind the doctor. It was taking everything I had not to return outside to watch the ship, but driving myself crazy wasn't going to do anyone any good.

"Take a look," Bishop said and gestured toward the microscope set up on the table.

Uncertain if I wanted to see what it would reveal, I took a deep breath and cautiously approached it. Bending down I peered through the lens to the slide before me. As I watched one cell began to mix and blend with another. The invaded cell shriveled like a raisin and appeared to die.

"What am I looking at?" I was happy that my voice didn't shake.

"Your blood cells attacking my blood cells," Bishop answered.

My knees shook as I stepped away from the microscope. "So my blood won't help to keep you moving if they do release another form of the gas?"

"It won't keep me moving; in fact it will kill me. I'd like to test the others though, especially your siblings."

I nodded as I glanced over my shoulder at Abby and Aiden. Aiden was sitting at the table with Bret, Jenna and Molly. Abby was curled up on the couch behind them; her hands were tucked under her head as she slept. She looked so young and vulnerable that it tugged at my heart. Her boyfriend, Matt was curled up on the other end of the couch with his feet entwined with hers. On the floor before them Barney had one eye open as the dog watched everyone.

Aiden leaned over and kissed Molly, his hand trailed over her cheek before he walked away from her and began to roll up his sleeve. "Bethany." I turned back to Bishop as he pulled out another syringe and began to prep it for Aiden. "There is one good thing going on right now."

"That is?" I prompted when he became more focused on Aiden's vein than what he had been saying.

"Your cells have completely stabilized. There are no new changes in them and they are no longer being taken over. Whatever changes your body was going through are over with now."

Relief filled me as I nodded. I didn't mind being faster and being able to see and hear better, who would? I didn't even mind the craving for red meat or blood as long as that was all I would have to deal with. It was a far better alternative to being frozen. But it was petrifying to think that my body may have just kept changing to the point that I became someone I might not recognize anymore; someone that started to attack and feed on people, someone that could no longer be trusted around my loved ones. I knew that Cade wasn't like that, but no one had known what it was that I would become.

Rosemary had said the others that had received blood were fine too, but there had been no way to know what would happen after more time past. Bishop had given me that answer though, this was who I was, who I would be from now on, and I was beyond happy with that.

"That *is* good," I whispered.

He offered me a small smile before focusing on Aiden again. Stepping back into the doorway my gaze instantly returned to the ship. *Cade had made it that far, that was something at least*, I told myself. This standing here, impotently waiting though was enough to drive a person mad as I swiftly moved down the stairs.

Lloyd rested his rifle against his shoulder when I stepped beside him again. His eyes remained distant and cold as his gaze ran over me. He'd never been the warmest of people but I'd considered him a friend, and ally. I would give anything to fix what was wrong between us but I didn't think that was possible. He had trusted me and I had betrayed that trust. I'd chosen my path and now I would have to accept the fact that I may never get his trust back, that I deserved his disapproval.

"Any luck?" he inquired dryly.

"No. Bishop's testing Aiden now."

He nodded as he turned away again. My eyes focused on the menacing alien vessel that had been marring our sky for far too long. I wished I could see through the damn thing to what was going on inside. The not knowing was the worst part but I thought I would feel it if something were to happen to Cade.

But what if I didn't?

I turned around and paced back to the house as Aiden appeared in the doorway. "Anything different with your blood?" I asked.

Aiden shook his head. "No."

My shoulders slumped, if my blood didn't help them than they were all screwed if the aliens decided to release a new gas. I could take a lot, but I didn't think I could take losing everyone that I loved and cared about. I turned away from them and stalked to the edge of the clearing. Deep within the shadows of the forest, I thought I spotted movement amongst the trees. Frowning, I brought my gun before me as I drew within myself like Cade had taught me to do. Searching amongst the shadows, I tried to pick out what it was that I sensed out there, but I didn't see it again.

A chill crept down my spine as I took a quick step back. "There's something out there," I hissed.

"Where?" Lloyd demanded as he appeared at my shoulder.

"I'm not sure."

Another shadow seemed to flit through the woods but I saw nothing as I turned to follow it. I was straining to see through the trees when screaming erupted at the encampment. Lloyd didn't bother to look back before running into the woods toward the people we had left behind. "Stay here!" I yelled at Aiden and the others before taking off into the forest after him.

I caught up and past by Lloyd before we were halfway to the encampment. I jumped and darted around the obstacles in my way as the woods raced by in a blur of tree trunks and branches. This new found strength and speed was amazing, and though I was frightened by what was going on, I was also exhilarated by the power that coursed through me. I wasn't even breathing heavily by the time I arrived at the compound.

It took me only a second to understand the source of the chaos as people ran screaming in multiple directions at once. Three of the giant octopus/tick like Seekers had invaded the camp and were in the process of hunting down as many people as they could.

I didn't know how they had discovered us, but the small bit of security we had found here was effectively ruined. I lifted my rifle to my shoulder and began to fire as one of the creatures picked up a young girl and slammed her viciously into the ground. More Seekers emerged from the woods as screams reverberated through the air and the monsters began to swarm us.

***

Cade,

I ducked down and moved rapidly through the hole into the room beyond. I hadn't known what to expect but I took a large step back as I found myself on a golden balcony that overlooked a tree with its roots embedded in a glimmering pool of water. The tree stretched almost to the top of the domed ceiling. Its boughs were full of thick green, red, and orange leaves that didn't appear to be about ready to fall from it but instead seemed to be the actual hue of the tree. Thick golden fruit that I didn't recognize hung from the lower boughs; the weight of them pulled the tips of the branches into the clear purple water below.

I didn't know what out of this would be considered The Fountain, whether it was the tree itself, the water, the fruit, or perhaps it was everything working together, but I was certain that we had just discovered the source of The Ancients immortality.

The room must have been designed to jut out of the side of the ship, instead of being nestled securely into the bottom like I had originally thought, as the domed roof was translucent enough to see the sun beyond. The rays spilling into the vast room caused a myriad of gold, silver, and blue colors to dance across the white marble floor. Tapestries full of vibrant colors and breathtaking scenes hung from the walls. There were strange animals on some of them. Some of the animals appeared docile but others looked like they could rip my head off with one swipe of their car sized paws. Other tapestries also depicted scenes from different planets, with strange looking species that most certainly weren't human, but I suspected they'd also fallen victim to my people.

There were three tapestries of earth within the mix of thirty or more. They depicted sparkling blue oceans, rolling fields, animals, the pyramids, Big Ben, what I assumed was the Grand Canyon, and one of people gathered before a fire with their heads bowed as if in prayer. A tug of longing pulled at my heart as my thoughts turned to Bethany. At least she was safe right now, and if we were successful she would continue to be so, for what I hoped was a very long life.

"This is not what I was expecting," Jessica whispered from beside me.

"None of this was what I was expecting," I told her. "Let's go."

These stairs didn't move but were more what we were used to as they wound down to the bottom in a twisting design that was beginning to annoy me by the time we were a quarter of the way down. Grabbing hold of the banister I kicked my feet up and propelled myself over the side. It was a fifty foot drop, but I barely felt the impact as one of my knees bent to rest on the ground.

Rising, I raced across the floor as I narrowed in on the tree and pond. I didn't know what I was going to do with it, blow it up or poison it, but I had the driving urge to get to it soon. Behind me, I heard the muted sound of the others shoes hitting the hard floor. Climbing onto the lip of the small wall surrounding the pool of water, I couldn't help but feel repulsed as I saw what the wall surrounding The Fountain had hidden.

The roots of the tree were fibrous and crimson in color as they moved like eels seeking a meal in the water. The fine hairs covering the roots rippled over and all pointed toward me as they seemed to sense me standing on the ledge. As one, the roots rushed forward and I swore I could almost hear eager chatter amongst them as they crashed against the wall beneath my feet.

"*This* is the source of their immortality?" Becky inquired in a low whisper from behind me.

"I don't know what *this* is, but it's awful," Jessica murmured.

"Is it the water or the tree?" Craig asked.

"It doesn't matter, we're going to destroy it all," I said as one of the roots began to slide up the wall toward me. I didn't move away from it as it broke free of the water. The fact that it was out of the water didn't slow it as it slithered upward and that odd sound of excitement continued to resonate in my ears.

"They feed it too," Jessica whispered. "They feed it humans."

"No," I said as I stepped off the ledge. "They feed it *us*. Our vitality, our life source runs this thing and in turn it runs *them*."

Betty inhaled sharply as Jessica's face scrunched up. Craig and Steve took an abrupt step back as the tip of the root thrust over top of the ledge and began to poke around. "That's disturbing," Craig said.

"And right, I believe he's right," Jessica croaked.

"They must have been crazy to drink or eat from this originally," Steve muttered as he eyed the fruit like it was going to bite him, which I wasn't entirely sure that it wouldn't.

"They're not exactly sane," I replied.

"Well that's not very nice." A cold chill ran down my spine as I froze in the act of pulling out another pipe bomb from within my shirt. My head came up as from behind the tree eight Tintagelians began to emerge. I hadn't seen them in years but I knew immediately that The Ancients had just arrived.

The pipe slid back into place as I released it and lowered my hand back to my side. I hadn't seen my parents since I was born but I knew immediately who my mother and father were. I don't know how I recognized them, but my gaze focused on them as they moved to the front of the group.

"Welcome," greeted the tall slender woman I recognized as my mother. She appeared to be in her mid to late thirties, her pitch black hair was cut just beneath her ears in a sleek bob that emphasized her angular features. Her cheekbones were high; her almond shaped eyes were the same hue as mine. The complexion of her skin was a faint olive that was a little lighter in color than mine. She wasn't stunningly beautiful but she was strangely mesmerizing as a smile spread across her full lips.

"And he *was* right." She was staring at me as if she expected me to say something but I remained mute as my gaze ran over the gathering of Ancients only thirty feet away. Their ages appeared to run from their late twenties to maybe early fifties, but there was an air of wisdom and age far beyond what their faces revealed surrounding them as their eyes ran over us. "About the tree, what it feeds on, what it *will* feed on."

My teeth clenched, my shoulders thrust back as I didn't miss the meaning behind her words. I'd blow us all up before I ever allowed her to feed me to that *thing*.

"You shouldn't be here." I remained focused on my mother; apparently she was the spokesperson for the group. The Ancients didn't look at each other but there was some strange rippling between them that I sensed was some form of communication. "But since you are, I think our friend will appreciate your presence, or should I say *essence*."

"The children Isis," another said. His skin was pale and there was a hunch to his shoulders that made me think of old men, fragile bones and death. I'd never seen one of our kind look like this, even in old age we tended to hold up well and more often than not we just passed away in our sleep.

"We will make more children Forseti. These two are too pathetic for us to even consider as leaders, or as our own. Feed them to the tree; let their life force nourish it," my mother replied with a dismissive wave of her hand.

I felt my gaze slide to the fiber still poking out over top of the wall. More roots had climbed up to join it now.

"Such a shame, the boy showed promise." My eyes slid back to them as the older looking man standing beside my mother raked me from head to toe with his charcoal eyes. *Osiris*, I recalled, *my father*.

"The boy is a waste of our time and effort," another woman stated. She reminded me of a pencil as there was little to her shape and her black hair had been pulled into a harsh bun.

"He is Kali," my mother agreed. "But he was strong."

I wasn't offended by these words; in fact I was as indifferent to them as these creatures were to me. "Sedna, Raijin why don't you grab your daughter?" my mother suggested. Sedna, a short, plump woman with ample breasts and her long hair pulled into a loose braid stepped forward. Raijin, a taller man with a hawkish nose moved to join her. I took a step to the side so that I was standing in front of Jessica.

"Oh let's not pretend that our offspring is the reason you're here," Raijin drawled.

My hands fisted at my sides as my teeth clenched savagely. There was no way they could know about Bethany but even so my anger prickled as a cruel smile twisted Isis's mouth. "Yes we're aware that some of you are faulty," another man said. He looked to be the youngest out of them all, barely twenty-one. I vaguely remembered him as Segomo and only because he had once yelled at me to get out of his way. "That the humans can affect you in some strange way, that they can ruin you."

"They don't ruin us," I grated from between my teeth.

"They've brought you to your demise," Isis replied.

"You're too afraid of death to understand, but that is *not* our ruin."

I must have pricked a nerve as her mouth curled into a cruel sneer and her eyes narrowed fiercely. "We fear nothing."

"You fear living, you fear us, and you most certainly fear death. You wouldn't be feeding this monstrosity and partaking in whatever it gives to you if you didn't."

There was a second when nothing moved, no one even breathed and then, before I could even blink, she was on top of me. I threw my hands up as she grabbed hold of my throat and spun me around. Jessica launched herself onto Isis's back but she threw an arm back and knocked her aside as if she were no more substantial than a flea.

"I'll give you something to fear," Isis snarled in my face.

I clawed at her hand as I tried to pry her strangling grip free but it was like a steel vice around my throat as she bent me even further over The Fountain. I'd known The Ancients would be powerful but I'd never expected to encounter this. Bright lights burst before my eyes as my air was completely cut off. Thoughts of Bethany suffused me; her smell engulfed me as her melodious laughter drifted through my mind.

Drawing on the last remnants of strength I had, and the suffusion of energy that thoughts of Bethany brought to me, I threw my arm up and slammed it against the side of her face. A startled cry escaped her as I proved to be even more formidable than she had expected me to be. Her hold was torn lose as she was knocked aside. Launching back to my feet I dodged one of the roots that nipped at me.

Isis's eyes were completely black; the veins in her face clearly visible as she rose up to glower at me. Noise from the front of the room brought the others heads up. I kept my gaze focused on Isis but when she glanced toward the balcony I couldn't help but look also. Gathered upon the balcony were a couple dozen Tintagelians that had been drawn to this level of the ship by the explosion and alarms.

"Get out!" Isis roared and thrust a finger at them.

They retreated through the hole like she had thrown a fireball at them. Using the distraction the Tintagelians had created I pulled one of the bombs from my pocket and snipped the fuse. I didn't give any warning as I lit the fuse and threw the bomb into the upper level of the tree. There wasn't enough time to get out of the way, not nearly enough time to escape the room as the bomb bounced amongst the branches and tumbled toward the water below. Throwing myself to the ground I covered my head as I braced for the explosion.

CHAPTER 22

Bethany,

I fell back as another creature burst from the woods and crashed into the campground. "Retreat, we have to retreat," Darnell panted beside me.

I scrambled to reload my rifle as we moved behind one of the buildings and took shelter in its shadow. People and Tintagelians ran by us, some of them were carrying others but both species were being captured and taken by The Seekers at an alarming rate. We had managed to take down three of them but there were at least four more running rampant through the camp.

I finished reloading and wiped away the sweat trickling down my face as I took a deep breath. My heart beat pulsed in my ears as adrenaline coursed through my body and I had to control the tremor that shook my hands. I refused to let panic get the best of me as I pressed the rifle against my chest and prepared to flee the temporary shelter of the building.

My gaze slid to the massive spaceship in the distance but since that first puff of smoke nothing else had occurred. *There may be nothing for them to come back to if they did survive*, I realized as pain twisted my heart. I absolutely refused to let them go through whatever it was that they were going through up there for nothing.

The ground shook as the creatures pounded across the earth. My ears began to ring from the echoing round of gunfire that pierced the air again. There was no more smoke from the ship, but the clearing was filled with a smoky haze that made it difficult to see as more screams rent the air. I leaned my head against the back of the building as my burning eyes met Lloyd's. Fear had pinched his mouth and widened his eyes but I also saw the same resolution in him that was creeping through me.

Not without a fight, there is no way they would take us without one *hell* of a fight.

"We have to get to the others," I said.

Darnell nodded as I took a deep breath and prepared to flee the shelter of the building. "Now!" Darnell commanded and rushed forward.

Lloyd and I stayed close on his heels as he plunged into the woods. I glanced back at the camp but all I could see were shadowy figures amongst the fog of smoke choking the clearing. Most of the contained fires had been knocked over and were beginning to spread amongst the buildings. The flames crackled as they leapt into the air and caught hold of the trees.

I could move faster than Lloyd and Darnell, but I was unwilling to leave them behind with those things stalking us and the fire spreading outward. Trees snapped and broke behind us as we scurried through the obstacles within the forest. We burst free of the woods and into the neighborhood where the research house had been established.

My mouth dropped, I skidded to a halt as I spotted two more of the monsters looming over top of one of the homes. "Please tell me you have some bombs left," I said to Lloyd.

"A couple," he panted.

"I think you better start digging them out."

One of the larger ones crashed through a ranch style house as if it were no more than a house of cards. Its crab-like eyes spun on their tall stalks and focused on us. My heart leapt into my throat, I lifted the rifle to my shoulder as it barreled toward us and began to fire. No matter how many bullets pierced it though it was determined to take us down and I wasn't sure that we could stop it. My heart was in my throat, I could barely see straight as it continued to close in on us.

I didn't see Aiden and Bret until I heard the gunshots from near one of the houses. The creature let out a strange wailing sound as blood exploded from one of its hind legs. Though it was injured it wasn't hindered much as it switched directions and honed in on my brother and Bret.

"Aiden run!" I screamed.

The two of them hurried to get out of the way but there was no slowing the momentum of the monster barreling toward them. Dropping my empty rifle I gathered every ounce of strength and speed I had within me. Unlike the mountain lion, I showed no hesitance here as I pulled my knife free. I raced at the creature and flung myself at its massive, silly putty like back. It bucked beneath me and tried to throw me off by rearing back on its hind legs but I clung as tenaciously as a tick on a dog to it as I climbed toward its head.

Bret dove through the doorway of one of the homes but Aiden was cut off from the doorway as the monster spun. A tentacle whipped wildly through the air and smacked into Aiden with a sound like that of a lobster shell cracking. I'd never heard the likes of that sound before but I knew I would never forget it. A scream of fury and agony tore through me as I grasped my knife with both hands and drove it to the hilt into the creatures head. Blood spurted over me but I barely felt it as I pulled the knife out and repeatedly drove it into the creature.

I hadn't been able to take down that mountain lion, but rage drove me now. Rage and a strength the likes of which I had never experienced before. I would *destroy* this thing. I would make it pay for what it had done to Aiden and I didn't care what I had to do to make that happen. Even if it meant diving into realms of myself that I had never known, or even expected, existed.

I wasn't aware of the black running through my veins, or the fact that I was still screaming, until the creature dropped out from beneath me. The breath was knocked from me, my screams silenced as I tumbled onto the ground. I caught a brief glimpse of the black threading through my arms as I rolled away from the creature and toward the prone figure of my brother.

I knew I wasn't supposed to move him but my driving urge to see him, to *know*, outweighed common sense as I rested my hand on his shoulder and cautiously rolled him over. A sob lodged in my throat as his head flopped to the side and his sightless eyes fell upon me. There was a moment where everything in me stopped, I didn't breathe, I was certain my heart didn't even beat as the world shattered around me.

Pain exploded through my chest, a heart wasn't supposed to feel like this, it couldn't continue to beat if it felt like this. There was no way a person could continue on when they felt like this, but even as I thought that I knew I was wrong. A person did continue on, they simply had no other choice. I most certainly didn't have a choice as my pulverized heart continued its pulsing rhythm and my breath found a way in.

"No," I choked. "No, Aiden no."

Tears spilled down my cheeks and fell upon his beloved face as my hands ran frantically over him. There was no blood but his head was flopped in that unnatural way and I could feel something jagged from his back pressing against my palm. A guttural cry tore from me as my tears fell more rapidly upon him and my hands clenched at his still warm cheeks. I bent my head and pressed my cheek against his as sobs tore from me. The tears I hadn't shed for my father and mother seemed to release now as a never ending stream poured from me. I wrapped my arms around my brother, my best friend, and buried my face in his neck as I clutched him against me

"I'm so sorry," I breathed as my fingers curled into his shirt. "Please, please don't leave us Aiden. I need you; I love you so much, please stay with me."

"Bethany, Bethy we have to go." Bret's hand fell upon my shoulder as he knelt at my side. Tears slid down his cheeks as he tried to pull me away from Aiden's broken body but I refused to release him. "We have to go."

I knew that he was right, but I couldn't leave my brother here, amongst this mess, amid this death and chaos. I hadn't been able to save him but I would *never* leave him behind. Bending low, I slid his arm around my shoulder and lifted him onto my back. "Bethany..." Lloyd started as I braced my legs and pushed myself to my feet with far more ease than I would have thought possible given Aiden's six foot frame.

"I'm not leaving him," I grated out between my teeth.

He stared at me for a minute before giving a brisk nod. "Come on, let's get out of here."

I could barely see or breathe but somehow I managed to keep going. The ground was beginning to shake again as we neared the house where we had left Abby, Molly, Matt, Jenna and Bishop. I had to get to my sister, I couldn't lose her too. I just couldn't.

We were almost to the house when another puff of smoke emerged from the ship.

***

Cade,

Scrambling back to my feet, I didn't give the others a chance to regain their bearings as I darted toward The Fountain in the center again. The blast had ripped the front of the tree off to reveal the hideous core of the monstrous plant. The inner part of the tree was made up of the same fibrous roots that filled the pond and were now oozing blood into the water beneath. The roots or tree, maybe even both, were releasing a high pitched scream that made me wince.

I grabbed three of the vials from within my jacket. Using my thumb, I flipped the tops off of them and heaved them into the water. I didn't know if it would have any effect on the tree, or the roots, but I was going to do everything I could to take the monstrosity down. The water began to froth and foam as the roots whipped back and forth in a frenzy that churned the reddening water. The roots shot up and began to whip rapidly above the water as the screaming increased to the point that I thought my eardrums would shatter.

Raijin leapt before me when I grabbed for another bomb from inside my shirt. My hand enclosed on the syringe Bishop had given me as Raijin seized hold of my throat. I threw my arm up to knock him off, but he knocked it aside and lifted me off the ground as if I weighed no more than a child. I faked going back at him with the same arm but instead I kicked him forcefully in the stomach. A loud grunt escaped him as he was knocked back a good foot. I grabbed hold of the hand squeezing my throat and snapped it back before ripping it off of me. With the full force of my weight I swung forward and drove the syringe deep into his neck. A smile curved my mouth as his eyes widened and I pushed the plunger.

Blackness bled into his eyes; a ferocious growl erupted from him as he thrust his face into mine. Before I could prepare to defend myself again though, his face went slack and he released me. His hands clawed at the syringe still sticking out of his neck as he stumbled back. All the color drained from his face, white bubbles foamed from his mouth and a strange gurgling sound escaped him as he fell away from me.

Isis reached for him but even as she went to grab him, his eyes were rolling back into his head and he was slumping to the floor. Foam continued to spill from his mouth but I sensed no heartbeat from him anymore. It took a moment for the realization to sink in that for the first time in over seven thousand years one of The Ancients had died, and I had been the one to do it.

Isis's eyes came up to me as she comprehended what I'd done to her friend, and what had been tossed into the pool with her precious tree. An enraged bellow ripped from her as she charged across the floor toward me. Snatching up a branch that had been blown off the tree and onto the floor, I swung it up and caught her across the face as she launched at me like a pouncing tiger with hooked fingers and a loud snarl.

Blood exploded from her mouth, her cheek caved from the force of the impact. The tree tore across my palms, slicing them open as the branch was ripped from my grasp. My arms were still shaking from the force of the blow when she landed with a big splash in the water. Like a school of hungry piranha, the damaged roots surged forward to feed as they had so many times over thousands of years. A blood curdling scream ripped from Isis as the water within the pool began to churn and her blood turned it an even deeper shade of red.

Jessica yanked the syringe from Raijin's neck and I tossed her some more of the poison to fill it with. She waved the syringe in front of Forseti when he took a step toward her. A sneer curved his lip but he looked toward the other Ancients spreading out around The Fountain instead of continuing toward her. An unnatural hush fell across the room as Isis finally became still.

I pulled another bomb out, but I didn't bother to cut the wick as I lit it and threw it across the room. "Run!" I bellowed.

"No!" Agrona, silent until now, screamed as the bomb spun across the room toward what remained of the tree. Her small, spindly legs moved remarkably fast as her desperate need for survival outweighed her apprehension of us. She tried to intervene with the bomb, but it was already beyond her reach.

Jessica was the first one to hit the stairs and dash up them as fast as she could with the rest of us right behind her. Osiris was lurching for the bomb when it went off. A spray of blood shot across the room as his hand exploded like a smashed pumpkin and the remaining half of the tree was rocked backward. A loud cracking filled the air as the tree began to twist to the side.

The force of the blow had knocked me over but I regained my balance and pulled myself back to my feet using the rail of the stairs. Malsumis let out a strangled cry and lifted a massive broken limb onto his shoulder. Holding it like a spear, he heaved it forward as if it weighed no more than a twig. It moved through the air with the deadly speed and accuracy of a heat seeking missile toward Steve.

"Look out!" I shouted as I lurched forward to grab Steve.

My hand curled into the bottom of his shirt and I jerked him back as he tried to twist out of the way of the limb. It was too late though, the branch pierced through his midsection and out the other side. His hands clawed at the protruding object in his gut, his mouth dropped as blood trickled from the corners of his mouth. The force of the branch had knocked him half over the railing and there was no stopping the momentum as his shirt tore within my hand and he toppled over the rail. The sharp sound of bones breaking reverberated through the room as his body bounced off of the stairs below before plummeting out of view.

I didn't bother to look back as I propelled myself up the stairs faster. Jessica had just made it to the balcony when the loud cracking of the tree became a splintering crescendo that reverberated through the room. The air whistled through the leaves as the tree completely gave up on maintaining its hold on life.

The tree slid down the side of the stairs and crashed onto the floor with enough force to rock the ship. I grabbed hold of the rail before I could be knocked over the side of it.

What was left of The Ancients scrambled to get out of the way of the tree as it bounced off of the floor. Osiris's head tilted back, he held his mangled arm up before him as he pinned me with his gaze. Even beaten and bloody there was nothing but murderous intent within those empty, shark-like eyes.

Grabbing hold of the banister, I kicked my feet onto it and braced myself as I prepared to jump off of it. The top part of the tree crashed onto the ground again as I launched myself off the railing and leapt for the balcony. My hands grasped hold of the floor of the balcony; my feet swung over open air as I tried to maintain my hold on the slippery floor. Discomfort slid through my arms as I moved myself down the balcony toward one of the rails bolted into the floor.

I was almost to the railing when hands grabbed hold of my arms. I swung my legs onto the floor of the balcony and pushed myself up while Jessica and Craig helped pull me the rest of the way over. "Go!" I shouted as I fell upon the floor and struggled to catch my breath.

I glanced back at the room, but most of it was blocked by the top half of the toppled tree. I didn't think there was any way they would be able to escape the room but to be on the safe side I pulled another bomb free and lit it. Pushing myself to my hands and feet I threw myself through the hole in the crystal as the ship heaved once more from the force of the bomb exploding.

A loud groaning filled the air as the ship began to shift toward the side. The ship had become a giant slip and slide as I fought to keep my balance on the smooth, moving surface. The Tintagelians that had been outside the door began to scream as most lost the battle against the tilt of the ship and crashed into the broken crystal door.

"This way!" Jessica cried.

Bracing my feet on the floor, I placed my hands against the wall and used the tips of my shoes to pull myself forward. Too confused by what was going on, the Tintagelians around us didn't try to stop our escape as we pulled ourselves toward the stairwell we had entered through. Betty let out a small cry as she lost her hold and started to slide by me. Somehow managing to hold on with one hand, I snagged her before she could get lost amongst the crush pressed against the back wall.

I pushed Betty behind me and waited for her to brace herself again before continuing on. Finally making it to the end, I pulled myself around the corner and fell against the wall. The screams and blaring sirens followed us as we made it to the stairwell. I stared doubtfully at the single stair before us. Unlike before though, the wall was pulled back to reveal the rail and open space beyond the stairwell. It must have been some sort of emergency precaution that occurred when the alarms were set off.

"Go Jessica," I urged.

"Go where?" she demanded.

"Walk the rail."

She turned the color of snow, but as she looked back toward where we had come from, it was obvious there were no other choices. Jessica stepped onto the rail as the first of the Tintagelians behind us turned the corner. Betty and Craig stayed close on Jessica's heels as she moved out over open space. I was just stepping onto the rail when the first Tintagelian reached the stairway behind me.

A part of me was tempted to punch him in the face but as of now they still didn't recognize us as the reason why the ship was tilting to the side like a boat taking on water. Giving them concrete proof by hitting him would only add to our list of troubles. Turning away from the man, I put my arms out beside me to keep my balance as I began to walk across the rail.

A low groaning echoed throughout seconds before the ship began to list even further to the side. My feet slipped, but I somehow managed to keep my balance on the six inch around rail. Thoughts of Bethany drove me onward with a growing urgency to escape this doomed vessel. I yearned for so much more time with her than what we'd had. I wanted more touches and kisses, more love, and I wanted *our* child.

Someone behind me cried out but I didn't look back as I heard the sound of their body bouncing off of something below us. With the grace of a deer, Jessica leapt off the rail and onto the next platform. Betty hurried forward, followed closely by Craig, and finally me. Jessica led the way down the hall, past the rooms with the crystal doors at a speed that would have beaten a cheetah but didn't seem fast enough for me.

Sirens and lights continued to blare around us as we ran. The doors surrounding us had stopped changing color; instead they had all opened to reveal a single, twin sized bed and a small chest within. Every room was the same white color; there were no identifying pictures or personal objects in them.

Jessica didn't even hesitate before scurrying onto the next golden rail with her arms straight out at her sides. Betty and Craig plunged out behind her just as the ship gave another jerking lurch to the side. More cries sounded from behind me but Betty's piercing shriek was the only one I heard as her feet lost their traction and she plummeted from view.

"Shit!" I hissed from between clenched teeth.

Craig stumbled before me and nearly fell, but he managed to catch his balance in time to save himself. I had come up here fully expecting to die, but I'd be damned if I went out like a tightrope walker in some sort of demented carnival. Drawing on the strength Bethany's blood and soul had given me, I poured on the speed as the ship began to tilt into a more downward angle.

I realized with absolute certainty that this thing was as doomed as the Titanic as Craig made it to the next platform and I leapt off behind him.

"Getting back to the container room is useless now," I said to Jessica. "There has to be an emergency way off of this thing."

Jessica shook her head as she looked at me helplessly. "There's a way off, but..." she glanced at the ever shifting environment surrounding us. "I'm not even sure it would still work."

"It's better than nothing. Just get us there."

She nodded and took off down the hall again. This time she bypassed the stairwell we had used to go over the massive central room. She leapt over the golden rail and dropped the thirty feet into the main room with the rest of our confused and panicked species.

CHAPTER 23

Bethany,

"Bethany what happened?" Abby cried as I stepped through the door.

"Are you hurt!?" Jenna gushed.

I shook my head as I barely glanced at the blood coating my body. "Aiden!" Abby screamed as she finally looked beyond the blood on me to who I was carrying.

I pulled Abby's hands aside before she could grab at Aiden and feel the lifelessness of the body pressed against my back. "Abby no," I told her with a small shake of my head.

Tears bloomed in her mahogany eyes, eyes that reminded me so much of Aiden's that for a minute I was almost unable to continue forward. "There has to be something we can do," she breathed forlornly.

I couldn't find any words for her. The tinkling sound of glass shattering thankfully distracted her as Bishop swept the microscope and blood samples from the table. I knew that the gesture was as useless as my newer blood samples had been but I couldn't bring myself to say those words as I gently placed Aiden's body on the table. Before Abby could get any closer I turned around and pulled her against me.

"Please," she breathed as her small fingers curled into my shirt and her tears wet through to my skin.

"Bethany..."

"I know," I cut Bishop off before he could state what I already knew.

Abby's slender shoulders shook as she started to sob harder. Bret pressed us against his chest and enfolded our heads with his hands. I took solace in the warmth and comfort he offered, but it did little to ease the shattering of my heart within my chest. Wrenching sobs escaped me, Abby pressed closer and Bret rested his forehead against mine. It was the wrong time to lose control, I knew that, but I couldn't help myself as my shoulders shook and I clung to the two of them.

The echoing fire of gunshots finally pierced the thick haze of grief enshrouding me as I recalled that there was no time for grief here, not right now. There was still a battle to be fought, still an enemy to kill. And I wanted to *kill*.

I wiped at my tears and reluctantly pulled myself from their embrace. Blood from my clothing and body stuck to their clothes and skin but they didn't seem to notice it through their misery. My gaze fell to Molly as she hesitatingly approached Aiden's broken form and took hold of his hand. Sitting on the stool beside the table she began to weep openly. I longed to comfort her but as she bent to press a kiss to his forehead I knew she needed some time alone right now.

The shaking of the earth tore me away from her sorrow as the windows in the house began to rattle. I took hold of Abby's shaking shoulders. "Abby, I need you to stay here, ok?"

"No!" she cried as she clutched my shirt. "No you can't leave me too!"

Those words tore at the already fragmented pieces of my heart. I would have given anything to be able to stay with her, but to cower in this house would do nothing more than put her life in jeopardy. Darnell and Lloyd were powerful fighters, but I was stronger than they were now, and they needed my help now more than ever.

"I'm not going to leave you Abby, I'll be back but Lloyd and Darnell need help. Please Abby stay with them. Molly really needs someone right now too."

Her lower lip trembled, tears spilled down her face but she didn't offer any more protests as she stepped away from me. Jenna hurried forward and pulled Abby against her chest. "Be careful," she mouthed.

I nodded and turned away quickly. Lloyd held a rifle out to me and Bret. "Ready?"

"I'm more than ready," I grated out as my sorrow began to ebb toward a growing fury.

I rushed down the stairs behind him and Darnell as gunshots rang out from somewhere down the street. I turned in that direction but didn't make it one step before two smaller Seekers burst from the side yard of the house next door.

Cade had taught me how to become still, how to feel within myself in order to hunt my prey, but something else came over me now as I focused on the enemy barreling down upon us. They had killed my mother, they had killed my brother, and now I was going to make them pay.

Blackness seeped through my veins once more, but it didn't frighten me, in fact I welcomed it as I felt its strength infusing my cells. I almost tossed away the rifle and leapt at one of them again, but I could only take one of them down and I would be putting the others at risk if I abandoned my position. No, instead I lifted the rifle to my shoulder and smiled grimly as I began to pull the trigger.

Disgust curdled through me as my stomach rumbled in hungry response to the blood that gushed from the wounds. Clenching my jaw, I adjusted my stance and shut out the world around me. I became solely focused upon destroying these monsters that had taken almost everything I loved. The only thing that mattered right now was killing them.

***

Cade,

My hands rested upon the floor as I landed silently beside Jessica in the cavernous room. Like a waterfall, water from the river spilled across the floor and rushed toward us as the ship continued its precarious tilt. The watermelon sized crystals fell to the floor and clattered like marbles in a jar toward us. It had been grueling enough to keep our balance with the sinking ship, but trying to stay on our feet in the water while dodging the crystals was worse than trying to rake leaves in a hurricane.

"This way!" Jessica shouted over the growing racket.

The water was completely out of the riverbed now; the olinades became projectiles as they tumbled by us and smashed against the back wall. I was on my hands and knees as I fought against the pull of gravity. Scrambling to the side, I barely managed to avoid being taken out by a tumbling crystal. Grabbing hold of one of the crystal bases I pulled myself up against it and braced myself carefully. Something within the ship fractured with a groaning sound that momentarily drowned out the screams around me.

There was little that surprised or unnerved me, but the back wall ripping away with a wrenching groan and spiraling toward the ocean was a disconcerting sight. Fresh air rushed in around us, the salty scent of the ocean drifted up to me as my hair was blown back. Screaming Tintagelians plummeted past me; they spiraled out of control as they tumbled out the back of the ship toward the unrelenting sea fifteen thousand feet below.

Shoving myself off the base, I lunged for a doorway over my head and pulled myself through. Jessica and Craig were each holding onto a base, their feet dangling in the air as the ship continued its precarious roll. Leaning out the doorway to my waist, I stretched out toward Jessica and clasped hold of her hand. She held onto me, her feet kicking in the air as I lifted her up and through the door. I took hold of Craig's hand next and helped to pull him up as more Tintagelians plummeted toward their death beneath us.

I took a deep breath and leaned against the wall. Jessica's chest heaved with the force of her breaths, her coffee colored hair straggled around her flushed face as she tilted her head to look at the hallway that was now directly above us.

"At least we succeeded," I said as I wiped the sweat from my brow. This wasn't where or how I wanted to die, but no matter what happened from here on out all that mattered was that we had won.

"They'll be ok," Craig panted. "They'll be safe after this."

"They will be," Jessica agreed as she looked out the door to the open area now beneath us. "If we can somehow make it to the other side there are emergency shuttles designed to hold one Tintagelian at a time. I have no idea which direction they would be pointed in now, we could get to them only to discover we won't have enough time to keep them from plummeting into the ocean. And it's that way." She pointed at the hall now directly above us as the ship had rotated one hundred and eighty degrees.

"Who knew chopping down a tree would cause so much damage," Craig muttered as he ran a hand through his disheveled hair.

"It's what we came here for, to ensure their survival, to give them a chance. To give them the life they never would have experienced if we hadn't. They'll have some peace now," Jessica whispered. "I hope Leo finds happiness with it."

"He will," I assured her. "And so will Bethany."

I knew that eventually Bethany would find some happiness, but I also knew that she would forever be broken, as would I if something were to happen to her. That thought drove me back to my feet. It may be nearly impossible, but I wasn't going to go down without a fight for her. I grabbed hold of the edge of the doorway above my head and pulled myself up. It was going to be one hell of a climb, but if the ship remained steady until we were out of this hall there was a chance we could make it.

Rapidly climbing up by using the doorways, I made it to the closed door at the end of the hall and pulled the golden handle down. I just barely managed to dodge the door as it swung toward me and crashed against the wall opposite of me. Crystal from the door shattered and spilled over Craig and Jessica before it tumbled into the void below us. I pulled myself through the doorway and looked back, but other than Jessica and Craig I saw no one below us anymore.

We continued to climb swiftly through the hallways as we made our way steadily toward the back of the ship. My arms and back began to throb from the strain, sweat trickled down my back and plastered my hair to my face but I refused to give up, refused to be deterred. The last door opened into another hallway that thankfully ran parallel to the one we were in. Craig and I helped to pull Jessica through and fell back against the wall. I glanced down the hall to the empty space beyond as the ship gave another heaving groan that set my teeth on edge.

"Let's get out of here." I ignored the twinge of my arms as I shoved myself to my feet. "Which way?"

Jessica pointed to the right and we broke into a run. Our feet thudded dully on the crystal doorways we ran across as we dashed across them to another massive crystal at the end. "There's no handle!" Jessica panted from behind me. "I don't know how it's supposed to open but there's no handle for it."

"The Ancients would want to make sure that no one was able to get off of this ship unless they allowed it," Craig said.

I could only hope the bomb didn't blow a hole through the floor as I pulled one out and lit the fuse. We ran back down the hall and darted through a doorway before it exploded. Debris and smoke blew outward and flew past the hallway we were sheltered in. I found myself holding my breath as I poked my head back around the corner. My shoulders slumped when I saw that the massive door had been blown outward but only a small hole had been punched into the floor.

Returning to the crystal I stepped carefully around the hole in the ground. Wind rushed in from outside to whip the hair back from my face and plaster the damp clothes to my body. My eyes watered as I took in the vast expanse of ocean and sky spread out before us. We were supposed to be near the top of the ship; instead we were stuck on the side of it with nothing but the sea below and the sky above in a dizzying array of blue.

The small ships that Jessica had been talking about were strapped to the side of the main ship. They were pointed straight at the sky instead of the land they were supposed to be directed toward. It didn't matter where they were directed though; we had no other choice but to use them. Stretching one leg down, my foot searched for the first pod before I stepped onto it. I braced myself against the side of the ship as I bent to fumble for the button on the side of the smaller ship.

My finger pushed it in and the top slid open. The wind drowned out all other noise as I turned to extend my hand to Jessica. She took hold of it and carefully slid down the side of the ship to join me. "Let's hope I don't end up hitting the sun," she said with a half hearted smile.

"You'll be ok," I assured her.

She settled into the driver's seat and I pushed the top shut for her. Craig took hold of my hand and helped pull me back into the doorway. Heat blasted from the small engines at the back of the oblong shaped object that Jessica sat in as the engine roared to life. I caught only a brief glimpse of her being thrown back against the seat before the small ship shot straight into the air. Craning my neck to look out the newly created doorway I watched it go until I couldn't see it beyond the wall of the ship.

Sliding back out of the doorway, I opened two more tops on the ships before rejoining Craig. "Go," I said to him.

He didn't have to be told twice as he scrambled out the door. I was reaching for the remaining two bombs when I saw his capsule shoot off the side of the ship. Lifting the lighter to the wick, I was about to ignite it when I felt something seize hold of my ankle. I went completely still as my gaze fell to the hand wrapped around me and the face and body that it belonged to.

Osiris's mouth was twisted into a ferocious snarl as he jerked on my ankle with enough force to twist it over. A loud popping sound rent the air as the joint was wrenched out of place and I was knocked on my ass. The Zippo tumbled out of my grasp and across the floor as Osiris jerked me toward the blown hole in the floor that he had pulled himself through.

A growl escaped him as he released my ankle and used his only hand to pull himself half out of the hole. Rage exploded through me and though my ankle felt as if it was only hanging on by a thread, I drew back both my feet and slammed them into his face. His nose twisted to the side with a loud crunch and a wave of blood poured forth.

A shout escaped him but he didn't lose his hold as he lurched forward and squeezed my dislocated ankle. Stars burst before my eyes, I was momentarily dizzy from the burst of pain I was fairly certain was going to shatter my skull. His hand scrabbled over my calf as he began to tug me toward the hole.

Reality returned as I jerked back and scrabbled for the lighter. My fingers brushing against it did nothing more than push it even further away from me. A sound of frustration escaped me as Osiris yanked me further into the hole. Spinning back around, I sent his head shooting back as I lashed out and drove my fist into his cheek.

His grip momentarily loosened on my leg and I flung myself backward in search of the lighter. A breath of relief escaped me when my hand finally wrapped around it. I didn't attempt to light the bomb again but brought it up to

Osiris and fired it up underneath his chin, and against the collar of his shirt. A roar escaped him; he completely lost his hold on me as he beat at the small flame against his neck.

Drawing my feet back, I smashed them repeatedly into his face. My ankle screamed in protest, my body fought against the repeated action, but my rage and my desperation to see Bethany again drove me onward. Bones broke and crumpled beneath my feet but I didn't stop, and I didn't look as he slid backward in the hole.

Gasping for breath, I finally took the time to look at my father's crumpled face. A face that no longer held any resemblance to my own, or to any Tintagelian anymore. A sneer curved my lip, I felt no pity as I pulled my legs back again and drove my feet forward with every ounce of strength I had. His head twisted to the side as he finally lost his precarious grip he had managed to retain on the floor.

A startled shout escaped him before he tumbled backward. Crawling forward I peered into the hole to watch him bounce against the halls and doorways beneath me. He crashed onto a wall three floors below and lay unmoving. I wasn't convinced he was dead, but I was going to make sure that he was as I gathered the remaining bombs and the grenade before dragging myself toward the crystal doorway above the pods. The dislocated ankle would take a couple of hours to heal, but it would be fine if I survived long enough for my body to be able to start repairing it.

Propping myself in the exploded doorway, I took the lighter to both wicks and pulled the pin from the grenade. I tossed them all over my shoulder before rolling to the side and throwing myself out of the open doorway and onto the open pod waiting for me. The breath was knocked from me as I landed on the plastician, a Tintagelian material that was harder than steel and that formed the smaller ships. Sliding inside, I didn't even give the top enough time to close before I hit the evacuation button.

I was thrown back against the seat as the pod exploded off the side of the ship. My hands grasped the control stick, the only other thing within the small container with me as I fumbled to control it. I jerked the stick back as I shot straight into the air. The blistering wind burned my face and eyes before the top finally slid to a complete close. I was just getting control of the pod when a blast rocked through the ship and fire shot out the side of it. I had only a brief second to see the debris racing toward me before the pod spun out of control and my vision was filled with the ocean rushing up to meet me.

CHAPTER 24

Bethany,

The last of The Seekers coming at us tumbled to the ground with a thud that vibrated the earth beneath my feet. My arm limply fell to my side when flames shot from the side of the ship and a nightmarish grinding noise resonated through the day. I couldn't breathe; my heart was in my throat. Fire and ice seemed to flow through my veins in alternating waves that left me shaken. The already awkwardly tipped ship turned even more in the air as parts of it exploded into the sky and plummeted toward the ocean. I'd already seen the bodies spilling out of it, but even more fell out now as fresh holes appeared in the ship and it began a strange but gradual descent toward the sea.

"They did it," Darnell breathed as more flames erupted from the massive spaceship.

I could only watch in some sort of remote, frozen horror as the first part of the ship plunged into the ocean. "He's ok Bethany, I'm sure he got out. I'm sure he's ok," Bret said as he rested his hand on my shoulder.

"It's over. It has to be over now," Lloyd muttered. "Or nearly over. If they managed to take the ship down it has to be almost over."

For the first time in months I actually saw a glimmer of hope in the young soldier's eyes as he turned toward me. It was that hope that made me smile; that hope that helped to ease the ache in my chest. Hope, Cade had told me once in a dream to keep hold of it no matter what. I'd thought that had been one of the bleakest times of my life, but though I'd lost much more since then, the hope within Lloyd's eyes was something to try and hold onto as desolation and rage threatened to consume me.

"It has to be," I agreed in a choked voice. Bret's hand tightened on my shoulder. I searched the woods even though I knew it was much too soon to expect their return if they had survived. I couldn't tear my gaze from the trees though as I struggled to keep breathing. "We have to find the others, see if there are other creatures out there, if there are any survivors."

"We will," Bret assured me.

"Are you like one of them now?" Lloyd asked as his gaze ran over me.

I frowned as my attention turned to my arms. I hadn't realized that my veins were still filled with black until he spoke. That had never happened to me before Aiden had been killed and I'd attacked that other creature. Apparently though my cells had stabilized, my body had still harbored one more secret.

"Are my eyes black too?" I asked as I tried to will my arms to go back to normal but they remained the same. Panic filled me as I lifted my head to meet Bret's confused gaze.

"No, they're the same."

I turned toward Lloyd. Though he didn't look as if he would like to shoot me, he definitely stared at me like I was something he'd never seen before. "I'm not one of them," I said. "Bishop said my cells had stabilized but I don't know what's going on now."

"It's ok," Bret assured me as he turned me stiffly toward the house. "I know it's difficult but you probably just need to relax Bethany. Let's get you back inside."

"I think I let my control go," I mumbled as I turned my arms over. "They killed Aiden and I lost it and now..."

"You're going to be fine. You just have to calm down."

He propelled me up the steps of the porch and into the shadowed interior of the house. Molly remained at Aiden's side with tears streaming down her cheeks. Jenna was in the corner by the window with Abby, who was still crying as she hugged Jenna. Matt was pale and shaken as he hovered in the doorway with Barney at his feet.

Bishop grabbed hold of my arms and led me away from the doorway. "Lloyd, take the body..."

"No!" Molly and I cried at the same time.

"Bethany, seeing his body is not going to calm you down any. Take some deep breaths, it's the only way you're going to regain control of yourself," Bret said.

"I can't believe they did it," Jenna breathed from the window.

"They'll be back," I whispered. "They have to come back."

"Yes, they'll be back," Bishop assured me. He nodded toward Lloyd and Darnell as he turned me away from the table. "Sit, Bethany."

I grasped my brother's wrist as Lloyd took hold of his shoulders. "You are not taking him yet," I grated through clenched teeth. I had Aiden's body, I had my chance to say goodbye. I may never get that chance with Cade and I wasn't willing to part ways with my brother just yet. "Please, leave him. It's not him causing this."

I closed my eyes as I bent my head and took a deep breath. "It's me," I whispered. "It's me."

Or rather it was the piece of me I was missing. A piece of me I was terrified had just been swallowed by the sea. I thought I would know if something had happened to him but I didn't know anything right now. There was nothing but anger and confusion inside of me, nothing but emptiness and loss.

I opened my eyes and was taken aback by the reflection of a woman I didn't recognize in the mirror behind Molly. The veins in my face were all clearly visible as the black I had seen within Cade seeped through them. I had been taken over and though I'd come to accept the fact that I wasn't completely human nor was I an alien, I was slapped in the face with the realization that I was something new, something different, and I had to get my act together.

I couldn't sit here and wallow in the desolation trying to consume me. It would only make me volatile and though I'd always remained mostly in control, this loss of restraint could get someone hurt. Someone else that I loved and cared for could die, and I could be the one that did it.

I had survived the wreck that had killed my father; I had survived the infusion of Cade's blood in my system, the loss of my mother, and the loss of my brother. If Cade didn't return I would grieve him every day for the rest of my life, I would never again know the peace and joy that only his arms and love could bring to me, but I wasn't alone in this world and I never would be.

I focused my attention on Abby and Jenna. I could feel the iciness that had settled into me after Aiden's death easing away as tears began to spill from my eyes and the blackness slowly receded from my face. My heart felt like it was shattering in a whole new way when my gaze fell upon the open sky outside of the windows and I realized that the ship had been completely consumed by the sea.

The ship had been there for so long now that I'd forgotten how clear and massive the sky could be. How beautiful.

My hand slipped from Aiden's wrist as fresh sobs wracked through me. So much had been lost today and yet so much had been gained. I clung to the hope that one of those gains had been the return of our freedom as Abby enveloped me with her tiny arms and pressed her cheek against mine.

***

After a final count we discovered that nearly a quarter of the compound had been lost to The Seekers, including Cory's mate, Blanche. Greg, Darnell and Arlene supervised the gathering of the bodies as Rosemary tried to comfort the broken Souls and Tintagelians that had been left behind. I knew how they felt as every movement was exhausting, every breath was a struggle, and every heartbeat felt fractured and off beat.

Bishop had taken some people to extract some of the venom The Seekers contained to keep on hand in case we ever came across more of The Frozen Ones again. It was a horrendous way to reawaken them and I thought the odds of finding more of them were slim given the fact that we hadn't encountered any in at least a month, but it was better to have the venom just in case.

I tried not to think about the death and melancholy surrounding me as I concentrated on shoveling dirt from the hole that would hold my brother. Bret worked beside me tirelessly, his head bowed as his bare shoulders bunched and flexed beneath the torchlight that illuminated the night. Sobs resonated throughout and though my chest felt as if someone had punched me repeatedly, I didn't shed any more tears. I wasn't sure there was enough water left in me for tears.

I glanced at the charred forest behind me, but most of the fire had burned itself out and what did still burn had been contained to a small area that others were working to put out now. The acrid scent of smoke and burnt wood clogged my mouth and nostrils making it difficult to breathe.

"How will we know if the other ships leave?"

I didn't know who had asked the question but it was Rosemary that answered. "They'll leave. If The Ancients are dead, they'll leave. They won't know what else to do and they'll be worried that their ships will be the next to go down. By this time tomorrow we'll know."

"The Ancients are dead," I said in a choked voice. "They didn't fail, I know they didn't."

Rosemary's deep brown eyes met mine and she gave a brisk nod. "You're right."

I turned away from her and resumed removing the dirt from my brother's grave. "Do you need a break?" Lloyd asked as he knelt before me.

I shook my head. "No."

My arms and shoulders were becoming increasingly sore but I was scared of what would happen if I stopped. The idea of having nothing to do, or focus on, was overwhelming and petrifying. No matter how sore I was, I wasn't going to stop. It was another hour before the hole was ready and Lloyd helped to pull me from it. I wiped the sweat from my forehead with the back of my arm and took a step away from the grave.

Molly and Abby had collected sticks and twigs that they had twisted into the form of a cross. Cloth and ribbons, scavenged from homes, had been twisted delicately into the cross. I was well aware of the fact that the ribbons were Aiden's favorite colors, royal blue and deep green.

Tears spilled down my cheeks as Bret hammered the cross into the ground and Lloyd and Darnell brought Aiden's body forth. Arlene followed behind with a small rock that had Aiden's name, birth date, and date of death scrawled on it in an elegant style that I never could have managed. Arlene placed the rock against the cross and nodded to me as she took a step back.

I took hold of Abby's hand while Aiden was lowered carefully into the ground. Darnell's head bowed as he recited a quick prayer and stepped aside. *It wasn't enough, it could never be enough, he deserved so much more than this,* I thought as I fought to keep myself together. But even as I thought it I picked up my shovel and began to toss dirt onto the body of my brother. It was more difficult this time as the tears clogging my nose and throat made it almost impossible to breathe.

After the last shovel full of dirt was tossed on the grave I gathered in a group with the others. The compound had been destroyed, but even though our only beds for this night would be the ground, I knew none of us would sleep. Tomorrow, Rosemary had said. Tomorrow we would know if it had all been for nothing, tomorrow we would know if we would have to continue to fight the monsters that had ruined all of our lives.

Though I'd thought that I'd never be able to sleep, exhaustion must have claimed me as my head snapped up sometime later in the night. I didn't know what had awoken me but I rose to my feet as a new sound drifted to me. Footsteps crunched within the woods seconds before Jessica and Craig emerged from the forest. Their hair stuck to their skulls, dirt streaked their faces, and scratches and blood marred their flesh. They looked like they had been run over by a bus, a few times, but they were alive and they were *here*.

Leo let out a strangled shout and shoved himself to his feet when he spotted Jessica. Cries of joy erupted from both of them as they embraced each other. Jodie leapt to her feet and raced to meet Craig. My heart soared, I frantically searched the woods behind them, but nothing else moved within the shadows.

"The others?" Rosemary asked when their joy over being reunited calmed a little.

I thought my heart was going to explode as I waited to hear what had happened to the others. Leo wiped the tears of joy from Jessica's face before she turned to face us. "Dead."

It felt like the ground had just been yanked out from under my feet. My heart plummeted; I took an unsteady step back as a wail of sorrow erupted from Steve's mate, Leighann. Betty's mate, Art, collapsed; his shoulders shook with the force of his sobs. Unable to support my weight anymore my knees buckled and I slumped to the ground. I pressed my fist against my mouth in order to suppress the scream of sorrow that threatened to erupt from me.

"We were separated from Cade just before the ship exploded. He may have made it into one of the escape pods, but he was the one that lit the last of the bombs. We were already away from the ship when they went off and the explosion..." Jessica's voice trailed off, her eyes met mine as she shook her head sadly. "I don't know what became of him."

All I wanted was for her to stop speaking and I was grateful when she finally did. Abby crawled up to my side and took hold of my hand. "There's still a chance he made it Bethany," she whispered.

"Yes," I forced myself to say. "Yes, there is."

***

My eyes felt like sandpaper as I tilted my head back to study the sky. They were gritty from tears and lack of sleep, but even so joy filled me as I watched the massive spaceship fading further into the distance. They were leaving, they were actually *leaving*.

Despite the heavy grief and oppression that had encompassed the survivors through the endless night, a loud cheer erupted from the gathered crowd. I couldn't help but shout along with them as fists pumped in the air and people hugged and embraced jubilantly.

Bret was laughing as he lifted me off of my feet and spun me in a circle. I hugged him back before he dropped me to the ground and happily embraced Jenna. There was no time to steady myself before Lloyd grabbed hold of my arm. I studied the soldier while I waited to see what his reaction would be to me. His youthful face split into a broad grin as he bent down and scooped me up.

"I had my doubts about him and you, but I'm glad you both proved them wrong," he declared as he held me close. "Don't lie to me again though."

I took solace in the strength of his arms and the forgiveness that he finally gave. "I won't," I promised.

"We'll always be here for you."

"I know," I whispered. "I'll always be here for you too."

He hugged me again before dropping me down. Darnell scooped me up and pounded my back so forcefully that I could hear the hollow echo of it rolling from my mouth. "I'm sure glad we found that ragtag group of yours!" he shouted in my ear.

I chuckled as I hugged his thick neck. "Me too!"

The large soldier finally placed me back on my feet. I didn't have much time to stay on them though as Bishop embraced me next. "Thank you," I whispered before he could speak. "Thank you for sticking by me, for trying to help me, for being Aiden's friend. Thank you for everything Bishop."

He chuckled as he kissed my cheek. "Thank you for keeping me occupied all this time, even if it was on a wild goose chase. I think I would have driven myself crazy otherwise."

"I think you would have driven us *all* crazy otherwise," I replied laughingly.

"True!"

He hugged me again and finally lowered me to the ground. I took a staggering step back before I was grabbed by someone else. I was beginning to feel a little dizzy as I was passed from person to person through what remained of our group. Tears of joy and loss slid down my cheeks as I was spun around and hugged by someone else.

My body reacted as if it had been hit by a bolt of electricity. All of my cells felt like they were filled with renewed life as they seemed to surge to the front of my body. A strangled cry escaped me, my head tipped back, but I already knew who I would find holding me. Cade's beautiful onyx eyes blazed down at me. His singed black hair was standing on end, there were burn marks and blood on his clothes and skin, but he was the most wonderful thing I'd ever seen.

A smile tugged at his lips. "I'm gone for one day and you're hugging everyone else?"

I couldn't get any words out as I flung my arms around him. My hands rapidly ran over him as I fervently tried to reassure myself that he was real, that I hadn't fallen asleep or was having some sort of hallucination. "Please," I whispered.

"I'm real love." His breath was warm against my ear as he kissed me tenderly. "I'm real."

He was real, he *was* here. I kissed his neck, chin and cheek before his head bent to mine and he took hold of my mouth. My body tightened and my pulse quickened as heat flowed through me. I allowed myself to drift into the pleasure and bliss that only he could give me. My body melded to his and I tried to pull him even closer, but it could never be close enough and no matter how badly I wanted him to, he couldn't erase the tragedies of yesterday.

He reluctantly pulled away and wiped the tears from my cheeks with the pads of his thumbs. "What happened here?" he asked.

"They found us," I managed to get out. "It was... it was awful. Aiden..."

Words failed me as I shook my head. "Oh Bethy," he breathed as he pulled me against his chest and cradled my head.

My fingers curled into his back, I savored in this miracle I had been granted for a second time as he swayed me soothingly back and forth. So much had been lost yesterday and yet so much had been gained today. The emotions coursing through me were confusing and chaotic but for now I simply wanted to celebrate the freedom we had reclaimed and the feel of his warm, solid body against mine.

EPILOGUE

One year later,

There was much to celebrate on the one year anniversary of the aliens leaving Earth. Though there was a lot of rebuilding left to do with homes and the human population, progress had been made in reestablishing towns and new centers of government. Cade and Jessica had been elected amongst their people to rule in our small area of the world, and Bishop and Darnell had been elected amongst ours to lead with them.

Though contact had begun to be reestablished with other areas of the United States and foreign countries, the population was still too small to establish any permanent communication that didn't involve traveling long distances. None of us had been shocked to learn that there had been other joint Tintagelian and human communities established throughout the world even before The Ancients had been taken out.

Cars and boats were up and running again but it would be years before the highways were in good enough condition to travel with any speed or guarantee of safety. Bridges were still mostly in ruins and planes, electricity, the internet or even phone lines were still a long way from being reconnected and brought back into use.

I was surprised to find that I was ok with this. There was something almost peaceful about this simple life that had been established amongst us and I wanted some peace after everything we had gone through. Though I really wouldn't mind being able to text someone again, or even call. It was a little inconvenient to have to walk or drive somewhere just to ask a simple question, but I also knew almost every person within the surrounding towns now.

We had even managed to find a few Frozen Ones, and though the reawakening process was exceptionally painful for them, the venom did bring them back to life. Bishop was working on recreating and trying to produce medicine and antibiotics in bulk. He was also working on teaching people in the surrounding areas how to create and use that medicine.

What remained of the enemy Tintagelians and Seekers on our planet were steadily being hunted down, but there were still some out there. I wasn't concerned about them though. Their friends wouldn't be coming back, Rosemary and Cade were certain of that. They would never take the risk of returning to the planet, and the species, that had managed to destroy their Ancient leaders. We'd find all the straggling Tintagelians one day but we had established ourselves enough so that I didn't lose sleep over the idea that they would overrun us.

"How do I look?" I lifted my head from the cake I was decorating to look at Jenna. She stepped through the doorway and spun in a circle.

"You look beautiful," I told her honestly as the simple dress drifted down to settle around her ankles again. The white of the dress emphasized her creamy complexion, reddened cheeks, and silky strawberry hair. "Just beautiful."

Her gaze fell to the cake. "That looks amazing Bethy."

I grinned at her, put the pastry bag of icing down and wiped my hands on my apron. "Who would have thought that I would be able to decorate a cake?"

"Most certainly not me," she admitted with a laugh.

"Well thankfully you didn't bake it," Molly said as she swept into the room. I had to agree with Molly on that one. I had a steady hand, and an unexpected talent for decorating cakes, but my baking skills were as awful as I'd always suspected they would be. Tears bloomed in Molly's eyes as she took Jenna in. "You look beautiful Jenna."

"Thank you," Jenna replied with a smile that lit the room.

"Bret's a lucky man," I assured Jenna as I squeezed Molly's arm comfortingly. "And it's a perfect day for a wedding."

There had been more than a few weddings over the year. Mine and Cade's one year anniversary was coming up in a few weeks, but I was truly excited about seeing two of my best friends get married today. It was also a bittersweet day as Cade was standing in as Bret's best man, a position I knew Aiden would have held.

I pulled the apron off to reveal the lilac cotton dress that was identical to the one Molly was wearing. Molly smiled at me, but sadness lingered in her eyes as she turned toward the window. Molly was moving on, I was aware that she'd been spending a lot more time with Lloyd, but yesterday had been the one year anniversary of the attack on the compound, and Aiden's death. The scars of that anniversary were still fresh in all of our minds as we prepared for the celebration of the world's Reclamation day, and for Bret and Jenna's wedding.

In another room the small squall of a baby began to sound. "I've got him!" I had only a brief glimpse of another lilac dress as Abby zipped out of the living room and down the hall.

I shook my head and tossed the apron over the back of the chair. Molly carefully lifted the four tier cake and made her way out of the kitchen with it. Abby emerged from the bedroom down the hall of the small house Cade and I had made ours with a small bundle in her arms. She was cooing softly while she played with the tiny hand wrapped around her finger. My heart swelled with pride and love as she stopped before me and smiled radiantly.

"Isn't he just the cutest thing ever?" she gushed.

"He is," I agreed as she slid my son into my arms. At only two months old he was nearly the spitting image of his father with his black hair and similar features. But when he opened his eyes they were the beautiful mahogany color that my mother, Aiden and Abby had all shared. My heart swelled with love when I found those beautiful eyes peering up at me. The pregnancy had been a month shorter than the average human pregnancy, but there had been no complications from it. He was a healthy baby and thankfully he hadn't been covered in scales. "Aren't you Aiden?"

"He may be growing fast but I doubt he's ready to talk yet."

I glanced up to find Cade standing in the doorway grinning at me. My heart melted at the sight of him leaning casually against the frame looking unbelievably handsome. There was little left of the distant, cold man that had pulled me into that antique shop and threatened to leave Jenna in the dump. Now his smile lit his eyes and warmed a room. Love fairly burst from him as he smiled proudly at the two of us.

He made his way over to us and bent to brush a kiss across Aiden's forehead before rising to kiss my lips. My toes curled and my heart leapt as the heat of his kiss seared through me. A small sigh escaped as he took Aiden from my arms.

I'd been so enamored with Cade that I hadn't noticed that Arlene had entered the room behind him. "I'll keep him occupied during the ceremony," she promised as she took Aiden from Cade.

Aiden waved a fist at her and released a small cry. Arlene laughed and hurried from the house as a man in his forties stepped through the door. "Are you ready?" the man asked Jenna.

Jenna's face lit beautifully as she hurried forward and slipped her arm through her father's. One of the best things that had occurred, six months after the aliens leaving, was the discovery of Jenna's parents. They had been in a town twenty miles away, sheltered in a half collapsed hotel when

Bret and Darnell had discovered them and brought them back.

Jenna and her father stepped aside to let Abby pass by them. Abby took hold of Darnell's arm and he led her down the steps of the house. Molly smiled sweetly as she took hold of Lloyd's arm and followed behind them. Cade held his arm out to me with a smile. "Are you ready Mrs. Marshall?" he inquired.

I slid my arm through his and leaned against his side. "I'm always ready Mr. Marshall," I assured him.

"You just remember that later," he told me with a wink.

A burst of laughter escaped me as we climbed down the stairs and around to the back of the house. An aisle and small trellis had been set up in front of the lake for the ceremony. Bret stood at the end, his shoulders thrust back proudly as he smiled at the two of us. Bishop stood beside him with his hands folded before him. The doctor had become the town magistrate of sorts and performed all of the wedding ceremonies for our area.

The two towns closest to us had joined us for the wedding, and the Reclamation celebration that was set to follow. There were a couple thousand people gathered within the field. I could feel the excitement in the air as Cade kissed my cheek and released my arm. Someone began to play a haunting melody on the violin as Jenna appeared at the end of the aisle with her father.

By the end of the ceremony I was wiping tears from my eyes but the festivities that followed quickly dried those tears. I found myself laughing and talking with everyone as I danced with Cade through the afternoon and into the night.

The aliens had taken a lot from us, but over the past year we had made a lot of valiant strides toward taking back all that they had robbed from us. We may never be able to reestablish the same kind of society that we'd once had, but as I kissed Abby goodnight, tucked my son into his crib, and crawled into bed with my husband I knew that, though so much had been taken from us, there were still many blessings and joys in our lives.

There was still so much hope and love.

The End.

Where to find the author

Website https://ericastevensauthor.com/

Facebook https://www.facebook.com/ - !/ericastevens679

Twitter @EricaStevensGCP

Blog http://ericasteven.blogspot.com/

Mailing list for Erica Stevens & Brenda K. Davies Updates:

http://visitor.r20.constantcontact.com/d.jsp?llr=unrjpksab&
p=oi&m=1119190566324&sit=4ixqcchjb&f=eb6260af-
2711-4728-9722-9b3031d00681

About the author

Though my name is not really Erica Stevens, it is a pen name that I chose in memory of two amazing friends lost too soon, I do however live in Mass with my wonderful husband and our crazy puppy Loki. I have a large and crazy family that I fit in well with. I am thankful every day for the love and laughter they have brought to my life. I have always loved to write and am an avid reader.

Made in the USA
Middletown, DE
03 February 2015